THE WAGES OF SIN

DAVID A. McINTEE

Published by BBC Worldwide Ltd,
Woodlands, 80 Wood Lane
London W12 0TT

First published 1999
Copyright © David A McIntee 1999
The moral right of the author has been asserted

Original series broadcast on the BBC
Format © BBC 1963
Doctor Who and TARDIS are trademarks of the BBC

ISBN 0 563 55567 X
Imaging by Black Sheep, copyright © BBC 1999

Printed and bound in Great Britain by Mackays of Chatham
Cover printed by Belmont Press Ltd, Northampton

For Gina, of course

Author's note

A word on dating: Russia used the Julian calendar until 1918, which means that all dates are twelve days behind the West.

Also, there is no set historical record for the precise events of Rasputin's murder. The main source of information about it came from Felix Yusupov's own books on the subject, but he changed his story with every telling. Maria Rasputin's version of her father's fate has definite inaccuracies in it, and no version quite accords with the official police report which establishes a base timeline for who entered or left the Moika Palace at which times.

So I've tried to use the different sources to construct the most feasible version possible, and squeezed our heroes into the gaps where the different versions don't chime.

As I write this, having finished everything, it's October 17th. Strange, that...

Prologue

Burning blue-white, and too bright to be viewed with the naked eye, the cylindrical fire blazed over the village of Nizhne-Karelinsk, passing high to the northwest. Though clearly moving fast, it took a whole ten minutes to burn its way down to the horizon.

As it finally neared the ground a small dark cloud appeared. This suddenly swamped the blue light, and a huge column of black smoke began to shoot up. Soon, a wave of sound rolled across the village. It was a swelling rumble, quite unlike the sharp report of an explosion. The village shook as the sound blasted through it and, in the distance, veins of fire rippled through the rising clouds.

This was two hundred miles away from ground zero.

Seventy miles from ground zero, the sky over Vanavara split asunder, and fire lashed out. The thunderclap knocked people off their feet in the rough streets, and earth rained from the sky as the village's buildings shook and cracked.

Thirty miles from ground zero, a wall of superheated vapour knocked the trees down like ninepins on the banks of the Chambe river.

The tents of a hunter were cast, burning, into the distance, and he himself was bowled over for what felt like several hundred yards. The reindeer and dogs he had brought bolted in sheer terror, but he couldn't hear their departure: the incredible sound had ruptured his eardrums.

* * *

Ground zero.

A body six hundred yards across, and massing around thirty thousand tons, burrowed into the Earth's atmosphere at supersonic speed. Five miles above ground, the density of the atmosphere finally proved too much for it: flattened against its own shockwave the body abruptly slowed, stopped – splashed, like a lead bullet on armoured steel. It tore itself apart in a gigantic, continuing explosion. Much of the force was expended downwards as well as outwards, into the great Siberian forest.

The trees for a few hundred yards directly under the explosion were stripped vertically of their branches, and charred, but remained standing as the air thickened around them. The earth at this point was slammed into a bowl-shaped depression a mile across, as the underlying permafrost and plant material were vaporised.

From this point, the shockwave spread out at hundreds of miles per hour, flattening the trees as it went. In a matter of seconds, nearly eight hundred square miles of forest were stamped flat.

Thousands of birds and animals were killed instantly, most smashed to a pulp by the shockwave. Every leaf in the devastated area was scorched away to nothing, leaving only hundreds of square miles of skeletal trunks lying bare under the churning smoke and dust.

It was June 30th 1908. The world would not hear of this devastation for another thirteen years.

Chapter One

No birds wheeled in the sky to disturb the sovereignty of the pale yellow patch that was the winter sun. The old Stock Exchange building, an abandoned but still imposing red-roofed acropolis, loomed against the clouds. From the wide steps and promenade that encircled it, granite causeways curled down to the ice where the surface of the Neva had frozen as it split around the headland.

The water that moved amidst the shattered ice was slow and dark, yet the ice also gleamed with the emerald flecks of broken champagne bottles that had become frozen into it. It was a wedding tradition that newly married couples would come here and break a bottle for good luck and, at this time of year, the fragments would be locked into place amidst the waves of ice.

Between the Exchange and the causeways were four huge rostral columns. They were red pillars over sixty feet high, with representations of ships' prows set into them. Beacons were lit atop them at holidays. Each rostral had carvings around the base representing a river: the Dnieper, the Volga, the Neva and the Volkhov.

The man who had just entered the Volkhov rostral was very lean, but not actually underweight. Rather, he was simply at a point at which he had no excess fat or muscle beyond that which his body needed. His planed features surrounded piercing eyes under dark brows. Neatly trimmed and combed black hair crowned his appearance. He was clad in a nondescript dark suit and overcoat.

Arkady Morovich thought the man looked like an

assassin. Not that he knew any assassins, but he was always watching out for them, just in case. He tried to stay motionless in the darkness a couple of turns up the rostral's interior staircase. The spiral staircase was used when the beacons were lit on special days, so he knew no one should be coming up here today.

On the floor below, the man who looked like an assassin opened the metal door to allow another man in. This one wore a Preobrazhensky Guard officer's greatcoat against the cold outside. He was shorter than the first man, and less fit-looking. Still, he looked fitter than Morovich felt. Morovich tried not to breathe, afraid that even that sound would give him away.

'You wanted to see me?' the first man asked. His accent was Russian enough, but somehow odd to Morovich. It sounded artificial, and he was sure this was not the man's native accent.

The officer nodded. 'I received new orders today – I'm to leave the city. I thought I'd better get things cleared up before I go.'

This was something worth reporting to Vasiliyev. Morovich could feel his leg starting to go to sleep, and shifted very slightly to try to alleviate the discomfort.

The first man was replying. 'We had anticipated such a possibility. It won't take long to activate an alternative route – in a few days your packets should reach you in the usual way. Things will take longer, but should still be worth while.'

The officer nodded again. 'I thought as much, but these days it's always best to check these things, yes?'

'Better safe than sorry,' the other man said with a smile. 'We look after our own – you know that.'

Morovich winced at the pins and needles in his leg. He had to stay still, but it was becoming more difficult.

'If I thought otherwise, I would not be here –' There was a tiny thud as Morovich's leg tapped the step below. Morovich hadn't even felt it move. A distant part of him knew that the sound was really only a tiny one, but it was so obvious that he doubted an artillery shot would have been any more noticeable.

'Who's there?' barked the officer.

Morovich momentarily thought of announcing himself and trying to explain his eavesdropping, but in that moment the officer pulled out his service revolver. Morovich's heart first seemed to stop, then raced away from him. They were spies and one had pulled a gun on him – if they caught him, they would obviously kill him. That instinct was enough to send Morovich bolting back up the tightly wound stairs.

Boots crashed on the metal steps below – they were following him.

In moments, Morovich was out on the square platform atop the rostral. A waist-high iron railing surrounded it, and a bronze basin was supported above for the beacon flame.

Panic-stricken and already imagining the bullets entering his back, Morovich climbed over the rail. The ground was at least sixty feet below, and looked like more than a hundred to his frightened eyes. He focused on the boat-prows at fifteen-foot intervals. If he could drop from one to the other, he should be able to get down alive.

The lean man's head emerged from the stairs, looking anxious. His eyes widened as he saw Morovich, and Morovich could tell that he was afraid his quarry might escape and expose him.

Hurriedly, he let himself drop to arms' length, hanging from the base of the railings. He looked down, and cursed fearfully. In his haste to escape, he hadn't judged where the prows were, and the nearest was a couple of feet to his right as well as eight or nine feet below his legs.

The assassin was at the rail, and Morovich almost screamed, knowing he was doomed for what he had seen and heard. He lashed out with his legs, trying to get in a better position to drop towards the first prow. Already the cold had robbed his hands of feeling, and he could no longer sense his grip on the rail.

With a sickening lurch, Morovich realised that he no longer *had* a grip of the rail. As he started to fall, he saw the thin spy's hand reaching out through the rails where his own had just been, as if to wave him goodbye.

His right shin caught the edge of the near prow, shattering the bone in an explosion of pain, but at least that mercifully blotted out the thought of the approaching granite promenade.

The two men watched from the top of the rostral as the eavesdropper's body thumped painfully into the column a moment before hitting the ground shoulders first. The thin layer of snow didn't provide any cushion for the impact. Both the cracking sound and the dark blood that started to freeze as soon as it pooled out around the fallen man's head suggested that he had been killed at once.

The lean man grimaced. At least no one was directly outside in this weather, but the scream would have attracted them. 'Dammit,' he growled. 'Let's get out of here before any soldiers or Ochrana turn up.' He looked down one last time. One of the corpse's legs was twitching, though he knew that was not a sign of remaining life. 'Always assuming he wasn't the Ochrana anyway.'

The morning had dawned cold and clear, and Josephine Grant woke in a chilly bed in a large and comfortable room. It was plain, but clean and well-kept. Though the snow had been thick in the air last night, today everything was calm, and the streets outside the window were snuggled under a blanket of snow – a dirty blanket. Most of it was now streaked and blotted with grey and black.

In spite of the cold weather, she was quite content. Her previous trips in the Doctor's TARDIS had generally taken her to horrifically dangerous places at the behest of the Time Lords, the Doctor's own people. Now that they had given him back the memory of how to operate the TARDIS, his first test flight had brought her to a time and place she was getting to enjoy.

True, it was a little primitive and there was no TV, but it was the past, filled with real people. She dressed quickly, pulling on the thick long dress and warm shawl provided by the TARDIS's inexhaustible wardrobe, and stepped out into the corridor. It was as well gilded and panelled as the furnishings inside her room, and there was a maid pushing a trolley along.

Jo approached the maid with smile. 'Excuse me?' She hesitated. 'I was wondering if there was a chance of any breakfast…'

'What would you like, Miss?'

Jo hadn't thought about that. 'A nice big greasy fry-up,' she suggested happily. Not normally her sort of thing, but in this cold climate she'd take all the hot and filling food she could get. 'You know – sausage, eggs, bacon…'

'I will take word to the kitchens, Miss,' the maid promised.

'Thanks.' Jo went and knocked on the Doctor's door.

'Come on in, Jo.'

She had doubted that he would have been asleep – he slept only rarely as far as she could tell – but was relieved all the same. She went through, to an identical room to hers. Like hers, it had a bed, a few tables and chairs, and a wardrobe and dressing table. 'We're being watched by a man down the hall, you know.'

The Doctor looked up from where he was tucking into a breakfast of his own. He seemed to have settled for hot buttered toast and marmalade. 'Well, of course, Jo. We're strangers here, remember – intruders, in wartime. The hotel staff probably alerted the authorities.'

Jo nodded. She'd forgotten that. The battlefields of the First World War were a long way from St Petersburg, and there were no warplanes to make air raids. To all intents and purposes the war was far away.

'Perhaps it wasn't such a good idea to spend the night here,' Jo said.

'And not sample a little of the flavour of your past? Come now, Jo,' The Doctor smiled. 'Think what a wasted opportunity that would be.'

'I suppose you're right,' sighed Jo.

The Doctor nodded. 'In any case, this afternoon we'll be back on course and out of their way.'

'Are you sure about that?' The TARDIS hadn't exactly performed admirably so far. They were supposed to be in Siberia in June 1908, not St Petersburg in December 1916.

'Completely,' the Doctor said. 'Now that I know the exact date –' he indicated the morning newspaper which had been delivered with his breakfast – 'it'll be child's play to make the requisite adjustments to the co-ordinates.'

In the room on the other side of the Doctor's, Professor Elizabeth Shaw had been awake for some time. She had been glad to see the Doctor again; perhaps more glad than she had expected to be. She had certainly intended to be courteous and friendly – he was an old friend, after all – but if he had any ideas about persuading her to rejoin UNIT, she'd have to be very clear about her stance on that. Something about snowballs in Hell ought to get the message across.

Huddled in an the long fur coat over a heavy woollen dress that she had brought from the TARDIS, she stood outside on the balcony of her room, wondering why she was taking so long to get used to the journey she had just made.

Liz had known during her time at UNIT that the TARDIS transcended its apparent physical dimensions. The complex hexagonal console which she had helped the Doctor work on was itself wider than the police box which contained it, so the truth had been rather obvious. That hadn't made it any easier to accept, in spite of the theoretical basis which she knew allowed it.

Once inside the TARDIS, though, there was no choice but to accept its paradoxical nature, as seemingly endless rooms and corridors branched off from the spacious white control room.

Somewhat perversely, Liz found it harder to accept the TARDIS's interior dimensions than Jo Grant seemed to. She supposed it was because Jo simply accepted that it was something beyond her understanding, while she herself felt an obligation to understand, since she was one of the most highly qualified scientists in Britain. She knew that there were many fields in which she wasn't qualified, but that didn't make things any more comfortable when she encountered one.

Now here she was, looking over the roofs of St Petersburg a good sixty years in her past, and she was uneasy. In many ways, it might actually have been easier to handle being in ancient Rome, or a Viking settlement, because then the facts of her journey through time would be simple and clear. But this city didn't look much different from the way it looked in her own time. That meant it was the small things that needled at her perceptions to tell her she was no longer in her own time.

There were no TV aerials on the roofs, and no jet-trails in the sky. Smoke from steam locomotives puffed into the air by the stations. It just felt odd and surreal rather than blatantly different. Somehow that seemed harder to get used to.

The sound of a horn on the Neva was a muted honk inside the grimy hospital. The expensive overcoat worn by Prince Felix Yusupov looked very out of place in what looked and smelled more like an abattoir than a hospital.

He himself seemed as finely wrought as his clothes, and certainly too delicate to be seen in such a place as this. Even so, he stood in the carbolic-scented morgue with unmistakable calm determination. He nodded at the slightly blue-tinged broken body that lay naked on a rough wooden table. 'Yes, that's Arkady Morovich.'

The other man with him, apart from the surgeons, was well-dressed, with features that seemed permanently tense, as if he was always ready to explode into anger. Felix had never quite decided whether this was truly the case, or merely a disguise he cultivated to impress opponents in court or in the Duma. Felix also wondered if perhaps Vasili Maklakov's apparent demeanour was a result of stress from juggling two such jobs. If ever anyone needed to get out and enjoy himself at the theatre or with a good meal, it was Maklakov. Maklakov signalled to the morgue attendants to wheel the battered body away. 'I'll see the forms are dealt with.'

'You said he was found at the foot of the Volkhov rostral?' Felix asked. He couldn't really believe this. Morovich had been so... *alive* the last time Felix saw him. Not just literally living and breathing, but vibrant.

'Some shoppers heard a scream, and when they arrived they found him at the foot of the column. It appears he jumped from the beacon platform at the top. From the condition of the body, and blood seen on the prows, he seems to have hit one or two on the way down. It looks like a fairly straightforward suicide.'

Suicide? That was so unlike Arkady. 'Was there no sign of anyone else in the area?'

Maklakov shook his head, and Felix sat down. He hated the loss of life anywhere, but that it should be someone he knew... And Arkady had been pleasant company: good-natured and soft-skinned. A pretty good balance of elements, all told. 'Grishka,' Felix muttered darkly. 'I should have seen something like this coming.'

'Grishka? Grishka Rasputin?' Maklakov frowned, glancing aside to make sure none of the morgue attendants were within earshot. 'But if Grigory Rasputin knew of our plans he would run to the Empress, surely, begging for your head.'

11

Felix waved a hand. 'How else do you explain it, then, Vasili? Who else could have swayed a man's mind so much as to make him climb a rostral and jump?' He shivered involuntarily. 'The man is… Not even a man, I think, but a devil come up from Hell to torment us.'

He knew exactly how much willpower Rasputin could bring to bear on a victim of his machinations. He knew only too well, from his own experience. Catching Maklakov's sceptical glance now, he felt his own wan, humourless smile.

'Never underestimate that monster, Vasili. Don't think I'm gullible – I tell you that mockery of a priest has some power, or something worse. You may think you know the danger in him, but I know more. I have already come up against his dark power, face to face. I have seen his eyes, Vasili, and felt them try to force me to do his will.' He took a deep breath. 'Poor Arkady…' Silently, Maklakov passed Felix a hip-flask with a small amount of cognac remaining in it.

As the prince took the flask, Maklakov said, almost diffidently, 'I am prepared to listen to you, if you wish to tell me. Do you wish it?'

Felix paused, flask raised, and gave Maklakov a slow nod. But after he took a first sip of cognac his glance fell and he remained silent, thoughts again less with the living than the dead. He wasn't surprised that Morovich had been unable to resist the sorcery that Rasputin must have put on him.

'It already seems so long in the past, Vasili…' When Felix had first visited Rasputin, on a scouting mission to see who this Holy Devil was, he had almost succumbed himself. 'Although, I suppose, it was hardly more than a couple of months ago. I wanted to see who this enemy of Russia was, and try to understand him better.' Felix gave a taut, bitter mockery of a grin.

'I saw all too much. And I understand nothing. You see, Vasili, I remember Rasputin stroking my head before making passes over my face with his hand, as a hypnotist does. I felt his power subduing me, and diffusing warmth throughout my body.' It had been an odd sensation; sinister and dangerous, yet strangely seductive.

'I still wonder, could he have drugged me? Somehow, without my realising…'

Under Rasputin's spell he had been paralysed, his tongue frozen numbly in his mouth. 'It was like being overpowered by opium.' Then he had seen Rasputin's eyes begin to phosphoresce quite unnaturally.

Startled by the intensity of memory suddenly relived, unprepared, it took Felix some seconds to become aware that Vasili in turn was staring at him now. He caught a long breath and steadied himself, head up again.

'Yes, it is a shaking thought. To recollect, and feel again… As Rasputin mumbled words that I could not make out, the glow from his eyes seemed to pierce me like rays of light, merging into a circle of power.'

He took another swig from the silver flask.

'Our holy man certainly believes in his own powers. Maybe he has reason to. He might be used to feeble minds. Or those who want to be easily mastered.' But Felix was stronger, and this attack had spurred him to fight off the influence.

Felix had sensed his own will struggle free, and the eerie light had faded as Rasputin came back into focus. 'When I gathered my will to slip free, I stayed lying still, so he would not know that I had defeated him.' Felix drained his cognac with a gulp. 'Vasili, he looked very smug, and spoke to me in the manner of a boor of a man who thinks he owns you.' Mastering the moment's anger he'd betrayed to the whole room, he quietened, saddened. 'Poor Arkady,' he said again.

Felix suddenly became more alert, driven by the anger and pain he felt. 'Vasili, I want to ask for your help in dealing with this demon among us.'

'Me?' Maklakov exclaimed.

Felix nodded enthusiastically. 'I've heard you in the Duma, calling for action to be taken against him. Inspiring words, Vasili, and courageous. I know you feel as I do about this.' And anyone who was against Rasputin would surely be in favour of his being dealt with. That was only natural.

Maklakov held up his hands, as if to repel an attacker. 'Feeling is one thing, but the law is my business, Felix. I am a lawyer; do you think I keep an office for assassins?' He grimaced sourly. 'I do not disapprove of what you are doing, of course, and I will not do anything that might interfere with your plans, but that is as far as I can go.'

'But you are a lawyer – you must have dealt in court with those accused of murder and assassination. You could help us find someone –'

Maklakov shook his head. 'I would not do that if I were you, Felix; it is a very naïve viewpoint. Assassins such as you describe owe their loyalty only to the highest bidder, and at court it would pay him better to betray you.' He glanced at the distant morgue attendants again, but Felix thought they seemed far enough away not to hear anything. 'But if you do decide to do it yourself, see me first and I may be able to warn you of inadvertent mistakes… Things to watch out for, just in case something gets out.'

Felix was disappointed, but decided against pressing the

issue. He had already enlisted one or two helpers, and Maklakov had a point. It would be much better to accept what little help he offered than to risk pushing him into refusing all contact, or even revealing their plans to others. 'Very well, Vasili. I will remember that, and visit you later. I'm sure whatever advice you give will be useful and valuable.'

Maklakov smiled. 'Just be thankful that I will not charge you my usual consultation fee.'

As they tramped through the snow along the Promenade overlooking the Neva, Liz was glad she'd availed herself of the TARDIS's remarkably comprehensive wardrobe. She didn't pretend to understand just how it could, apparently, provide suitable clothes for any occasion for any period; she was just grateful she had more than her customary trouser suit to combat the cold. What's more, she couldn't resist a sneaking feeling that as she and Jo swept along in their rich full skirts, boots and furs, they could have been extras in *Doctor Zhivago*. The real Doctor, wearing a full-length ulster, strolled along as if they were on a spring morning's constitutional.

Ahead, as they walked westwards, the forbidding grey walls of the Peter and Paul fortress loomed, guarding the city's southern approaches. Between them and the fortress, the cruiser *Aurora* was moored at a small dock. It was a little over three hundred feet long, with three funnels set between its fore and after masts.

'Does the TARDIS always get this lost?' Liz asked.

The Doctor paused in his strolling. 'What do you mean?'

'I mean that we're thousands of miles and eight years away from where we were supposed to be going.' Liz wasn't a historian, and hadn't thought about whether she would have accepted an offer to see a past city. But the chance to see the immediate aftermath of the great Tunguska blast of 1908 was too good for a physicist specialising in meteorites to turn down.

'Well, the TARDIS has been trapped in the one point in space and time for a while, you know. She has to get back into the habit.' Liz noted that he *didn't* say whether its navigation had been particularly accurate before his exile, and she was developing suspicions that it hadn't.

Jo, meanwhile, had kept walking, and reached the corner of the row of warehouses that lined the inland side of the promenade. 'Doctor,' she called, sounding alarmed. 'Look!'

The Doctor and Liz hurried over to join her. Liz had the sinking feeling that she somehow knew what Jo was going to point out, even before she reached the end of the warehouses.

The Doctor halted. 'Good grief, that's all we need...' As she had feared, Liz saw that the road ahead was empty, but for a flattened patch of snow about four feet square.

The TARDIS was gone.

Chapter Two

There were a few sea birds hovering around the *Aurora* waiting for the crew's discarded table scraps. The two civilians leaning on the rail of the shelter deck ignored them. Their eyes were focused on the man and two women who were leaving the embankment further along. The man wearing the long heavy overcoat was tall, with hair that must have been prematurely white – for he had a youthful air about him. One woman seemed no more than a girl, slight and blonde, while the other was a redhead, a few years older and with rather more poise.

'Is that them?' the middle-aged observer asked.

His pockmarked companion nodded. 'I think so. I'm sure it's the same man. Harder to tell about the women, but I think so.'

'That saves us the trouble of looking for them, then. Follow them, Mischa. See if you can find out who they are.'

'Could it have dematerialised on its own?' Liz asked, staring at the flattened snow where the TARDIS had landed the previous day.

The Doctor shook his head. 'No, and no one else could have got in, either.'

'Perhaps it slid down the bank and into the river,' Jo suggested.

The Doctor gestured down to the frozen Neva. 'Wouldn't it have made a rather large hole in the ice?' He shook his head, and knelt beside some tyre-tracks in the slush. 'Look at these. Some kind of vehicle stopped here, and men got out.'

'And took away the TARDIS?' Liz deduced.

The Doctor nodded. 'Exactly. Stole it, to be precise.'

'But why? I mean, they couldn't have known what it was, could they?'

'That isn't very likely,' the Doctor admitted.

Liz sighed, and Jo couldn't blame her. Standing around here talking about the problem wouldn't get anything done to solve it. 'The first thing to do, then,' Liz said, 'is report it stolen. There can't be too many British police boxes in the middle of Russia.'

The Doctor rubbed at the back of his neck, as if trying to ease away the predicament. 'Yes, I suppose you're right, Liz.'

'I'll go with you,' Jo said quickly.

'And we should extend our stay at the Astoria,' Liz said. Jo was relieved; she had no intention of being left out on the streets in these temperatures, especially while there was a swanky hotel to be had at sixty-year-old prices.

The Doctor nodded. 'Police headquarters isn't that far away – we should go there now.' The two women looked at each other, shivering slightly despite their coats, but the Doctor was already marching along past the southern wall of the city zoo. They hurried to keep up.

The police headquarters was a large, buff-coloured building at the riverside end of Kronversky Prospekt. Opposite it, a grey swathe of the Neva cut across the grounds of the zoo, and the threatening mass of the Peter and Paul fortress jutted out of the frozen water.

A uniformed desk sergeant was taking complaints in the main hall inside, though most people in here seemed to be men in identical plain clothes. That, Jo thought, was always a bad sign, and she wondered vaguely whether the KGB existed yet, though she was reasonably sure it was founded

18

after the Revolution.

'What is it?' the sergeant asked without interest.

'I'd like to report a theft,' the Doctor said sharply. 'In fact, from just along the road there.'

'What was stolen?'

'Yes, well, that's rather difficult to explain… A large blue box about eight feet high and four feet on each side, with a lamp on top.'

The sergeant stared. 'Are you the guests at the Astoria?' he asked.

'That is correct,' the Doctor replied. He went on to explain, 'We're travellers – somewhat out of our way, I'll admit.'

'Travellers? Gypsies,' the sergeant growled, in the sort of tone Jo associated with skinheads saying 'nigger' or 'Paki'.

The Doctor glared at him. 'We are perfectly innocent travellers, who –'

'What is happening?' a new voice demanded. This voice was female, but stern and commanding. A woman approached from the stairs, buttoning up her overcoat in preparation for going outside. The woman was only a little taller than Jo, and thickset, her tied-back hair giving her an appearance of severity. In spite of that, something about the depth of her blue eyes, the slimness of her nose and the fullness of her cheeks carried with them the visible echo of former beauty. 'These do not look like gypsies from the islands.'

'Indeed not, madam,' the Doctor agreed, turning on the charm. He bowed slightly. 'My companions and I were travelling, and some of our property has been stolen.'

'You are English?'

'We came from England, yes. I'm the Doctor, and these are

19

my travelling companions. Miss Josephine Grant is my secretary, and Professor Elizabeth Shaw is a scientist from Cambridge.'

'Anya Vyrubova. Do you expect me to believe that you just happened to be in the area, or are you here by invitation?'

The Doctor's eyes glinted. 'Bertie Stopford is an old friend of mine. In fact we're members of the same club in London.'

The woman nodded thoughtfully. 'Ah, and you were on your way to visit him to discuss the progress of the war?'

'Yes,' the Doctor said quickly. 'Our car has broken down – stuck in the snow, to be precise. Rather than stay in the car and possibly freeze before morning, we thought it would be better to seek shelter and find alternative transport in the morning.'

'Understandable, but foolish,' Anya replied. 'There are still two-legged wolves in the city just like the four-legged ones outside.'

'Forgive me for asking,' the Doctor went on, 'but are you the same Anya Vyrubova who attends the Empress?'

'Yes. Why do you ask?'

'Perhaps you can help us find our property. If the Empress would pass the word to her soldiers around the city, to look for this, er, diplomatic cargo... And we certainly can't leave without it.'

Anya's eyes narrowed, and at first Jo thought she was going to ask more questions. She herself wondered who this Bertie Stopford was, and how the Doctor knew about him.

'Very well,' the woman said at last. 'I will telephone the Honourable Mr Stopford and check that you and he really do know each other.'

Once they were back at their suite at the Astoria, Jo began to relax. It was just so good to be back inside in the warmth again. 'That was a stroke of luck,' Liz was saying to the Doctor, 'knowing that the Honourable Bertie Stopford was the British Ambassador here.' Not that there was anything unusual in the Doctor seeming to know something about everything.

'Well, not exactly,' the Doctor admitted. 'Lethbridge-Stewart happened to mention it, before you joined UNIT.'

In a narrow corridor that passed between the two rooms, Mischa considered what he had just heard, and slipped quietly away.

The Doctor's statement surprised Jo. She hadn't thought the Brigadier was much of a history buff. Except for military history, at least. 'The Brigadier? But how could he know?'

'Because his grandfather worked with Stopford in Military Intelligence just before and during the First World War, up until the Revolution.'

Jo shuddered. She didn't really know much about the Russian Revolution, beyond the fact that it was a rather bloody affair. 'Well, I hope we're not going to get caught up in the Revolution.' In fact, she reflected, that was quite an understatement.

'Don't worry, Jo. According to the newspaper here, we're a good couple of months too early for that.'

Jo was relieved, but then looked at the paper, which had a date of December 12th on it. 'But I thought the Russian Revolution was in October. I've seen all those big parades on the television news.'

'That's a common mistake. In October the Bolsheviks overthrew the provisional government set up by the people's revolution in February. Or will do, rather.'

Jo understood that confusion quite easily. These things hadn't happened yet, but they also had. 'I don't know how you keep track of it all,' she said.

The Doctor beamed at her. 'Practice!'

Alexandra Fydorovna, wife of Tsar Nicholas II and Empress of All Russia, didn't wince in the slightest as the needle found its way into the vein in her arm. Having been trained as a nurse, as part of her duty to help the people of Russia during the war, she knew what she was doing. She didn't like to look as she pressed the plunger, though, and instead looked out across the snow-clad dawn.

Outside, the lawns were carpeted with beautiful unbroken snow, amidst which statues and fountains were dotted. The fountains weren't running at this time of year, of course, but they still made impressive pieces of art. Through a curtain of trees, she could see an enormous palace, which ran for almost a quarter of a mile, with curved stables arcing in behind the impossibly lavish façade. The pristine white columns stood out against alternating stretches of maroon and sky-blue walls of the Catherine Palace. Alexandra had long since become used to that sight, but it still made her happy.

For Alexandra, it was always the crowd of nurses milling around the wooden-walled ambulances parked outside which caught her attention. They were the flipside of the coin that was a soldier's lot. As in so many countries, young men marched off to the front lines in neat ranks heralded by stirring martial music. And in return they came back in tattered rags, heralded by moans of interminable pain that chilled the blood.

The wounded and their care were a heavy burden, but one which Alexandra was willing to bear if it kept her beloved husband's people from the death of the soul that defeat would bring. Alexandra had no love for the war, any more than Nicholas did, but she had no intention of allowing her son to become the ruler of a defeated Russia.

Of course, she wished that the war was not against her German homeland, but it wasn't her choice. Her brother, Ernest, was among the leaders of the German military, and her sister was a member of the British royal family. Some nights, especially when Nicholas was off directing the war, the prospect of her loved ones fighting each other drove her to despair.

When the depression took her, it threatened to rob her of her focus and her confidence. The mild cocaine solution helped that, for a while, as it dulled any other pain in the body.

She looked up as Anya entered the bedroom. Even at this hour, Anya was impeccably dressed in a suit that would have needed only some rank insignia to be turned into a military uniform. Alix still didn't quite know what to make of Anya. She had once thought the woman was her husband's lover, but that had been a mistake and her loyalty was unquestioned. Alix would simply have been happier if she knew *why* Anya was so loyal. People never really gave of themselves without wanting something in return.

'Did you call Ambassador Stopford about these strangers you mentioned?'

'Yes, Majesty,' Anya replied. She looked troubled about something. 'The British Embassy says that their Ambassador will vouch that the Doctor, as he calls himself, and the two women are who they say they are.'

'You sound unsure, Anya. Did they say anything else?'

'No, but... They did not seem very interested in answering my questions until I mentioned that the Doctor spoke of a Lethbridge-Stewart. Then they vouched for these people.'

Alix shrugged. 'And?'

'The Doctor did not speak of this man when he was found. One of the guards overheard him speaking to one of the women. That suggests that they hoped to keep their links to "Lethbridge-Stewart" a secret from us. If they have one secret, then how many others?'

Alix suppressed a smile. 'You have a very devious mind, Anya. It is most likely that they simply didn't think it was worth mentioning. But it's better to be safe than sorry. As British envoys travelling abroad in time of war, they must be... protected.'

Anya smiled, showing the merest hint of her former beauty. 'I will see to it.'

'Good. Also arrange an audience for them later this morning. If they are acquainted with English society they may know Alice, and it would cheer me to hear some news of her.' Alix exchanged letters with her sister in Britain regularly, as well as with her brother in Germany, but the mail was slow, and conversation with these people might help ease her over the time between letters.

What with that prospect, and the effect of her... medication, it looked like being a fine day.

Chapter Three

Liz had woken up later than her travelling companions the next morning. Though she knew there was no reason for it, she felt a momentary pang of jealousy when she saw Jo and the Doctor chatting.

When the two of them had come to Cambridge to invite Liz along on the Doctor's first post-exile trip, she would have taken the blonde girl in the flared dungarees and turtleneck for a student. She had that slightly excitable look of the sort of person who spent more time at the various action and pressure groups attached to the student union than at lectures. The Doctor, of course, hadn't really changed. His hair was a little longer, but he still had the same eyes, youthful and sparkling. She remembered him always wearing black jackets, but here today he had a double-breasted burgundy velvet smoking jacket over the inevitable frilly shirt.

She knew the reason why that green-eyed monster was prowling about. Jo was her own successor, and part of her was already slipping back into thinking that it was she who should be discussing plans with the Doctor, and helping him complete whatever the assignment was. Old habits, however uncomfortable they could be, died hard.

It was doubly foolish, considering that there was no job to do here; they were simply visitors, or tourists, to the past. She hoped the Doctor or, more importantly, the TARDIS, could fulfil his promise to return her on the afternoon they had left Cambridge. It wouldn't do for her assistant, Singh, to have to report her missing on the very day she was supposed to talk to the appropriations board about money to build a small observatory.

In spite of her concerns, she smiled as she emerged into the sitting room shared by the three bedrooms. 'The Kraken wakes,' the Doctor said. 'Did you sleep well, m'dear?'

'Like the proverbial log. I think it must be something to do with being away from students and budget meetings. They serve a good breakfast here, though.'

'They certainly do,' Jo agreed.

'Most important meal of the day,' the Doctor assured them. 'Skip any meal you like, but not breakfast.'

'The Doctor and I were just talking about where we are,' Jo said. 'In time, I mean.'

'Yes, and I begin to wonder if you failed History, as well as Science,' he replied. From his light tone, he could have been joking, but Liz frowned. 'I hope I'm not being rude, but did you really fail Science?' she asked.

'At O level, yes,' Jo agreed breezily.

Liz blinked, looking at the Doctor. She really didn't want to be rude, and tried to think of a diplomatic way to phrase her concern. She had expected her successor to be from the cream of British science; surely nothing else would be much use to the Doctor? 'I had thought that another scientist…'

'Jo is one of the Brigadier's staff,' the Doctor said smoothly. 'He seemed to think that a UNIT undercover agent will keep me out of trouble.'

Liz understood now: Jo was one of the Brigadier's cloak and dagger types. Or, more likely considering her fashion sense, one of his feather boa and dagger types.

* * *

Interior Minister Protopopov hadn't welcomed the early morning call. The telephone was a relatively recent invention that he could have done without in pre-dawn hours. Even the fact that the caller was Anya hadn't improved his temperament.

The news that three foreigners had arrived at Tsarskoe Selo had silenced his protests. He didn't like this at all. These strangers turned up on the 13th, and he could hardly ignore that inauspicious date. They were most assuredly bad news, as far as he was concerned.

Once Anya had rung off, Protopopov dialled the number of the St Petersburg Ochrana headquarters. He didn't have to worry too much about waking its chief, Viktor Vasiliyev, as he doubted the man ever slept. He was like a vampire, always prowling around in the dark.

The phone was answered quite promptly. 'This is Interior Minister Protopopov. Put me through to Chief Vasiliyev.'

Protopopov wasn't at all surprised that Vasiliyev answered equally promptly. 'Vasiliyev here. What can I do for you, Excellency?' Protopopov could hear the flippancy in the last word. He knew he wasn't popular but, to his mind, that simply meant he was doing his job well. Medicine always tasted bad.

'There are three British envoys newly arrived. A man and two women. The police are aware of their presence, but I want you to keep an eye on them, Viktor. I have a bad feeling about them...'

The sounds of the morning were only slightly muffled by the falling snow as the car that had been sent for them drove Jo, Liz and the Doctor out of St Petersburg. Nobody made any comment at the solo tenor that rose in the frigid air. This voice led to a bass chorus from the members of the Preobrazhensky Regiment as they marched to its cadence. As they did every morning, the soldiers marched past the bronze statue of their founder, Peter the Great.

Elsewhere, the bright red trams gathered a coating of snow in the middle of the streets, since the electricity which powered them had failed yet again under the winter weather. They now formed occasional obstacles, around which the many horse-drawn sledges had to steer carefully.

Lines of sullen women stretched away from shop doors, and this looked more like the image of Russia that Jo was used to from the TV news. Without so much as a word, she imagined she could feel their silent anger at having to bundle themselves up to stand around for bread before Christmas.

Small groups of men were clustered around outside grim factory buildings, carrying banners written in Cyrillic. Over the gentle sound of the car engine, she could hear their singing of the 'Marseillaise'. Jo frowned. 'Why are they singing a French song?'

'To show their discontent, Jo,' the Doctor replied. He pointed at the banners. '"Peace, Bread, and Work" those say. They're not quite revolutionaries yet, but the mood's there. In this decade, French is still the main international language, and a song so closely linked with the French Revolution makes a pretty obvious point.'

'And those men with the notebooks? KGB?'

'The Ochrana, Jo, which amounts to same thing. Secret police, taking names.' The Doctor's voice carried a hint of distaste.

There was a sound of hoofbeats from ahead, and the strikers moved out of the centre of the road. A dozen mounted Cossacks moved down the street at a walking pace, lance butts resting on their stirrups. For all the strikers' obvious apprehension at their passing, the Cossacks ignored them, and jingled past in an orderly fashion.

Viktor Vasiliyev wasn't superstitious, like the Interior Minister, but he did have the incipient paranoia that was a requirement in a chief of the secret police. The only people he didn't suspect of something were the dead, and he wouldn't have put it past them to be up to something if they could.

He had arrived in the wood-panelled coffee lounge at Donons at first light. Even at that time of the morning, he had to dodge the bourgeois coming for breakfast in this most exclusive of St Petersburg restaurants.

Vasiliyev sat in the corner as usual, watching the door, while nervous staff brought him coffee and croissants. He doubted that any of them were guilty of really serious crimes, but the minor ones were enough to keep them wary of him. Some people liked that sort of passive power, but Vasiliyev found it a nuisance as often as it was useful. It was remarkably difficult to get true respect from someone who thought you only wanted to send him to a gallows at Schlusselburg.

A lean man in a neat, dark suit and overcoat entered the lounge, looking around. Vasiliyev beckoned him over. He had planed features and dark brows, but his easy smile dispelled any suggestion that he could ever look sinister. Brushing the wet snow from his trimmed dark hair, he came over and sat opposite Vasiliyev.

'Kristoff – Kit,' Vasiliyev greeted him. 'I have been waiting for you.'

'Not too long, I hope. The trams are stopped again, and I had to walk half the journey.'

Vasiliyev shrugged. 'If I don't have my driver, I sometimes find it faster to just walk than take the trams.' He snapped his fingers at an obsequious waiter and curtly ordered tea.

'I need that,' the man called Kit said thankfully. Vasiliyev was glad to hear the gratitude in his voice; the true professional cultivated such friendships with the smaller, more subconscious rewards. That bred reliance and trust, rather than greed. 'How are things with the Ochrana?'

'Busy.' They always were, of course. When he was young, Vasiliyev might have entertained the possibility that crime and sedition would dry up if you removed enough of their perpetrators, but it wasn't true. The ranks of both the underworld and the politically undesirable were like hydra heads: remove one and two replaced it. If nothing else, it at least made for steady work among the police.

'I'm glad to hear that. Wouldn't want you to get bored.' Kit smiled. 'Your message sounded rather urgent – has something happened?'

'Please, Kit,' Vasiliyev protested. 'It's not right to be so businesslike before we've finished the formalities…'

'Sorry, Viktor. My brain isn't at its best either in the early morning or in the cold. You can imagine that a mixture –'

'Yes, I can imagine easily. I remember being your age.' The other man wasn't that much younger, but Vasiliyev allowed himself the comment on the grounds of rank. 'This is what endless late nights bring you.'

Kit yawned agreeably. 'Two in the morning isn't that late. At least the cognac keeps me warm when I'm alone.'

'That's what I call devotion to duty.'

'Please don't, my father would be horrified if someone

made me sound respectable. I have a family reputation to uphold, you know.' The waiter returned with a samovar of hot tea, and Kit took a cup. 'Have we completed enough formal chit-chat yet? It does have a certain *je ne sais quoi*, but isn't that easy to keep up for long before breakfast...'

Vasiliyev sighed. He had long tried to make this sort of clandestine meeting into an art form of misdirection for observers. If truth be told he quite enjoyed the ritual for its own sake, and was rather depressed when actual work finally caught up with its own trappings. 'I'd like you to check around for me about something.'

'Oh?' Kit sipped his tea with an interested expression.

'There are three British envoys newly arrived.' Kit paused in his sipping. 'Yes, I thought that would interest you.' Vasiliyev tolerated a small amount of what, for want of a better word, he still called espionage. It was simply the way of the world, and he had quickly seen how it could be turned to domestic advantage. 'This morning they reported the theft of some of their property – a large box, what seems to be a "police box".'

'Go on.'

'The descriptions and reports are in here.' Vasiliyev passed an envelope to Kit. He hesitated then, knowing that discussing a breach of security was in itself something that could compound that breach. 'I'm concerned that these three people were able to make their way so far into the country, and bring such a large cargo with them, without being challenged. The time of their arrival is also odd.'

'And you'd like me to find out whether they are who they say they are –'

'Or have an ulterior motive.' Vasiliyev sat back. 'We're sure they're not assassins, but at the very least they've shown up a gap in the border patrols, and I'd like to be sure that this is not something they will lead others to exploit.'

The man called Kit pocketed the envelope without looking at the contents. 'I'll keep my ear to the ground.'

Vasiliyev smiled. 'That's what you do best, and that's why I called for you.'

'Meet me at the Errant Dog at four. You're buying.' With that, Kit rose and buttoned up his coat.

'If you have good information for me,' Vasiliyev corrected. 'If not, the food and drink go on your bill.'

Kit sighed. 'Somebody ought to tell you that gambling on duty is illegal in most police forces, Viktor.' With a mock salute, he left.

Vasiliyev shook his head in wonder that any government would allow its staff members to be so easily swayed. Still, their loss was his gain.

The car had brought the Doctor, Liz and Jo out of the city, and through a small village before turning into a huge snow-covered park. A set of Chinese pagodas could be seen in the distance, but the car drove past them. Eight or nine buildings were arranged in a question-mark layout around a central pagoda.

'A Chinese village?' Jo wondered aloud.

The Doctor shook his head. 'Catherine the Great had these decorative follies turned into homes for runaway serfs.' The car had already left the pagoda behind, and drove past an enormous palace, which ran for almost a quarter of a mile, with curved stables arcing in behind the impossibly lavish façade. Pristine white columns stood out against alternating stretches of maroon and sky-blue walls. Jo had never seen anything quite like it, and thought it made

Buckingham Palace look like a lodge cottage.

The palace to which the car eventually pulled up was only about half the size, though no less impressive. Rows of trees divided the expansive gardens of each palace from the other, though they were mostly skeletal guardians, having lost their leaves for the winter.

As they emerged from the car, the palace door opened and Anya emerged. 'I shall escort you to your audience with the Empress. If you will follow me?'

Anya led the Doctor, Liz and Jo to a room decked out in lavender, pink and mauve. The wallpaper and upholstery were of matching chintz, and the walls were covered in small framed prints of landscapes. Vases of flowers filled the room, and Jo wondered where they got them at this time of year.

The Empress, wrapped in layers of nursing uniform, was sitting comfortably in a large armchair. Jo could see that she had also clearly been beautiful; but where Anya had become stout, the Empress had taken on an icy and hard-bitten air. She was prematurely aged, too, her skin dry and tight. Determined eyes looked out of a pale face that Jo thought would edge towards gauntness if she wasn't careful. Together with the uniform that left only her hands and face showing, she resembled nothing so much as a hardened mother superior at a convent school.

'Your Majesty,' Anya began. 'May I present the visitors from Britain. Miss Josephine Grant, Professor Elizabeth Shaw, and Doctor John Smith.' Liz tried hard not to smile as the Doctor stepped forward and kissed the Empress's hand gravely.

'We are at your service, Your Majesty,' the Doctor said. 'This is an unexpected honour.'

'Unexpected for us too,' Alix said drily. 'Normally such

33

visits are arranged well in advance.'

'As I explained yesterday, we were simply travelling, and became lost. When we took residence at the Astoria overnight, our property was stolen.'

'Where were you on your way to?'

'Irkutsk.'

Alix laughed. 'Irkutsk. In the dead of winter? You set yourselves a difficult task.'

'Purely out of scientific curiosity. Crossing Siberia in winter is a logistical and engineering problem.'

Alix considered. 'And you like problems?'

'Well, I wouldn't have put it quite those terms, Your Majesty, but I enjoy a challenge.'

Alix maintained her poker face. 'I see. And Miss Shaw is a professor?'

'From Cambridge, Your Majesty,' Liz said. She realised that female scientists must be rarer in 1916 than the 1970s, and hurriedly added, 'With all the men being at the war...'

Alix's face cleared a little. 'Of course. The war...'

'I quite understand,' the Doctor said, more gently than usual. 'This war can't be easy for you, with a sister in England and a brother in Germany.'

A spark flashed in Alix's eyes, though Jo couldn't immediately tell whether it was good or bad. 'You know my sister?'

'I have had the pleasure of meeting the Princess Alice on one or two occasions, yes.'

For the first time since they entered the room, Alix smiled. 'Sit down, all of you. Anya, have some tea brought in.' She turned back to the Doctor as he sat on a nearby chair. 'Tell me, what news is there of Alice?'

* * *

34

Anya had served the tea as the Empress chatted with the three newcomers. She listened intently to every word, not out of a desire to eavesdrop, but as part of her duty to beware of any possible threat.

For the most part, it was the Doctor who had spoken for the new arrivals, telling Alix about recent developments in Britain, and the interest he and his companions had in the Russian landscape. Though Alix's expression rarely changed that much, Anya could tell that she was quite happy with her visitors. Anya was glad of that. Nothing pleased her more than keeping the Empress happy.

Alix broke off from her conversation to call Anya over. The Doctor and his companions withdrew to a tactful distance as the Empress gave Anya her orders. 'Have the description of the Doctor's stolen property passed to the Guard. Arrange accommodation for the Doctor and his friends in the city.'

'The Astoria should have a suitable suite free –'

Alix shook her head. 'No. I will not have friends of my sister waste any more of their money staying amongst the whores and playboys at the Astoria. Give them a suite at the Winter Palace.'

Anya glowered slightly at the thought of compromising her mistress's security. 'Is that wise?' She lowered her voice, glancing at the three visitors, who were busily and appreciatively studying the landscape outside. 'They may yet be spies or assassins with hostile intent…' Having looked into their eyes, Anya didn't actually believe that herself. But she did believe it was her duty to beware of any possible threat to her Tsar and Tsarina.

'Then it will be easier for the guard to observe them when they are close, than it would be if they were staying elsewhere. And they will pose no extra threat to myself or the girls, while we are out here.'

That was true enough, Anya saw. Keep your friends close, and your enemies closer… an old saying, but old sayings were generally the wisest ones. By definition they had to be, or they would never have been remembered for so long. 'I'll see to it.'

The Empress beckoned the Doctor to rejoin her, and acquainted him with the arrangements.

'That's most kind of you, Your Majesty,' the Doctor said gravely.

'It is nothing,' Alix responded. 'But I regret that I must leave you now. I have business to attend to. As you may have noticed, most of the buildings here at Tsarskoe Selo have been converted into hospitals for the war effort, and I and my daughters have nursing duties.'

'Setting a fine example,' the Doctor said approvingly. 'If only others were as willing to get their hands dirty…'

'And if only others were as willing as you to understand. We may speak again later in the week.'

Once the visitors were gone, Alix moved to her writing desk. It was true that before long she would have to join her daughters Tatiana and Olga on duty in the Catherine Palace. Many disliked her practical approach, thinking their leaders should be above the blood, but Alix ignored them. Just as Nicholas had gone to take personal charge of the headquarters at Mogilev, so she must show that she was willing to do her part.

In truth, she also felt that it helped to take her mind off the absence of Alexei. Her little boy was staying with his father at Mogilev, surrounded by the best protection possible, but still it troubled her. His bleeding could be triggered by the slightest bump, and she would not be there to look after him herself. That made her feel guilty; how could she look after others if not her own son?

Even her dearest friend, Grigory, could not get to Mogilev in time if anything happened. She could only pray that there would be no need. But she could also remind her friend that she appreciated his help. His holiness made his prayers undoubtedly more effective than her own, and she would feel better knowing that she and Alexei were in his thoughts.

My Beloved, unforgettable teacher, redeemer and mentor, she wrote. She certainly didn't want him to get the impression that she listened to any other staretz. Only the one who had saved her son had proved his worth in doing so. And these holy men were always open to ritual flattery.

How tiresome it is without you, she continued. *My soul is quiet and I relax only when you, my teacher, are sitting beside me. I kiss your hands and lean my head on your blessed shoulder.*

He wasn't quite a pope or archbishop, but nevertheless Alexandra could see the power that God had imbued him with.

Oh, how light do I feel then. I only wish one thing: to fall asleep for ever on your shoulders and in your arms. What happiness to feel your presence near me.

Spiritual support was desperately lacking in the palace these days, and she had no desire to let that blessed protection for her son fade away. It was better to be safe than sorry where this faith was concerned.

Where are you? Where have you gone? Oh, I am so sad

and my heart is longing. Will you soon be again close to me? Come quickly, I am waiting for you and I am tormenting myself for you.

Well, she told herself, she was no flagellant, but the reference would surely display her religious loyalties.

I am asking for your Holy Blessing and I am kissing your blessed hands.

Since he wore no bishop's ring, this was the best compliment she could think of, to praise his abilities. *I love you for ever.*

The car had now brought the time travellers back not to the Astoria, but to Dvortsovaya Square, and passed though a huge archway set into a sprawling four-storey palace that was every bit as impressive as the Catherine Palace they had seen at Tsarskoe Selo.

Like that palace, this one had crisp white pillars and window frames, with gilt highlights, against a light sky blue background all along its quarter-mile length. Something about it all reminded Jo of icing sugar, and she felt it was very much like being driven into an enormously complex wedding cake.

'Part of the palace here has also become a hospital,' Anya said from the front passenger seat. 'We will put you in a suite at the top floor, in ambassadorial suites furthest from the hospital area.' Jo was quite relieved to hear that.

Anya twisted round in the seat to face the Doctor. 'The Imperial Guard has been given the description of your missing property. If it's still in the city, we will find it. In the meantime, the city is yours to explore.'

Empress Alexandra had gone off to her nursing duties in

the Catherine Palace, but the mauve boudoir didn't remain empty for long.

The door opened silently, and a man in a Guard's uniform slipped inside. Working quietly and carefully, he searched the room, until he found the letter to Rasputin in a locked drawer of the writing desk.

He almost gasped when he saw its contents. His masters would be delighted with this finding, and that made him feel a little better about an act which was surely treasonous.

Knowing exactly where his duty lay, the man quickly folded up the letter, and slid it into a pocket. Then he relocked the drawer, and left the room as stealthily as he had entered it.

Chapter Four

The snow-capped Urals overlooked Pokrovskoe from the west with lofty disdain, Grigory Efimovitch Rasputin had always felt. Even in summer, when the heat turned the air to dust and caused shimmering haze on the horizon, their peaks remained aloof and frosted.

Much of his homeland was boggy, as three rivers cut their way through the land. Stands of fir trees grew up from some parts of the boglands, which froze solid in the eight-month winter, and unleashed clouds of accursed mosquitoes and blackflies in the brief and dusty summer. Forests stretched from horizon to horizon, until they got too far north for any tree to survive the cold.

Rasputin remembered the steamers and barges that plied their way along the Tobol, all the way to the Caspian. As a boy, he used to watch them from the banks upon which Pokrovskoe was built. The sailors were all hardy men, fond of drink and women, either of which could persuade them to tell of the far off places they had been, like Armenia, or Turkey.

Rasputin had often wondered what it would be like to go there, where the maidens were duskier. At least it would get him away from his father, Efimy. Sharing an izba with that violent drunk was very wearing on Grigory's patience, perhaps because there was only room for one violent drunk in the family, and not both of them.

The izba was a single-storey log cabin, very simply built. However, the window-frames were carved very ornately. In winter the family slept in the heat of the tiled stove. In one corner were the family icons, lit by candles. Visitors first paid their respects to the icons before kissing the master of the house, and Rasputin didn't envy them that.

Most of the villagers had a couple of horses, some chickens, geese or maybe one pig or cow in a bare fenced yard. In winter the animals were brought indoors, and spread their fleas throughout the house. But Rasputin hadn't minded that, for the simple reason that he knew no other life at the time. It was simply the way things were.

Yet for all its faults, he would almost prefer to be living in such a place now. He hated the dirt of the city. Natural, God-given dirt like earth and dung was one thing, but he loathed the artificial dirt that clogged St Petersburg. The soot, and the oil, and all that was discarded.

Thinking of the dirt reminded him of how he used to love the eves of holy days. Then, the whole village would steam out the grime in the communal bathhouse, and Rasputin would try to peek in at the women's session. On the next day they would drink, dance and sing. Rasputin preferred those occasions when he managed to slip away with a girl, to the ones where his father got quick with his fists.

Governments always tried to curb the drinking, but it never worked. The villagers hated officials and tax collectors, and took no notice of their attempts to enforce depressing laws. None of them blamed the Tsar, though. It was generally considered that their 'Little Father' would surely understand a man's problems if he could talk to him without corrupt officials getting in the way, and Rasputin had discovered that this belief was correct. The Tsar himself was a fine and reasonable man; it was those self-serving incompetents under him who did the damage.

Rasputin enjoyed watching them panic, falling from grace when the Empress sided with him against them. On some days, he even let himself think that his agreements were what pushed them off. Funnier still, that there were people – generally those incompetents who wisely feared for their own positions – who truly believed that he had power over them. He enjoyed rubbing their noses in their foolishness.

It had not always been pleasant in Pokrovskoe. Apart from fighting with his father, he had enemies even there. Those enemies had struck at his head and his heart, but still he survived.

He fell to the ground. Kartashev, another farmer, had hit him with a pitchfork for stealing a fence to pay for vodka. His head spun in pain, but it couldn't distract him from the agony erupting in his stomach. He knew without looking down that the woman Gusyeva's knife would be protruding there…

Around him, the simple buildings of Pokrovskoe blurred, merging into other walls, or fading into the darkness of the morning in his bedroom. He could feel the warmth from the bodies of the two pretty girls who slept on either side of him, wrapped up in his red fox-fur bedspread. He had resisted the temptation of their charms, and that pleased him. It had been a test of character and willpower, which he felt he had passed.

Of course this meant they had not been purified by his embrace, but there was always time for that. He would leave a note for them to return for that tonight.

Soon his sister, Matriona, would serve his scalding-hot tea before he went to church for prayers, so Rasputin pulled on a dressing gown, and wandered out into the study. His secretary, Aaron Simanovich, was there already, working on some paperwork or other.

'Father Grigory,' the diminutive man said. 'Morning.'

'And the light was good,' Rasputin murmured. 'Is there any mail today?'

'No, but Anya called. She said she had to come into the Winter Palace today, and that she could drive you out to Tsarskoe Selo on her way back if you like.'

Rasputin smiled. Anya was always ready to serve both himself and the Tsarina. 'Very well. I shall go after morning prayers.'

The Winter Palace was very much like Liz had imagined it. She had made one or two academic trips to Russia before, and was used to the impressive buildings that were used as museums there. This complex had much the same air, its marbled halls filled with priceless treasures from Europe and the Near East.

The palace was actually built connected to the Hermitage, a building designed as a museum in Catherine the Great's time, but Liz knew that treasures from other parts of the palace must have been moved to this part when the rest of it was converted into a hospital for wounded officers.

Anya found her in the Malachite Room, on the first floor, which was far too sumptuous to be converted into a part of the hospital. The fireplace, tabletops and pilasters were all made of malachite, and there was a huge and comfortable divan to one side. It was odd being here, knowing that this was the room where the Provisional Government would meet for a while prior to the October Revolution.

Though Liz had visited such places before, being in a historic room before its place in history was assured somehow felt different to being there after the fact. For one thing it made her wonder how the furnishings could survive such troubled times. She supposed it proved the truth of the old French saying that the more things change, the more they stay the same.

'Professor,' Anya said. Liz could sense distrust from Anya, and couldn't really blame her. They were uninvited guests, after all, and that had to be a worry in time of war and civil unrest. 'I have received a telephone call from the Academy of Sciences. Academician Kuznetzov wishes to come and meet you. Apparently you and he work in similar fields and have interests in common. Some of his past research results might reward your attention, also. When I mentioned that you had been travelling to the Tunguska region, he told me he has been there too, and would like to compare notes.'

'Thank you,' Liz said. 'I'm sure I'll be honoured.' More than honoured, she'd be fascinated. She had always thought that Leonid Kulik was the first to visit the site of the Tunguska blast but, with a war on, who was to say someone else hadn't been, and died before they could tell anyone. She'd been disappointed to be off course, but she might yet learn something about the destination she had selected for her trip in the TARDIS, even if it was only second-hand. She supposed it would be the next best thing.

There was no time like the present, Liz thought wryly, and accompanied Anya towards the door. They passed the Doctor and Jo, who were on their way in. The Doctor was chattering away like a tour guide, and had obviously been here before. Or would be, which amounted to the same thing. On seeing Liz, he came over to her, still volubly expanding on the historical beauties of their surroundings. After shifting impatiently in place for a few moments Anya's shoulders spread and relaxed a trifle in the nearest she'd ever come to a shrug. 'I shall go and see if Academician Kuznetzov has arrived,' she announced rather stiffly, and strode off.

When she was safely out of earshot, the Doctor asked Liz, 'Well, now, what do you think of your first trip through time?'

'It sounds odd, I know,' she said, 'but this doesn't *feel* like the past.'

'Feel like the past?' the Doctor echoed. 'In what way?'

'Oh, I don't know exactly... It's just that I kind of expected to feel more... out of place. I mean, I haven't even been born yet!'

The Doctor chuckled slightly. 'I see what you mean. You thought it'd feel like a dream, or some dangerous experiment?'

'Well, yes, I suppose so.'

'The TARDIS isn't just projecting you into the past, you know. It brought you here just like any other vehicle could bring you to any other place.'

'I imagine you must get used to it eventually.'

Along the corridor a click of assertive heels announced the return of Anya Vyrubova. The Doctor simply smiled and answered, 'Eventually, yes.' Then smoothly switching gear to say, 'I gather you have an appointment soon?'

Liz nodded. 'With an Academician Kuznetzov. Apparently his expertise lies in a similar field to mine, and I'm told he has actually visited Tunguska. So something might come of this after all.'

'He's visited the site?' the Doctor asked disbelievingly.

'Yes.' Surprisingly, it was Anya who had answered. 'The Academy has a train at Varshavski Voksal which he took on an expedition to Irkutsk recently.' She turned back to Liz. 'This way, please.'

A man in an expensive tailored coat was waiting for them as they descended into the huge entrance hall. He resisted the fashion for full beards, and settled for having a walrus-like handlebar moustache squatting under his pointed nose. Hair the colour of roadside snow curled around his head, and his chin was rather heavy.

Anya launched straight into the introductions. 'Academician, this is Professor Elizabeth Shaw, from Cambridge. As a scientist and astronomer, she is particularly interested in the Siberian explosion eight years ago. And this is the Doctor, and Miss Grant.'

'Ah, I see.' The Academician seemed taken slightly off his guard.

'I mentioned to Professor Shaw that you had been in the Tunguska area a few months ago.'

Liz nodded. 'I'd be very interested to know whether you made any discoveries there that might lead to discovering precisely what the cause of the blast was.'

Kuznetzov still looked rather fazed. Pulling himself together, he asked, 'So you are a professor? I had not realised the extent of your scholarly attainment.'

Liz was momentarily puzzled, but then realised that Kuznetzov probably hadn't seen a female scientist before, let alone a full professor. She resorted to what was becoming a useful formula: 'Yes... with all the men off to the war...'

Kuznetzov held up a hand. 'Of course, I understand. I should have realised that at once.' He looked over at the other time travellers. 'And what of you, Doctor?' Kuznetzov asked. 'Are you a scientist too?'

'That's right,' the Doctor said bluntly.

'Specialising in what field?'

'Oh, every field. Well, many fields, anyway. And what about you?' the Doctor continued. 'What's your speciality?'

'Ballistics,' Kuznetzov said absently. 'Something of a martial discipline, I'm afraid, but these days we're encouraged to specialise in things that will aid the war effort.'

'That's hardly surprising,' the Doctor said understandingly, 'given the circumstances.'

Kuznetzov smiled. 'Of course, I'd prefer a less warlike area of study. That's why I'm so fascinated by your friend Miss Shaw. Meteors and meteorites are a field of study that I can understand, given the similarity of our fields.'

'You both study trajectories and impact effects.'

'Precisely,' Kuznetzov agreed warmly. 'But we must go now – I have a tour arranged. I trust you won't object?' he added, as he opened the door and motioned Liz to his waiting car.

'Not at all,' the Doctor said. 'I have to help with a search for some missing property of mine.'

'The city gets less safe every year,' Kuznetzov said sadly. He nodded to the Doctor. 'I hope you find your box.'

The Doctor looked up, his head tilted, as Kuznetzov left, ushered out with Liz by the attentive Anya. 'I didn't say that my property was a box...'

'Well, it's a reasonable guess,' Jo pointed out. 'If a scientist is travelling with his equipment, he's bound to keep it in something – probably a box. I suppose that's what he assumed.'

The Doctor frowned. 'I suppose it's possible, but I know history.' He put his hands on his hips, a move Jo recognised as heralding a lecture. 'The first person to visit that site was a man called Leonid Kulik, in 1921.'

Jo canted her head. 'You mean Kuznetzov lied?'

'That's right. Also, his train is at Varshavski Voksal – Warsaw Station. That station only services trains running westward. If it really ran between here and Irkutsk, it would be at Moscow Station.'

'Voksal? Sounds like Vauxhall Station, back in London.'

'That's right, Jo. Russia took that as their word for "railway station".'

'But wait a minute... This is Russia before the Revolution, right?' The Doctor nodded, and Jo went on. 'So, maybe this Kuznetzov *did* go to Tunguska, but got killed in the Revolution, before he could tell anybody about his discoveries, or write them down.'

The Doctor looked dubious, but considered it. 'I suppose it's just about possible...'

'But if not, then what would he want to talk to Liz about?'

'Exactly.'

Chapter Five

Across the street the watching man known as Kit saw Academician Kuznetzov emerge from the Winter Palace with a woman he didn't recognise. Her description matched that of one of the new arrivals from England. He considered following them, but decided against it. The man would be the leader, and he was still inside. He was in for a further surprise, as Grigory Rasputin walked around the corner. Other pedestrians gave him a wide berth.

Kit wondered if Rasputin had been summoned by the new man. If so, he had certainly wasted no time. Rasputin normally went to the public baths after church, and didn't drag himself along to a palace until after lunch, when his hangover had cleared enough to be unnoticed by the Empress.

He hoped that, whatever happened, the Doctor would come out of the palace before long. It was far too cold a day to stand around on street corners.

The Doctor and Jo had started back up to the Malachite Room after Liz and Kuznetzov had left, but had hardly gone more than a few paces when they heard someone else enter the building. Jo looked round, hearing the Doctor mutter some sort of old alien exclamation.

'What's wrong?'

'Nothing exactly wrong, Jo – I'm just surprised to see *him* here.'

'Who?'

The Doctor nodded to the newcomer, now being

effusively greeted by Anya. Keeping his voice low, he said, 'That, my dear, is one of the most notorious figures in your planet's history. Grigory Efimovitch Rasputin.'

Jo wasn't quite sure what to expect Rasputin to be like. All she really knew of him was from the movies of his life, and she was more or less expecting a suave and demonic Christopher Lee to walk in.

When Rasputin did step into the hall, she was surprised that he was only of average height, perhaps an inch or two shorter than the Empress herself. His broad-shouldered frame was strongly built, though. His long lank hair was tied back and an equally unkempt beard hung from his thin lips. Above his large nose, blue-grey eyes gazed piercingly back at her, with almost enough physical presence to make her flinch.

For a moment, his eyes seemed to drill into her soul, and she was reminded of the way the Master sometimes considered people, but then she saw that it was more like he was mentally undressing her. Though that was irritating, it was also slightly relieving – it was such a human failing.

She recalled the film she'd seen, and the song she'd heard. She might have failed history as well as science, but she still knew of the black-hearted Rasputin who was so brutally murdered. Somewhere around the time of the Revolution, wasn't it?

While her thoughts whirled, Rasputin had switched his gaze on to the Doctor, who seemed singularly unfazed by the attention. After a frozen moment, Rasputin turned back to Anya, who led him out to the car.

A shiver tingled its way along Jo's spine. In a way, she had hoped to escape his notice, and yet being noticed by such a well-known historical personage was somehow exciting.

She was not just a ghost of the future, or a vision, but a real person from his future. She suddenly felt more overwhelmed by the TARDIS's power than she ever had on a trip to the future or a different planet.

Rasputin was amused by the younger girl's reaction – like so many of the gentler classes, she feared him. The other two were more of a mystery; the woman he had passed on the steps had seemed wary, and the man wasn't reacting much at all.

Rasputin wondered what sort of man would have no particular reaction to meeting such a noteworthy – or infamous – person such as himself. He would have expected either fascination, fear, hatred... something. In a way, the white-haired man's lack of reaction was in itself unusual, and Rasputin wondered what he meant to convey by it.

Anya had always felt comfortable in the presence of Rasputin. When her husband had died, it was Rasputin's support that kept her sane. They had a lot in common, not least their devotion to the Tsar and Tsarina. She knew that satirists said he was Alix's lover, but she also knew that wasn't the case. Since she had once been accused of being the lover of both the Tsar and Rasputin, she understood the strain he must be under.

Once in the car, Anya continued another train of thought, one that seemed to be occupying her mind more and more frequently.

'What do you make of this Doctor, now you have seen him?' she asked her companion. She had kept Rasputin up to date with the recent incursion by these mysterious foreigners.

Rasputin considered. 'His face and white hair are indeed signs of age, and from what you have told me of his words, he speaks with what seems to be much accumulated wisdom. And yet... he did not appear to have lost any of the fire of youth. It still burned brightly in his eyes. His eyes show me his soul, Anya. There is steel there, and I do not doubt he can be dangerous to those who oppose him, but I also sense that he is a good man. Certainly he can bear the Tsar and Tsarina no ill-will.'

'I sense a "but".'

'Not exactly. The younger girl –'

'Josephine Grant.'

'Josephine,' Rasputin said slowly. 'I should like to meet her.'

Anya gave him a sidelong look. 'Taken your fancy, has she?'

Rasputin grinned. 'Both the women have. But there is something else about her. I saw her eyes when she first saw me. She looked as if she was having a premonition, a vision.'

'Of what?'

Rasputin sighed impatiently. 'How in damnation should I know? But I would like to ask her about it...'

'And hope that she will open her legs for you at the same time?'

'There's plenty of time for that,' he answered.

'Rasputin had converted the cellar room of their house in Pokrovskoe into a little chapel. There, he would preside over rituals of the Khlysty, his congregation beating each other before they fell upon each other for...' Kuznetzov's voice trailed away as he sought the correct words. From what he had seen of this English woman of science, she did not seem likely to an attack of the vapours, but you could never tell with the fair sex. He cleared his throat and continued. 'For – please excuse the indelicacy, my dear Professor – for acts of an unnatural nature.'

Having negotiated this tricky piece of the narrative, he went on with more confidence. 'By committing sin, then confessing it, they believe they can gain true forgiveness and become closer to God. The local priest of Pokrovskoe made charges about him to the Bishop of Tobolsk, over these things.' Kuznetzov didn't bother to mention that the Bishop had, upon investigation, declared the charges false. Everyone knew there was no smoke without fire, and how did one even know that the Bishop wasn't Khlysty himself?

'How did he get that idea in any case?' Liz asked, drawing her eyes away from the mural of the Battle of Poltava, which was on the upper landing of the Academy of Science's grand staircase.

'He picked it up, along with some thoughts of the Skopsty, at Verkhoturye Monastery when he was sent there instead of prison for stealing a fence.'

'The Skopsty?'

'Another bizarre cult. They think that by prayer and deprivation they can become holy, so then they can't be judged as sinners. Just to be on the safe side, they consider chastity to be the sin of pride.' He smiled faintly. He would have thought that if someone wanted to bed women, he would not become a monk. What could be simpler?

He had brought Liz to the Academy of Sciences, which was directly opposite the old Admiralty building on the other side of the Bolshaya Neva. Next door to it was a quarter-mile-long university building called the Twelve Colleges. Most of that building was devoted to classrooms, and there really wasn't much actual physical science to observe. Kuznetzov had then brought her into the Academy building.

'I certainly didn't like the way he looked at me when he passed us.' In fact, she'd half expected him to make a grab at her. 'I should hardly have been surprised if he had tried to...' Liz tried to imagine the kind of expression acceptable at this time. '...force his attentions upon me.'

'Nor should I. But during daylight you're probably safe.'

Liz laughed. 'You make him sound like some kind of vampire.'

Kuznetzov laughed too. 'He drinks more heavily in the evenings, and his behaviour deteriorates. It wouldn't be the first time he's molested a woman in public.'

'And people still respect him?'

'Not many.' Not many who mattered anyway. The peasants did, because he was one of them, and it amused them to see him cause such a stir among their betters. He had to admit, it sometimes amused him too. But, like others, he felt that something needed to be done.

'"The staretz is he who takes your soul and will and makes them his. When you select your staretz you surrender your will. You give it to him in utter submission, in full renunciation,"' Liz quoted. 'Or so Dostoevesky wrote. Frankly, I imagine you'll be better off without him.'

'Really?' Kuznetzov observed her more closely. An English scientist... She could be a worthwhile addition to Felix's group, as well as offering some answers to questions of his own. He was sure his friends would see the value in that, when he told them... Felix tended not to be impressed by women, though, apart from his mother and his wife Irina, so he wasn't sure whether she would make a good enough impression.

Still, it was better to try and fail than never to try.

'I've been thinking... I have an errand to run to a friend of mine. Would you care to accompany me?'

'A friend?'

'A prince.'

'Yes, I see,' the Doctor said into the telephone. 'Thank you.' He put the receiver down. 'Another interesting coincidence regarding our friend Kuznetzov.'

'Like what?' Jo asked.

'I just telephoned the Academy of Sciences to ask where he had been working most recently. According to them, he's been working on the main guns of the *Aurora* all week.'

That name rang a bell in Jo's memory. 'Isn't that the ship down by –'

'Down by where the TARDIS was. Which means Kuznetzov might easily have seen it from the ship.'

'Then maybe he saw who took it,' Jo said hopefully.

'Precisely. But if he saw something, why not say so?' The Doctor pulled on his checked ulster.

'Where are you going?'

'Varshavski Voksal.' The Doctor settled his cloak on his shoulders. 'To find out more about this "Academician Kuznetzov", such as what he's really up to, starting with his train.'

'Why not the Academy?'

'Because he's there with Liz, remember. You can't be covert right in front of the person you're investigating, can you? I'd like to know where that train has really been – and whether the TARDIS might be on board.'

'Why would it be?'

'Imagine you're a scientist in a country at war. Suddenly you see a box materialise out of thin air. Might you not think it could make a new weapon or transport for your soldiers?' He paused at the door. 'Look, Jo, stay here, would you?'

'Can't I come with you?'

'Not this time, Jo. This is a very large city, and you'd be easily lost. Besides, I need you to do something for me.'

'What?' She hoped it was something worthwhile. If he planned to just keep her out of the fun, she would follow him to wherever he was going, no matter what.

'Call Anya at Tsarskoe Selo. Ask her to give you as much information on Kuznetzov as she can. Press-cuttings, anything.'

'Why?'

'Just in case. What if he saw the TARDIS arrive and recognised it for what it was?'

Jo was confused. 'What, an English police box?'

'No, Jo.' The Doctor looked grimly at her. 'A space-time machine belonging to a Time Lord.'

Chapter Six

From the outside, the Yusupovs' Moika Palace was impressive but still blended in with the style of the buildings that lined the rest of the embankment. Inside, however, it could hold its own in the grandeur stakes against the larger complexes at Tsarskoe Selo.

Liz and Kuznetzov were greeted in the entrance hall by Thesphe, the lanky African butler. A wide staircase led up to a landing, then split in two to double back up to the first floor. An enormous crystal chandelier hung from the stuccoed ceiling.

'This way, please,' Thesphe said, indicating that they should follow him to one side of the staircase. The visitors did as they were bid, and he led them through a maze of corridors and then into a room that seemed to belong in a different building altogether. It was very reminiscent of the Alhambra Palace in Spain. A spectacular mosaic was set into the marble floor, and painted screens divided up the room. Low sandalwood furniture was mixed with huge cushions for sitting on. An onyx fireplace, decorated with arabesques, was set into one wall. Inscriptions from the Koran were set into panels around the cornice, and there was an onyx fountain in the centre of the room.

Liz found that the gentle splashing of the fountain's eight jets of water was quite relaxing. 'It's very impressive,' she said, to no one in particular. She dreaded to think how much it all must have cost, and how better the money could have been spent.

'I sometimes feel it is a mausoleum.' A young man's voice

announced his presence in the Moorish room. Prince Felix Yusupov was tall and slim, with deep blue eyes and long lashes that enhanced his almost feminine features. Like many golden-haired people, he had very pale smooth skin. Just as some women were described as handsome rather than beautiful, Liz could imagine the reverse was true of him.

He greeted Kuznetzov with a warm handshake and bear-hug, then nodded politely to Liz. 'Welcome, Professor Shaw. Nikita Georgeivich here has told me a lot about you.' Although he was polite enough, she sensed a certain cool distance between them.

'I'm honoured,' Liz said, feeling that it was the sort of thing she'd be expected to say. She suddenly realised that she really didn't know quite what the etiquette was here. It wasn't just a foreign country, but a foreign era, and anything she might do or say could be anachronistic for a woman in this time. She was momentarily hesitant, but then decided that she wasn't going to let maybes or could-bes stop her from being her normal self – within limits – and the moment passed.

'You are a scientist?' Felix went on.

'Yes, from Cambridge. I study meteors and meteorites.'

'Ah…'

Smoke and steam belched out from locomotives as they pulled into or out of the grey platforms of Varshavski Voksal. Their boilers seethed and their pistons' gusting exhaust made Herculean heartbeats as they hauled their carriages of wood and steel through the grime of the industrial part of the city.

From the solid old footbridge that crossed the lines

between platforms, one could watch the crippled and dying being unloaded from the hospital trains. Their wounds and stains were clear, but at least the height and the sulphurous coal-smoke clouds exhaled by the locomotives masked the stench of blood, sweat and gangrene.

Soldiers helped their comrades off the trains and led them to the waiting nurses, who were swathed in conical white dresses that made them look very much like nuns.

There were plenty of both civilian and military officials directing things at the station, so the Doctor didn't look particularly out of place. The man called Kit didn't think so anyway, watching from a tea stall.

He didn't know what the Doctor was actually doing here, but it was clear that he was working to a purpose. Either he was looking for something or someone, or he was out to gather some sort of specific information. Kit had to admire the old boy's dedication, even if he thought it was a bit too much like hard work. Kit was firmly of the opinion that if you wanted to dig up information in St Petersburg, the best way to do it was to take the relevant official to one of the restaurants or nightclubs. Get them drunk and they'd tell you anything. It was also a lot more comfortable than tramping around in the snow.

The Doctor crossed over the footbridge, and Kit hastily followed.

The small talk – for Liz recognised that was what the conversation about her work was to Felix – had passed by pleasantly and blandly, as it always did.

'Our arrival seems to have attracted a lot of attention,' she was saying.

Kuznetzov agreed. 'It's only natural – the people with positions to guard are interested in our allies' perspective on the war.'

'I'd love to say I had a perspective on that,' Liz admitted, 'but I confess it seems rather... distant, to me.' She was amused at the thought of how they might react if they knew just how distant, but she knew better than to say anything. Even though she wasn't experienced at travelling through time, she was educated enough to understand the paradoxes that could be caused. As a result, she tried to think especially carefully about everything she said.

Felix smiled faintly. 'War has always been distant to me. Have you made many acquaintances since your arrival in St Petersburg?'

Liz shrugged slightly. 'We were granted the honour of an audience with the Tsarina. We've been exploring the city all day today, so we haven't seen many people to talk to. Though we did see Rasputin.'

Felix's expression stiffened. 'Rasputin?'

Liz realised that she had better think even more carefully about her responses now. She knew enough history to know that Rasputin would be murdered within a few days, and enough science to know that she mustn't do anything to prevent it. 'He was getting a lift from Anya Vyrubova, apparently.' She glanced at Kuznetzov for corroboration. 'I didn't actually see much of him. He seemed...' She paused in thought. She refused to feel intimidated by the man, but there was something unmistakably crude and threatening about him. 'He seemed to be the kind of man who would stop at nothing to get his own way, who would commit a dreadful crime and then bribe the judge to get released,' she said, finally.

'That would not be the first time,' Kuznetzov murmured.

'True,' Felix agreed. 'There was that fracas at Yar... Then Rasputin's infamy has spread wide? I have heard that his behaviour is reported in the English press.'

'He's probably the most notorious figure of this decade,' Liz opined. 'Where I come from, his name is synonymous with manipulation and debauchery. There are even songs about him.'

Felix relaxed a little, and sat beside her. 'That doesn't entirely surprise me. I would quite like to hear them.'

'I... don't remember the words,' Liz said, flushing slightly. She guessed that the two men would assume she was embarrassed by rude lyrics, rather than that she had almost quoted a song that wouldn't be written for sixty years. 'What happened at Yar?' she asked, hoping to divert their attention.

Felix grimaced. 'Yar is a nightclub in Moscow. Grishka Rasputin had gone to pray at the Cathedral of the Assumption in the Kremlin. Later he turned up at Yar, got roaring drunk, smashed up a dining room, and tried to assault a woman right there in the restaurant. Because everyone is so frightened of his influence over the Empress, no one dared to throw him out. Eventually the police were called, and he... excuse my frankness, Miss Shaw, but there is no other way to describe his action – he exposed himself to them and the British Ambassador, before he was dragged away. He also told everyone present that he regularly has his way with the Empress.'

Liz was incredulous. 'Surely he must have been punished?'

Felix shook his head. 'He spoke to the Empress, who then dismissed the police chief, to save Rasputin.'

Liz was momentarily taken aback. She'd heard of Rasputin as the Empress's lover, but hadn't thought that court intrigue would be quite so blatant. 'It sounds like he deserves all he gets…' she murmured to herself.

With the occasional patient 'Excuse me' the Doctor forced his way through part of the station crowded with busy nurses and their injured soldier patients to a more sparsely populated platform. Here the great iron hulk of the University's own train was waiting, like a thoroughbred in the starting gate. The carriages behind it had clearly once been plush private carriages, but were now worn and stained with more practical use.

Although a few wisps of steam were clouding around the engine, it didn't look like the train was preparing for an immediate departure, and there were few enough people around that the Doctor could slip on board the last carriage unnoticed.

Inside, the carpet and wood panelling remained, but the rest of the space had been turned into a workshop of some kind. Small lathes and drills were bolted to the floor, while the tables that ran along either side were replete with clamps and vices. The Doctor judged it to be for repairing or making small arms, which would fit with Kuznetzov's interest in ballistics.

None of it provided any clue to the whereabouts of the TARDIS or Kuznetzov's true activities, though, so he moved onwards, into the next carriage.

Felix was quite pleased by Liz's attitude to Rasputin. 'He is certainly no demagogue,' he agreed. 'I cannot imagine what his followers see in him.' That wasn't strictly true, but he doubted that Liz would know otherwise. Though Rasputin was just a common peasant, Felix had always found that there was something in him that attracted attention. Perhaps it was the way his behaviour was so unconstrained by etiquette and protocol. Felix had been brought up in a military and aristocratic environment where etiquette and protocol were twin albatrosses around his neck. There were times when the desire to hurl down those burdens, trample them and allow himself free rein became almost unbearable.

There had been a time, in his teens, when he been able to do so, while disguised. He and his brother Nicholas would go out to the clubs and theatres, with Felix disguised as a girl. No one ever thought that a society girl should be bound to the same rules as a prince.

That had all ended with Nicholas's death, of course. Felix still sometimes expected to hear Nicky's voice, or see him enter the room. There were times when he would see a picture, or meet someone, and make a mental note to tell Nicky about it. Then he would catch himself, and be momentarily nonplussed by the sudden emptiness.

Thesphe suddenly reappeared from behind a partition. 'Your Highness, the Grand Duke Dmitri Pavlovich is asking to speak with you.'

Dmitri's timing could have been better, Felix thought, but he wasn't going to turn him away. 'If you will excuse me…' Felix said.

'Of course, Your Highness,' Kuznetzov replied.

Felix met Dmitri in a small anteroom, filled with treasures that had been moved out of the west wing when that area had been converted into a hospital. Most of the other palaces around St Petersburg had since done likewise, but

Felix prided himself on being the first. It was a minor drain on the family fortune, but they could more than afford it. In any case, Felix had never been particularly interested in riches. He enjoyed his comforts, yes, but familiarity bred contempt, even for wealth. His aunt had learned that long ago, and Felix had always valued her wisdom. She even understood his tastes, which no others - save Irina, who had to - really did. Not even himself sometimes. When he first met Rasputin, he had actually thought that the staretz might ease his confusion, but the Holy Devil had merely tried to make him his puppet. It no longer troubled Felix the way it once did.

Dmitri himself was in his Third Guards overcoat. Like Felix, he was tall and slender; quite elegant, in Felix's eyes.

Felix smiled for the beautiful Dmitri. 'What is so urgent that you risk being seen to come here?' Some time ago, the Empress had forbade Dmitri to see Felix, fearing that the latter was a bad influence on the former. As it was, neither of them could bear to give up the other, so they simply became more discreet.

Dmitri handed Felix a small envelope. 'I thought you'd want to see this at once.' Dmitri shifted uncomfortably.

Felix wondered what could be so important, and opened the unsealed envelope. Inside was a letter, which he read quickly. The contents of the letter inspired both horror at the implications and a certain grim satisfaction at the fact that this evidence proved they were right to take action about Rasputin.

Felix blinked a couple of times. 'Powerful evidence indeed. Has Vladimir seen this?'

'Not yet. I thought you'd want to take the decision on that.'

'Yes… I'll bring it to the meeting on the train. Lazovert and Sukhotin can see it then as well.'

'Very well, Felix.'

'Did you come in your car?'

'Yes.'

'Then I'd like you to escort Professor Shaw back to the Winter Palace, or wherever else she wishes to go. That at least will provide a reasonable excuse for why you are here today.'

'That is a good idea,' Dmitri agreed. Together, they went back into the Moorish room.

'Professor,' Felix said apologetically, knowing that his charm would soothe any disappointment she might feel. 'I'm afraid something has arisen which requires my attention. However, I hope to see yourself and Academician Kuznetzov again soon. I will telephone the Winter Palace when I can arrange another meeting. In the meantime, Grand Duke Dmitri has offered to drive you back to the Winter Palace, or any other destination you wish.'

'I understand,' Liz said. 'In any case, I do still have my research studies to continue.'

'Of course.' Felix could hear a telephone ring, somewhere in the vicinity, and wasn't surprised when Thesphe appeared again.

'A call for Academician Kuznetzov,' he said simply.

Felix looked at Kuznetzov. 'Thesphe will show you to the telephone.'

'Thank you.' Kuznetzov turned to Liz. 'I'm sure this will only take a moment.'

The telephone was in a small gallery room filled with ornamental glassware. Kuznetzov lifted it, and checked to see that Thesphe had vanished again. 'Yes?'

'It's Mischa,' the voice said. 'The Doctor was seen at the station.'

The Doctor? Professor Shaw's friend? Kuznetzov thought immediately. 'Doing what?'

'Looking over your train, and asking about where it had been.'

'Why?' If it was mere curiosity, he could have accompanied Liz and himself here today. Kuznetzov had a healthy case of paranoia, and the thought crossed his mind that the Doctor may have let Liz accompany him as a diversion. The box, he realised. Hadn't he referred to the Doctor's property as a box? Damn himself for being so careless…

There was a deep breath from the other end of the line. 'We have it on good authority that this Doctor works for British Intelligence.'

Kuznetzov looked around, relieved that no one else was in the room. 'Are you sure?'

'Only that it seems reasonable to assume so. The word among the palace staff is that he came to see Ambassador Stopford, who we know works for them. Also, the superior officer he mentioned is highly placed in the Military Intelligence branch of the British War Office.'

Kuznetzov could see that the evidence was somewhat circumstantial, but worrying. Even if the Doctor was not in Intelligence work, it was likely that Stopford and his superiors would want to hear all his tales… He grimaced. This was a nuisance, to say the least. 'Did he find out anything?'

'Impossible to tell.'

'Better to be safe than sorry… Pick him up, and eliminate

him. Just to be on the safe side,' he added. He didn't want the hired help to think there was any real danger, lest they seek more profit by changing their allegiances. 'He's a rich-looking aristocratic foreigner in a place of unrest... I'm sure it's not beyond the bounds of possibility that he could be caught up in a fatal street robbery.'

Mischa hesitated. 'I don't know...'

Kuznetzov cut him short. 'Not sure? Mischa, if I fall, you fall with me. But if we are to protect ourselves...'

Mischa sighed slowly. 'Very well.'

'If it makes you feel any better, you can keep whatever money or valuables he's carrying. Just try not to get caught with them, all right?'

'Such thoughts had occurred to me.'

Chapter Seven

Kit had lost sight of the Doctor time and again as they struggled across the thronging railway platforms yards apart in the human tangle. More than once he'd been sure that was the last of him, but then glimpsed the white head and vigorously working shoulders still easing a way through the crowd of nurses' head-dresses and walking wounded's uniform drab.

Reaching clearer parts of the station Kit picked up the trail more confidently again. He'd watched the Doctor enter the university train. He'd had to divert a certain amount of care to not attracting unwelcome attention on his own account, but that hadn't stopped him keeping that train under observation. Now and again a less grimy carriage window allowed glimpses of a white-haired head within, bowed over less distinguishable objects or apparatus in the converted coaches or making a methodical way along the train without coinciding with the uniform-capped or bare-headed figures who also passed along the carriages.

He allowed his unknown colleague high marks for professionalism. He didn't know which branch of Military Intelligence he might belong to, but it obviously wasn't the first time he'd conducted a clandestine survey under the noses of the occupiers. Not one of the railway or University staff who'd briefly all but shared a window with him had shown a sign of noticing that the Doctor was aboard. And the Doctor hadn't shown a sign of being done with his search, whatever it was for. Kit didn't reckon he would be coming back out just yet. He wondered exactly what the Doctor was looking for. In any case, common cause proved, it was perhaps time that he made contact...

Kit's finely tuned sense of self-preservation suddenly alerted him to a group of half a dozen muscular men marching down the platform. Though they were in scruffy civilian dress, they moved with that involuntarily co-ordinated purpose that was second-nature to military men. Kit didn't like the look of them at all. Only too clearly they were some sort of security for the train. Sure enough, three of them boarded at each end, and the engine almost immediately started belching out larger clouds.

Thinking quickly, Kit turned, and with a last glance fixing the latest position of the shock of white hair and flamboyant caped surcoat hurried back the way he had come.

The Doctor had gone through several carriages, searching for anything that would suggest that Kuznetzov might have either been to Tunguska, or be preparing to take the TARDIS out of the city.

So far he had found nothing but traces of cordite and other explosive compounds. That in itself wasn't surprising or suspicious, since Kuznetzov was working in ballistics, but it was odd that he had lied about it. If he wanted to hide his trade, then why not deny it altogether, instead of saying that his most recent journey wasn't associated with it?

By the time he reached the second from forwardmost carriage, he had all but given up on finding anything useful. In itself, he suddenly thought, the carriage was unusual. It was wood-panelled like the others, but maintained its former glory. Plump leather armchairs were dotted around. A private bar was against one wall, with champagne already in an ice-bucket. A chaise-longue was opposite it.

More interestingly, there was a locked filing cabinet in one corner. The lock was too primitive to be opened by the sonic screwdriver, but the Doctor was confident that a bent safety pin would do the trick.

As he worked on the cabinet, the Doctor suddenly heard the connecting door to the next carriage open. 'It seems we were just in time,' a gruff voice said. 'Turn around, Angliskii... Slowly.'

Irritated, the Doctor turned, and was not the least bit surprised to see that his discoverers were armed. 'Ah.' He ran his fingers through his hair. 'Now, I know how this must look to you, but I assure you there's a perfectly reasonable explanation for my presence.'

The floor jerked slightly, but not enough to tip any of the men off balance. The train was moving. 'I'm a reasonable man,' the Doctor persevered. 'Perhaps if I could explain...' But no one seemed interested in hearing what he had to say.

Kit had never much liked running, and the strain of drawing breath as he hared through the stockyard was made even more painful by the cold. It felt like hordes of rats were trying to claw their way through his rib cage.

The train with the Doctor aboard was already starting to pull away from the platform. With a curse, Kit turned, darting up on to the footbridge. He climbed over the rail carefully, all too easily remembering the fall of the man at the rostral. Even though he held his breath, the steam and smoke that enveloped him choked his lungs with the acridity of hot metal. He briefly reviewed his plan – if that wasn't dignifying a hasty improvisation too much: he'd land on the train's roof, climb down between two carriages and get inside, or –

And here came the carriage the Doctor must be in. The thought flashed through his mind that this sort of action should only be taken by fictional types like Tarzan or Richard Hannay, and not someone who enjoyed life's little luxuries so much. But his body wasn't listening to any of that, and leapt off the bridge.

The Doctor was carefully judging the odds on his making it to either door before one of his assailants could shoot him. They weren't good. 'You know, if you'll just put your guns down, I'm certain we can come to some arrangement. There really isn't any need for violence.'

'There is for us, Angliskii, if we want to get paid what we're owed –' A shower of glass fragments burst noisily down from the skylight as Kit crashed feet-first into the carriage, knocking down one thug with a perfectly accidental glancing blow of his foot and landing from his already half-broken fall on one of the overstuffed armchairs.

The Doctor took advantage of the distraction by jabbing at a nerve point on the chest of the man closest to him, who stumbled back, his gun dropping from his suddenly numb hand. Before he could recover, Kit had smashed a small footstool across the back of his shoulders.

The thug Kit had knocked down was struggling up, aiming his revolver, but Kit cracked the gun-hand with a heavy champagne bottle. Kit's free hand on the back of the thug's head sent his face into the mahogany bartop with a

74

loud crack, just as the Doctor overbalanced the third man with a flick of the wrist.

The door at the far end of the carriage opened, disgorging three more armed men. The Doctor snatched the chipped champagne magnum from Kit, and shook it hard, then threw it headlong at the edge of a cabinet just in front of the men.

The bottle grazed the cabinet just hard enough to crack the glass, and the pressure of the effervescing gases inside did the rest. It exploded like a grenade, forcing the men to cover their faces to ward off the flying shards of glass.

The Doctor grabbed Kit, and pulled him through the nearer carriage door, moments before the first shots from the men split the wood. 'They're shooting at us!' Kit gasped.

'Yes,' the Doctor agreed. 'They don't seem very friendly at all, do they? We have to get off this train as quickly as possible.' They were now on a little open-air platform between carriages, and the train was still among the stockyards.

'What?' Kit was still trying to let his mind catch up with what had just happened. 'How? We're moving –'

'Jump, man,' the Doctor continued exasperatedly, and shoved Kit off the train.

Kit was too busy gasping for breath to give vent to the screaming curse he wanted to deliver to the Doctor for throwing him off a moving train. Yes, the train was moving very slowly, but the Doctor's peremptory action still didn't show much gratitude for Kit's having saved his life. And he'd already misjudged one jump by hitting the skylight… Then he slammed into the gravel ballast alongside the rails and was tumbling aside.

The Doctor landed beside him, and both of them dived headlong under a rusting tender on a neighbouring track. Kit didn't like this at all; his was the world of courtly gossip, and secrets told over sweet tea and cognac. Running around in the cold and getting shot at by anarchists were two of the very things he'd taken this job to avoid.

'Well,' the Doctor began. 'I don't know who you are, but your intervention in the carriage was most timely, thank you. I do wonder why you went to such efforts to save a man you've never met before?'

'Powell, Christopher Powell. Kit. It looked like somebody had to.' He'd much rather it had been someone more experienced at such things. Or at least someone with more of a taste for it. 'You're lucky I got to you in time. If I hadn't been following you –'

'Following me? Why?'

Kit sighed. The Doctor's sudden ingratitude was depressing. 'Because luckily for you, Doctor, the chief of the St Petersburg Ochrana came to see me to find out who you were. Otherwise I might not even have known you and the ladies were in the city.'

The Doctor frowned. 'You know who I am?' he asked warily.

'Your arrival has generated something of a new rumour mill in the upper echelons of life here.' Kit had been listening out for any pursuit, but didn't hear any. With any luck their pursuers were too nervous – or sensible – to jump as the train gathered speed, and were on their way to Warsaw. And this was no time, as far as he was concerned, to sit around talking in the middle of the tracks. 'Come on, the sooner we get you properly briefed, the better.' He scrambled out from under the rusting tender, and led the Doctor across several sets of rails.

Without warning, the Doctor pulled Kit back between two disused carriages. Two of their pursuers, with revolvers drawn, were walking slowly along between the tracks. 'Shouldn't we go back now?' one of them asked.

The other shook his head, looking around. 'You heard what Kuznetzov said. The Angliskii is to be killed in a street robbery.'

Kit was surprised. The only Kuznetzov with enough monetary clout to hire such thugs was Academician Kuznetzov, but he surely wouldn't have any reason to. He glanced at the Doctor, questioningly. The Doctor merely put a finger to his lips, and motioned to Kit that they should move silently along the opposite side of the disused cars.

For long seconds, the pair moved stealthily along, careful not to disturb any stones that would give away their position. It didn't matter anyway, since a third assassin suddenly appeared between two carriages on his own initiative.

He looked as surprised as Kit felt, but that didn't stop him from raising a pistol, no more than about six inches from Kit's nose. 'Say goodbye, *alik*.'

Kit suddenly pushed the gun away, stepping inside to elbow the thug in the face. The gun went off, almost deafening Kit, but the bullet heading harmlessly skywards. The thug staggered back as Kit twisted the gun out of his grip. 'Amateurs,' he muttered, hitting the thug behind the ear and knocking him cold. 'If you want to wave something in someone's face and not have it taken away from you, use a knife.'

But the shot had brought their other pursuers haring

back towards them. There was a section of thick iron chain by the tracks. Instinct made Kit snatch it up with unthinking speed. As the nearest attacker slowed to aim, Kit swung it at him, letting it fly out to full length so it whipped at the man's head with a hollow moan of icy air.

Ducking and sidestepping the man sprang, inside the chain's swing, pistol tucked in close to his chest, ready to ram it at his victim's midsection point-blank. Kit yanked, caught, brought the heavy metal links down on the thug's head with both hands, knocking him out cold. Out of the corner of his eye, he saw the Doctor dispose of his opponent more elegantly, a slight tug on the wrist sending him head over heels across the stockyard. Kit was impressed, and more than a little bewildered.

He was rudely dragged away from his ponderings by a half-seen jackknife's blade, blurring with motion – too close, the cloth at his side ripped as he swerved aside. The blade bedded in a wagon's timber side, then cracked off short with the thin, high snap of steel brittle with cold. As its owner cursed, Kit flung a desperate chain-wrapped punch. A pair of strong hands slammed him into the side of a wagon. Pain exploded outward from Kit's spine, wrapping around his ribs as he struggled to stay upright.

He fell, but the weakness saved him, as the attacking thug's boot crashed into the wood just above Kit's head. Kit forced himself forward, changing the fall into a dive and driving his head into the thug's stomach. Both men tumbled painfully across the frozen rails, but Kit had the distinct impression that it was worse for his opponent.

Kit rolled aside and to his feet. In the moment before his opponent rose also, Kit managed to swing a kick at the side of his head. The thug rolled with the blow, sprawling across the track. He rose, grabbing Kit's lapel with one hand and preparing to club him with the other. Kit's breathing sounded massively amplified in his own ears, and he knew that was the fear of death gripping him.

Only as the assassin's eyes widened in horror did Kit realise that the sound wasn't his terrified breathing, but the huge dark hospital train bearing down on them.

Then two hands latched on to his shoulders, pulling against the thug's grip. The Doctor hauled Kit to safety just in time, but as he reeled one way the assassin stumbled backwards, slipping on the ice of the frozen rail as he lost his grip. His scream barely started before a wet smack and the screech of metal drowned it out. Hot steam enveloped the Doctor and Kit as they backed away and, when it cleared, there was no sign of the man other than a severed foot a dozen yards down the line. Kit was glad that the train was stopping over the mangled remains of their would-be assassin. He doubted his stomach would hold up to the sight of that right now.

'Are you all right, old chap?' the Doctor asked.

'I will be, yes,' Kit replied unsteadily. He pulled himself together with some effort, and looked at the Doctor. 'Academician Kuznetzov?'

'Yes. For a man of science, he has some decidedly odd friends.'

'And for a man of science, you have some rather odd skills.'

'Touché,' the Doctor admitted. 'Come on then. We don't want to wait around here for them to send someone else after us, do we?'

'No,' Kit agreed. 'Ah, an academic dispute? I think you'd find a nice boat race a more civilised way to settle things.'

Not that he expected things to be settled the civilised way outside of the Home Counties.

'Believe me, I heartily agree with you, old chap.'

'Still, if you have some idea who, then you must have some idea why.' At least the affair wasn't a total loss if they had gained some information.

'Well, I'm not too sure about that,' the Doctor admitted, scratching his nose. 'I thought he might have seen the theft of some of my property, and I also believe he lied about visiting the Lake Baikal area.'

'Lake Baikal?' That meant nothing to Kit, since there was no danger of the war going that far into Siberia. There was nothing of military importance there. 'Hardly something worth killing over, even these days…' A thought struck him. 'Unless he's afraid that being caught out in one lie means he could be caught out in others. Or that he's afraid you might know where he was when he wasn't in Siberia, if he was somewhere more… incriminating.'

'Yes, that thought had occurred to me as well.'

'This property that was stolen – Vasiliyev tells me the report you made mentioned a large blue box. Was it War Office property?'

'Well, it certainly had some assistance from the Ministry…'

'And I presume it's something we wouldn't want the locals getting a good look at?'

'You could put it that way.'

'Why would Kuznetzov be interested in it? Assuming he even is?'

The Doctor grinned cheerily at Kit. 'I wonder if we'll live long enough to find out.'

Chapter Eight

Jo had been amusing herself by trying on a variety of expensive and luxurious dresses that she had found in some wardrobes. She supposed they belonged to the Empress's daughters, but assumed that they were intended for the use of guests, otherwise they would surely have been removed from the rooms.

Amused though she was, she didn't think any of them particularly suited her – and she was scarcely planning to go to a ball anyway – so she had changed back into her rather more practical costume from the TARDIS. As she was doing so, she heard the sound of an engine outside. Jo looked out the window, and saw that a car had arrived in the central courtyard.

Rasputin had remained in the passenger seat for a few minutes, watching the girl who had come down to collect the bundles of files from the driver. Like her comrades, she was intriguing. Normally, Rasputin could tell at once whether someone would be a friend or an ally, a help or a threat.

In the case of the three newcomers, he could not. As he had told Anya, there was something odd about them, as if they had seen more than most men could.

Josephine was, of course, also an attractive girl. He emerged from the car while her back was turned. She was smiling sweetly at the driver, who responded with a rather nervous smile of his own. That look became even more nervous when he saw Rasputin, and he suddenly found other things to do. Nobody joined the army to be lazy, if they knew what was good for them.

Jo turned at the reaction, and again Rasputin saw that flash of fear in her eyes, but it was quickly hidden. 'What do you want?' she asked.

'Only to oversee delivery of your... files.' He indicated the stack of folders the soldier had just unloaded. 'I was returning from Tsarskoe Selo and needed transport back.'

'Oh, I see.'

'You fear me? You don't need to, you know.'

'Don't I? You are Rasputin, aren't you?' She spoke as if that explained everything.

'I am,' he agreed. 'The Garden of Eden has many serpents, but I am a man of God. I simply wondered whether I could speak with yourself or one of your friends.'

'Why?' She looked puzzled, as if this wasn't the conversation she had expected.

'I like to hear stories that travellers tell. Ever since I was a boy.' He saw another flash of surprise cross her face. 'Yes, even I was a boy once.' Now she relaxed slightly. 'Your name is Josephine, is it not?'

'Yes, but people call me Jo.'

'Walk with me, Josephine. I like to have company when I walk. Someone to talk to.'

Jo looked hesitant but finally nodded. 'Let me put these things inside and get a warmer coat, first.'

Kit Powell reflected on the day's events. Being chased and shot at while uncovering schemes and conspiracies was something that many of his generation would like to be involved with. In this war, that would be an honourable occupation.

Kit wanted nothing more than to see the world, and mix with people his forebears hadn't even imagined. Since his family wasn't particularly rich, there had been three main options open to him after university: join the navy and sail the world, join the army and fight abroad, or join the Foreign Office. Since Kit got terrible seasickness, and had no desire to let opposing armies shoot at him, the third choice had seemed the most comfortable.

He had spent a year at a consulate in Norway before being moved here at the outbreak of war. It had mostly been an improvement; though the winters were more severe, St Petersburg had a cosmopolitan air that Oslo lacked. It also had remarkable architecture and palaces full of some of the world's greatest art treasures. Kit loved that.

The white nights, in June and July, were his favourite time of the year here. It didn't get quite fully dark for those four weeks or so, and the city's parks and boulevards were tranquil and restful. It was easy to forget that the rest of Europe was being consumed by the war.

He and the Doctor had managed to leave Varshavski Voksal unmolested, and Kit had insisted on coming to a private room at Donons. To his surprise, the Doctor had agreed, saying that he too had worked up an appetite.

'Now,' the Doctor said, having removed his ulster to reveal a rather natty double-breasted burgundy velvet jacket. Kit was immediately envious. 'You have told me your name, but I hope I won't sound too ungrateful if I ask just why you intervened to save my life on the train, Mr Powell.'

'Nobody likes to waste valuable agents, Doctor. And you can call me Kit.'

'Thank you, ah, Kit. But that still doesn't answer the rest of my question.' The Doctor's steady gaze was calm, but not going to be distracted.

'I was sent to contact you, and provide you with some local assistance. Intelligence-gathering isn't as solo an occupation as –'

'I assure you I'm not a spy,' the Doctor said mildly.

Kit didn't believe a word of it, of course, and riposted, 'Well said. You never know who might be listening.' He turned to pour a couple of drinks from a bottle of fine imported cognac, and so missed the Doctor's wearied expression. 'But I assure you these rooms are perfectly safe. I assume Alistair briefed you about the situation when you saw him last?'

The Doctor frowned. 'Alistair?'

'Lethbridge-Stewart. He *is* your superior officer, isn't he?' Or so he had been told.

The Doctor looked surprised. 'What do you know about Lethbridge-Stewart?'

'He analyses all the reports that Bertie Stopford sends back.'

'Of course,' the Doctor said thoughtfully. 'Of course!' He grinned. 'Yes, in a way. Though I'm a civilian myself. Special scientific adviser to... Lethbridge-Stewart's unit. And you, I presume, work for Stopford.'

Kit nodded. 'Though the Ochrana chief here in St Petersburg will swear blind that he's the only person who runs me.'

'That must be something of a juggling act.'

Kit smiled. 'I have had easier tasks in my life, yes.'

The Doctor relaxed slightly, and took a sip of cognac. 'Well, to tell you the truth, I shouldn't really be here at all. I was on my way to Irkutsk, but seem to have come rather off-course.'

'Irkutsk?' There wasn't much of interest there that Kit could think of. 'Still, it's handy that you're here. The whole city is even more on edge than usual.'

'Any particular reason why?'

'Well, if the satirists are to be believed, the Empress herself is a German spy at the behest of that bounder Rasputin.'

'Don't the Russian authorities have more to be concerned about than that? The Empress is hardly a threat to Britain's national security.'

'Not in the way you mean, no,' Kit admitted. 'But she is the King's cousin, and the granddaughter of Queen Victoria. Any wrongdoing on her part could certainly damage confidence in our own Royal Family, and we can't afford that, especially in wartime.'

'Ah… So Bertie Stopford brought you out here to investigate these rumours, eh? The devil's in the details, and all that.'

'Exactly.'

'And what about you? D'you think she's giving away secrets and plans to the Germans?'

Kit considered long and hard. 'No. She, her sister and her brother all send letters to each other, but they're above-board.' He shook his head at the strangeness of the heads of state of three warring countries all remaining in touch with the other members of the family, while at the same time sending their subjects out to get killed in their millions. 'Someone is, though, and my money's on Rasputin.'

'Ah.' The Doctor waggled a finger at him. 'But do you have proof or are you just believing too much of what you read in the papers?'

Kit shrugged. 'The main German agent here is a man

called Manus – he's a banker operating out of Sweden, and has visited Rasputin a few times. Last year a strategy map that only the Empress had access to turned up in German hands, and only Rasputin has that much access to the Empress. If you'll forgive the expression.'

The Doctor leaned back, steepling his fingers, and looking along his nose at Kit. 'That hardly constitutes proof of conspiracy. It could have been stolen.'

'True,' Kit admitted. 'But it seems reasonably unlikely.'

'And what are you planning to do about it?'

'Same thing I've always done. Keep my eyes and ears open.'

'Ordinarily that's excellent advice, but the problem with it in this situation is that you have no control over what you're shown and told.'

'If you have a better idea, I'm willing to hear it.' That was, presumably, the whole reason for putting him in touch with such a more experienced agent.

'Of course I have a better idea. Quite frankly, Rasputin's in enough trouble as it is. In fact I'd say we could probably leave him to others, and concentrate on what Kuznetzov is hiding. He has one of my companions, Miss Shaw, with him. If he is involved in anything, I'd like to make sure she is kept out of any danger.'

'If he has your box, he probably hopes to lead her into giving him information about it. Quicker to charm a woman than torture the man.'

Kit began to shake. It started with his hands, and he looked down, wondering what was wrong with them. Then it dawned on him that they had been grappling with a man who died as a result. Kit could feel his soul desert him, having committed the cardinal sin of taking someone's life.

God knew, the nightmares about the man at the rostral were bad enough, and that had been a pure accident – he had even tried to save him...

The Doctor saw what was happening. 'You've never been in a fight to the death before?'

'No.' Dammit, he shouldn't be shaking like this. 'Something's wrong with me, I think.'

The Doctor shook his head. 'If there was something wrong with you, you wouldn't be feeling so shocked.'

Jo couldn't really tell why she went with Rasputin. He hadn't coerced her, or forced her in any way, but she had still felt that she really ought to walk with him. She supposed it was because he wasn't quite what she had expected. Or maybe he had hypnotised her in some subtle way, to make her think so? The Doctor had told her to stay, after all, but...

But why should she always stay behind? She was a trained agent of UNIT, wasn't she? Perhaps she should be more independent...

Rasputin had the deep and vaguely threatening eyes, that sense of darkness about him, but he was also... human. She hadn't expected someone like him to say he felt like company for a walk. So she had gone with him, wondering what else was different from what she'd expected.

He had spoken about the Empress for most of the walk, telling Jo how much he cared for both the Tsar and Tsarina, and she suspected he was inflating his own importance a bit to impress her. That seemed so mundane she almost laughed. Of course the occasional mis-remembered biblical quote that he threw out made her wonder if maybe he was unbalanced after all.

But then, he *was* supposed to be a holy man of some kind, wasn't he?

'Ah, home,' Rasputin said suddenly.

Jo thought the apartment block at 64 Gorokhovaya Ulitsa was much like any other lower-middle-class terraced housing. The architecture was strange, but she recognised the familiar air from London.

'I thought you'd live somewhere flashier,' she commented.

'Flashier?' Rasputin echoed.

Jo realised he wouldn't be up to date with future slang, but that didn't dampen her cheer. 'You know, something a bit more up-market. Richer.'

'Dear child,' he said, 'why would I wish to live in a money-changer's temple?' He shook his head. 'The people here in this area are like those at home, so I *feel* at home here.'

Rasputin led Jo past the door of the building's main foyer. Inside she could see a wrought-iron staircase. They went through an archway into the small courtyard, and through a door in the far corner. There, a narrow staircase led up to the third floor. 'This way is quicker,' he said. 'The front stairs will be filled with people who wish to see me.'

Jo wondered what he meant by that – he was hardly a pop star to be mobbed. When they emerged on the third floor, however, she saw that there was actually a queue of people waiting outside apartment number 20. A poker-faced man in a dark overcoat at the far end of the corridor was writing something in a notebook. He was so much like the Ochrana agents they had seen in the streets that Jo couldn't believe he could be anything else. A small man in shirtsleeves and glasses was holding the queue back, insisting that they would be called when Rasputin was ready for them.

Then they were inside, and Rasputin was grinning broadly. 'Welcome to my humble quarters, Josephine. I thank you for walking with me, and will have tea brought to fortify you before you leave.'

'Thank you,' Jo said heartily. She would need the warmth of a hot drink before going out again, and Rasputin didn't seem as bad as she had expected. 'Simanovich,' he called, and the man with glasses appeared at the door. 'Bring tea, and wine.' He slumped a little. 'I need wine.' Jo didn't like the sound of that as much. Alcoholics weren't her idea of fascinating company.

'Isn't it a little early in the day for drinking?' Jo asked.

Rasputin looked at her. 'If I was truly drinking, I would bring vodka. Wine is good for the soul – it cures many ills.'

'You're ill?' Jo was concerned in spite of herself.

Rasputin smiled grimly. 'Sick of the war, perhaps. And I have not always been so beloved, Josephine. More than once, someone has tried to kill me, but the Lord watches over me as he does all his flock. One of those attempts kept me in Siberia when the war started.' He shook his head, and she could see anger building in him. Slightly afraid, she stayed seated at the table.

'If I had been *here*!' Rasputin snarled, 'I could have added my voice to Mama Alix's and perhaps pulled back from entering this war.'

Jo was astonished. 'You want Germany to win?'

'God's teeth, woman, of course not!' He scowled. 'But I also know that we cannot win. Let the British and the Germans fight it out, but why should our sons –' He hesitated, and Jo thought she saw his mask slip for a moment. 'Why should Russia's sons die for a squabble over Serbia? Even if we could win, what is there to gain? Nothing!'

His determination suddenly reminded Jo vaguely of the Doctor's pugnacious stand for his beliefs. They were very different beliefs, obviously, but there was that arrogant determination to bloody-mindedly stick to his guns no matter how crazy it might make people think he is... That did remind her of the Doctor.

'No more sons,' he muttered, trailing off. 'We are sacrificing the first-born instead of the sacred calves...' Jo felt a pang of sympathy for him then, and could tell that he was not just quoting or imagining things this time.

'Do you have a son?' she asked. 'Is that what you're saying?'

'I...' He shook his head, driving out the hesitation. 'Yes, I had a son once.'

'Had? You don't mean he...' Jo couldn't imagine how she'd feel if a child of hers died.

'He was still a baby,' he said. 'The Lord takes away as freely as he gives, but...'

Rasputin remembered it clearly. He had rushed out into the fields, confused and angry with God for taking his son. He had hoped that, at the very least, some hard work would take his mind off his grief.

He had toiled for hours under the sun, until he stank, though there was no one near enough to be bothered. As the day wore on, and his head began to throb around the old pitchfork wound, Rasputin had felt an urge to look up into the sky.

There, descending from heaven, the Virgin Mary appeared to him. She was draped in shimmering robes of liquid silver, and pointed to the southern horizon. To Rasputin, who had fallen to his knees, consumed with religious ecstasy, this was a clear instruction that he should make a pilgrimage to the Holy Land.

He understood, suddenly, that there was more to his soul than his grief, and that turning to God would honour the son who was now with Him.

The very next morning, he had gathered up a few possessions in a bag, and set off on his long pilgrimage. That was after one last fight with his father, who was convinced that God was merely Grigory's latest excuse for his laziness.

'Did you ever get there?' Jo asked. 'The Holy Land, I mean.'

Rasputin shook his head. 'I walked two thousand miles, all told, and eventually found my way to the monastery at Mount Athos, in Greece. That is where I learned about God. My father may have been right about one thing – I always wanted to be a staretz.' Rasputin said. 'The visit of such a wanderer was always interesting in Pokrovskoe. They would tell us about their travels in distant lands, and in return they would be given a place to sleep by the stove, and a meal.' He smiled, not altogether pleasantly. 'I always imagined myself being welcomed in by a young and pretty widow, or the sister of an absent householder, whose gratitude for my tales and wisdom would be warmer still.'

'And did that ever happen?'

'Hah! All the time. I tell you, the steppes are scattered with villages full of women who haven't seen a *real* man in years. And to be purified by a Holy Man at the same time… Hah!'

Chapter Nine

Dmitri had dropped Liz off at the Winter Palace, then drove Kuznetzov across the Dvortsovy bridge to the Academy of Sciences. Kuznetzov had lived here for almost a year, and still hadn't quite got used to the house he had inherited with his post.

He shared it with several other scientists, but had an apartment – number 12 – to himself. The apartment was dim as he entered, and he switched on the light. He really wanted to lie down, having been up all night working on a new paper until past three in the morning, but he knew he had other things to do first.

For a start, he had the Englishwoman to consider. The professor from Cambridge was certainly interesting company, but Kuznetzov didn't feel quite comfortable around her. He knew that there had been a few women scientists over the past few decades or so – everyone knew Marie Curie, for example – but he was a little uncomfortable with the idea that a young woman would know more about science in general than he did.

Kuznetzov's father had gone to great lengths to get an education for his son, and Kuznetzov remembered being looked down upon at university. He didn't have the same privileged background as most other students, and so he had to work twice as hard, to be better than the others, just to show them. And that was without the others even knowing that his education was paid for with defrauded money. With that in mind, it was difficult to feel at ease with anyone who was a better student than himself, or more knowledgable.

He poured himself a shot of vodka, then lifted the telephone receiver, and dialled a number.

'Koba. It's Kuznetzov. I've spoken with Felix, and it looks like he will go ahead with his plan. So we can be ready. There are even some newcomers around to get the blame if anything goes wrong.' He laughed. 'Yes, I thought you'd appreciate that. I'll call later.' He rattled the receiver, then dialled another number. 'Mischa, come up here. I have a job for you. One that you should be able to manage without being beaten by old men.' He hung up the phone.

While he waited for Mischa to walk across from the Academy building, Kuznetzov opened his large and cumbersome wardrobe. Inside, he opened up a small hidden panel and took out one of several canvas bags that were inside.

Tossing the bag on to the bed, he then opened a briefcase and started filling it with wads of banknotes from the bag. When there was a neat layer of money – still with the bank's wrappers around the wads – inside, he closed the case.

There was a knock at the door and he opened it to Mischa, who was now sporting a black eye and a bandaged hand. Kuznetzov gave him the briefcase and a key for it. 'I want you to slip into the Winter Palace, and place this somewhere in the suite occupied by the new English visitors. Leave the key where it will be seen.' Kuznetzov knew that if someone found a key lying around their own room, they would generally pick it up on the assumption it was one of their own which had been dropped. If not, then the authorities would find it in a search anyway. 'And, Mischa, don't try to open it. It wouldn't be good for you.'

Mischa looked at the case fearfully. 'What is it? Some kind of bomb?'

'Something like that.' He chuckled slightly. It would certainly be explosive, if he wished it.

'Do you know anything about Kuznetzov's recent activities that could seem odd in any way?' the Doctor asked Kit, when the latter had steadied himself.

'He got a whole bunch of locksmiths to visit the Academy yesterday. No one knows why.'

'That's it,' the Doctor said with satisfaction. 'Every locksmith and safe-cracker on this planet couldn't open the TARDIS – my property – but he'll keep trying. Do you know where they were taken?'

'To Kuznetzov's apartment first, then we don't know where.'

'The first thing I have to do,' the Doctor said, 'is to find out all the places that Kuznetzov frequents, where he could have taken the TARDIS.'

'Couldn't you just confront him?'

'He'd only deny it, and no doubt provide plenty of witnesses to prove he's never seen it. Then he'd know we're on to him, and we'd never see the TARDIS again.'

'I'll find out for you, Doctor. Gathering that sort of information is what I'm here for. I'll have a quick perusal of Kuznetzov's apartment. You'd be better off returning to the Winter Palace to get some rest –'

'I'm perfectly awake and alert, thank you,' the Doctor said sharply. 'Besides, I want to make sure that no harm comes to Liz – Professor Shaw.'

Kit looked at him for a moment, but the Doctor's face was determined, and Kit had the distinct impression that there was no way to change his mind. 'Very well, but… Be careful. I'd hate to make a habit of jumping into the line of fire to save you. That just isn't me at all.'

The Doctor was looking at him sharply, but not unkindly. Then he gave a quick and slightly abashed smile. 'I'll try not to involve you in any needless heroics.' Which didn't inspire much confidence, Kit thought. With that, the Doctor buttoned up his ulster, and left the dining room.

Kit remained seated to watch him go, and thoughtfully finished off the Doctor's cognac for him. He had the nasty suspicion that the Doctor was going to get into danger of some kind. Perhaps that was what Bertie brought him over for – better that than to risk his own people.

For now, he had another appointment, at the Errant Dog. A glance at his watch showed that he had just enough time to get there.

Neither the Doctor nor Jo was at the Winter Palace when Liz returned – at least, not as far as she could tell.

For the first time since she had arrived, Liz allowed herself to relax and soak in the reality of having travelled through time. She had no need to worry about budgets and pleasing the Whitehall bean-counters here – hell, most of them probably hadn't been born yet.

Although she recognised that the St Petersburg of 1916 had all sorts of rules and restrictions, she felt strangely free. A change was as good as rest, or so they said, and this was as big a change of scenery and pace as she could ever imagine.

Kuznetzov would be round soon to collect her for dinner, so she knew she ought to get changed into something a little more formal. Like Jo, she too had discovered a rail of gowns in her wardrobe – though elaborate confections had never really been her style.

Given the choice, in her own time, she'd have opted for a slightly jazzy trouser suit. But this was 1916, so she'd have to try to be a little more *comme il faut*. To her relief she found a more suitable dress tucked away at one end of the rail – plain and tailored almost severely. Liz felt she would look strait-laced, even academic – just the impression she wished to foster this evening.

She wondered if she should tell the Doctor where she was going, feeling for a moment like a child on a school trip wanting to confide in the responsible teacher. Then she shrugged and started her last preparations before leaving.

The Doctor strode purposefully through the Strelka. He felt quite at home there for some reason. As the Doctor turned the corner of 7-ya liniya, he saw Kuznetzov's car sitting outside a large house, its engine running.

The Doctor slipped back into a doorway, and after a few minutes Kuznetzov emerged from the house and got into the car, which drove away. The Doctor watched in thought. If he remembered correctly, this house had been home to several Academicians over the last 150 years or so, which made it reasonably likely that Kuznetzov lived there too.

Once the car was out of sight, the Doctor went into the Academician's house. A message board in the lobby indicated who lived in which apartment, and so the Doctor went straight up to Kuznetzov's rooms.

The door was, of course, locked, and the Doctor wasted no time putting his bent pin to work.

The apartment was quite typical – bathroom, two bedrooms, a study, lounge, and kitchen. The Doctor moved slowly through the apartment, uncertain what it was he was even looking for. All he knew was what his instincts told him, that something about Kuznetzov was very wrong.

The kitchen and bathroom were clear, as was the lounge. The study was cluttered with books in and out of bookcases, but there didn't seem to be anything out of the ordinary. By the time he reached the second bedroom, the Doctor sighed heavily, beginning to wonder if there was any sort of evidence here at all.

The Doctor opened the wardrobe in the room, ruffling through a few suits and jackets. Actually Kuznetzov's dress sense wasn't that bad, he decided, for the era. A clothes hanger shifted, and bumped against the back wall, with a hollow boom. The Doctor stopped immediately, listening for any sign of anyone coming to investigate.

No one did, so he tapped quietly on the wall. The back of the wardrobe was hollow, but the Doctor doubted that it led to anything C S Lewis might have imagined. His fingers quickly found the edges of the hidden door, and opened it.

Beyond was a hole in the wall, filled with little sacks. The Doctor pulled a couple out, and opened one. It was filled with bundles of money, still with the bank's wrappers around them.

The Doctor hefted a few wads of bills, thoughtfully. In his experience, money that had paper wrappers around it usually belonged in a bank vault. And if such money was in private hands, then it was generally stolen.

The telephone rang, and the Doctor stuffed the money back into the bag, and back behind the wardrobe. On impulse, he lifted the phone. 'Yes, who is it?' he asked, his voice a perfect mimicry of Kuznetzov. As he spoke, he noticed a small drawer set into the telephone table.

'It's me,' the caller said, which wasn't very helpful. 'Koba has approved your plans. Things are difficult for him, but

100

he says he can move when you give the signal.'

'Thank you.' The Doctor wondered what all that meant, but could sense it was nothing good. 'I'll continue as agreed.' He slid the drawer open, and shuffled through the papers inside. One of the diagrams on one sheet caught his eye.

'Understood.' The caller hung up. The Doctor remained holding the receiver for a few moments. 'Koba,' he murmured to himself. 'Where have I heard that name before?' Folding up the sheet of paper that he had found, the Doctor slipped back out of the apartment.

Rasputin eyed Josephine thoughtfully. She was young, her skin soft and warm... It was said that a temptation resisted was a sign of character, and Rasputin could understand that. He wondered whether he would pass such a test with her. If he took her to bed, would he be able to resist the warmth of her body, and the scent of her hair... Or would the desire to feel the touch of her soft skin under his palms lead him to sin?

Not that it mattered much; if he gave in to temptation, he would be purifying her, and that could hardly be considered a sin at all. 'Do you still fear me?'

'No,' Jo admitted from a seat by the window.

'Good.' He sighed, taking a huge gulp from his wine glass to deaden the pain in his gut from where that whore Gusyeva had stabbed him two years ago. He remembered the days when she provided harmless pleasure for the farmers and merchants of Pokrovskoe, back before she got religion.

He grunted at the thought – religion, and a pouch of roubles from Illiodor, in return for shoving a knife into a former customer on the very day that this stupid war had started.

He had healed, eventually, but the wound was deep and still ached in the cold. And here the cold was very intense and lasted for so long. Wine usually did the trick of imparting some warmth to ease the pain, but it took more with every passing month. He could imagine the day coming when no amount would be enough.

If he lived that long, he thought wryly. He had no shortage of enemies, who couldn't see what vital services he provided to his beloved Alix. But that was hardly unusual for a religious figure, he reminded himself. Hadn't Jesus made enough enemies to get himself crucified?

In a beautifully marbled, but otherwise cold and empty hall, the TARDIS stood, with a few tables clustered around it. Two men in overalls were tending to the variety of drills and cutting tools that were scattered over the tables.

Kuznetzov paced around the strange box. It wasn't too dissimilar to police boxes he had seen in England. When he touched the wooden door, it didn't feel like wood, or even stone. It was smooth, and tingled slightly. If he listened closely enough, there was a faint humming sound – like an electrical generator, but far quieter than any he had ever heard.

The sound did suggest that he was right about one thing, though: whatever caused this box to move instantaneously was somehow contained within it.

'I planted the bag as you said,' Mischa said, entering the hall through a large set of doors at one end. 'And the key.'

'Good. Were you seen?'

Mischa shook his head. 'Your friend Professor Shaw was

arriving just as I left.'

'Excellent.' He thumped the side of the unusual police box in frustration. 'This is intolerable. How can it still be locked, after all we've done to it?'

Mischa frowned. 'Why shouldn't it, if it has a new type of lock? That is the purpose of such things.'

'Why not? Because I'm a genius, that's why not!' Kuznetzov exclaimed. 'A mere puzzlebox should be child's play for me to open.' Kuznetzov glared at it, as if it were a conscious enemy. He had seen it, from where he was examining the bore of the *Aurora*'s rear guns. It had split the air with a strange mechanical howl, and appeared from nowhere. He had barely managed to keep enough wits about him to send Mischa to follow the three people who had emerged from it, and to have it loaded on to a truck so that he could examine it at his leisure. As a scientist, he knew that it had to be something astounding.

When Mischa had returned with the news that the occupants seemed to be from British Intelligence, Kuznetzov had been surprised for more reasons than the obvious one. He had excellent scientific contacts in other parts of the world, and found it unlikely that such an invention could have been kept so secret that he wouldn't have even heard rumours of it. Even the outrageous scientific romances of Wells didn't offer any suggestions as to how such a transport could be made, and yet here it was, mocking him with its inscrutability. 'We must get it open, Mischa. The power to transport objects instantly around the globe would be worth...' He tailed off, lost in the possibilities.

Mischa frowned. 'Maybe it's just a container, and the power for it came from whatever sent it, like a bullet from a gun.'

Kuznetzov shook his head. 'I considered that, but it's obviously unfeasible. For one thing, there's that sound, like a generator, inside. Also, the Doctor and his friends want it back, which implies that they expect to go home in it. Since we have nothing that could transport a capsule instantaneously, it *must* be self-contained.'

'At least you're safe,' the Doctor said, relief evident in his voice, when he returned to their suite in the Winter Palace. Liz was on a chaise-longue examining the files and press cuttings when he came in. 'Where's Jo?'

'I thought she was with you. I take it this means she doesn't stay out of trouble when she's told to either?'

'No one ever does,' the Doctor said with a sigh. 'Is that the material on Kuznetzov I wanted?'

'Yes, but what's it all for?'

The Doctor sat down. 'I hate to break it to you like this, but I don't think Kuznetzov is quite what he appears to be.'

'If this is about his claiming to have to visited Tunguska –'

'No.' The Doctor unfolded the paper he had taken from Kuznetzov's apartment. 'It's about this.' The sheet of paper contained plan views and measurements of a police box. 'This was in Kuznetzov's apartment. At the very least he must have seen the TARDIS – and probably for quite a detailed examination, to have got these measurements.'

'Couldn't these be the blueprints for a real police box?' Liz asked. 'Just to play devil's advocate for a moment.'

'If so, then it's an anachronism. This type of police box –' he tapped the blueprint with a fingertip – 'which the TARDIS resembles won't be produced for at least another decade. At this point in time they look relatively different, and vary from city to city.'

'Perhaps it's his own design,' Liz went on. 'I mean, maybe he flees the Revolution, settles in England, and invents the TARDIS-type police box?'

'Decidedly unlikely, don't you think? Surely this type would have appeared in 1917 or 1918 if that was true?'

Liz waved the paper at him. 'Not if you've stolen his design,' she said with mock severity.

The Doctor grinned. 'It's a fair cop, WPC Shaw.'

Liz stared at the diagram. 'But how...?' She suddenly realised, and felt like a fool. 'The same way he knew we were here. He called Anya asking about us, which meant he already knew about us...'

'Yes, exactly. And I believe he's planning to try to wheedle information about the TARDIS out of you.'

'Doctor... He's coming to pick me up for dinner tonight.'

The Doctor scratched the back of his neck.

'Well, then you must go, of course. I don't think he intends any harm, and so long as he doesn't realise that we're on to him, you might be able to find out from him where the TARDIS is.' He looked sombrely at her. 'Without it, we're marooned here for ever!'

Chapter Ten

Rasputin seemed to sink into himself and, in doing so, he no longer was the bear-like figure that held Russia in a fearful grip, but a passionate man who strayed out of his depth. Jo clasped his hand reassuringly.

'Sometimes I can see my death, Josephine,' he said softly. 'You would think that the virtuous would be spared, to carry on their work... But that is not true, is it?'

Jo shook her head, thinking of the various members of UNIT who had been killed in action since she'd joined. Many of her colleagues there had become a sort of extension of her family. 'Where I come from, there's a saying that only the good die young. I don't think it means that the good *only* die young.'

Rasputin gazed deeply into the dregs of his Madeira. 'I do not feel very young, Josephine. I have walked this Earth for forty-seven years. I am not yet truly old, but... Did they tell you about my gifts?' he asked suddenly. 'My... talents?'

That, thought Jo, was certainly one way of putting it. Rasputin's animal magnetism was legendary.

'The "gift" of second sight,' Rasputin went on. 'All the great prophets had this. Jesus knew that he would not return from Gethsemane. Nostradamus foretold his own death. And I see mine.' He certainly sounded convinced, and Jo shivered. Foreseeing your own death didn't sound like much of a gift as far as she was concerned. 'Go back to your friends, Josephine. Simanovich will drive you. I am in no mood for your arms tonight.'

'My arms?' Jo stood in shock, not sure whether it was at

the dismissal or the implication that he thought she would... Well, she just wasn't that sort of girl. 'If that isn't conceit, I don't know what is! Whatever makes you think – Oh, never mind.' Angrily, she grabbed her coat, and flounced out.

Kuznetzov had brought Liz to Donons, one of the more expensive and cultured restaurants in St Petersburg. He had seemed a little disappointed in her choice of outfit; it didn't bother her. He just wasn't her type. Her type didn't steal things and lie about it.

'What were you doing out at Tunguska anyway?' Liz asked. She didn't think research into meteorites was that common yet.

'Impact research,' Kuznetzov replied, pouring the wine. 'We always knew that some huge explosion had occurred there, larger than any man-made detonation. Since I led a team of ballistics experts, it was felt that there may be something worth investigating for the war effort.'

'I see,' Liz said. 'And what did you find?'

Kuznetzov sat back, thinking deeply. 'Flattened trees, mainly. Mile upon mile of flattened trees. There may also have been great fires there.'

'What makes you think that?' Liz smiled. She was so tempted to tell him he was right, and share her later knowledge, but she knew that if her credibility was destroyed, he'd be a lot less willing to share his findings... Or be lulled into revealing whatever he might know about the TARDIS's whereabouts.

'I've seen forest fires before, Elizabeth. Afterwards, the mosses and ferns grow back more rapidly than they had before. I saw just that sort of growth colouring the ground there too.'

Liz nodded slowly, knowing that he was quite right. But she had to wonder how he could be, when she knew that Leonid Kulik would be the first person to visit the site, in another five years' time.

'But,' Kuznetzov said slowly – here it comes, Liz thought – 'I did not bring you here to… Is it "talk shop" you say in England?'

Liz nodded. 'That's one way of putting it.'

Kuznetzov smiled. 'Ah, good. I didn't bring you here just to talk shop. It's rare that I get the chance to meet such a beautiful woman in my circles.'

Liz held up a hand. 'Please. I didn't come here to be flattered either.'

'Of course… And you must be upset by the theft of your property…'

At last, Liz thought. 'It's certainly inconvenient,' she admitted. 'But we have every confidence that the police will find it.'

Kuznetzov frowned in thought. 'My students come from all over the city. Perhaps if you could tell me something about it, one of them may have seen something…'

Liz smiled, hoping he'd take it as relief for the offer of help. 'It's a large blue cabinet about eight feet high, with the words "Police Box" written above the doors. It's locked, so they won't be able to get in.'

'But, of course, you and your friends have keys?'

'The Doctor does.' Liz watched as Kuznetzov nodded, slowly.

When Rasputin's secretary dropped her off at the Winter Palace, Jo hurried up to the suite, and huddled in front of the huge blazing fire. She was beginning to feel that she would never be warm again. The staff had brought in a huge samovar of boiling tea, which Jo helped herself to gratefully. No wonder they needed it this hot if this was what the winters were like.

Not that there was anything cold about being indoors – the fires in the fireplaces, and the heating pipes that threaded through the building, made it quite hot and stuffy. So much so that she was soon sweating uncomfortably. Presumably the Russians were used to it all.

The floor of the main room was strewn with papers, and the Doctor had a large sheet with some sort of blueprint spread across the table. 'Welcome back, Jo. Been exploring the city?' he asked drily.

'Not exactly. I've been hobnobbing with the stars of history just like you always say you do.' She was quite proud of that. After all his frequent references over the years to having known many famous figures from the history books, she could now do it back to him.

'Oh, who?'

'Rasputin.'

'Jo!' the Doctor exclaimed in a mixture of shock and dismay. 'If I took you to thirties Berlin would you go and look up Hitler as well?'

Jo frowned. 'Rasputin's not a dictator, though. I mean, I know there are stories about him being wicked, but he's just a *man*.'

' I suppose most of the stories about him were written by the people who killed him, after all,' the Doctor admitted. 'They're hardly likely to have written "Rasputin a very nice chap; killed him anyway." So what did he say then?'

'He told me all about his life in the country. Some of it

was terribly sad. Actually,' she said slowly, knowing it would needle him in a friendly way, 'in a lot of ways he reminds me of you.'

'I'll trust that's a compliment to him and not the reverse to me.'

'Of course it is!' she grinned, having got the reaction she was aiming for. 'He stands up for his beliefs, no matter what it makes people think of him.'

The Doctor nodded gently. 'Always a dangerous thing to do in an era such as this.'

'You'd like him,' she said. Certainly she didn't imagine Rasputin would try to chat up the Doctor. 'And I'm sure he'd love to hear all the stories you could tell him. Stories were the thing he loved most from his childhood, he said.'

The Doctor shifted uncomfortably. 'Ordinarily I'd be happy to oblige, Jo, but now that I've found some evidence that Kuznetzov may have stolen the TARDIS, I'm afraid I'll be rather busy.' He indicated the police box blueprint in front of him.

'Oh.' Jo was slightly disappointed. 'It's strange,' she said, 'meeting someone you know is going to die...'

The Doctor cleared his throat awkwardly. 'I understand, Jo.'

'And yet, he knows too... He said he'd had visions, and felt sure he would die soon.'

'Well,' said the Doctor, rather brusquely, 'I'm afraid he's right.'

Jo sighed. 'I know you don't believe in that sort of thing, and I'm not so sure I do, but –'

'You'd be right in that assumption, Jo. Visions are very subjective things. D'you know who Nunquawuse was?'

Jo shook her head. 'Some sort of visionary? On another

planet?'

'Actually she was a girl who lived in South Africa in the last century. Over several days she experienced some visions in her garden, which told her that if her tribe, the Xhosa, were to be great once more, they should slaughter all their cattle, and burn their crops. Of course, at first people were doubtful, but over time, she amassed quite a few followers, and eventually got the backing of the Xhosa king, who gave the order for the cattle to be slaughtered, and the crops to be burnt.'

'And did the vision come true?'

'No, Jo. Forty thousand people starved to death, and the rest were absorbed by the British colony of what is now Rhodesia.'

'But Rasputin can see his own death,' Jo insisted.

'Jo,' the Doctor protested. 'Precognitive visions, whether accurate or not, are relatively common in your species. But quite frankly, he would have to be blind not to know that something was up. His brain may filter it as messages from God, but in reality he can hardly be failing to pick up the mood of the city. He must have seen the looks on a hundred faces, and overheard fragments of dozens of conversations, all wishing him harm.'

'I suppose,' Jo said doubtfully. 'Well, I'm going to bed anyway.' She started to leave, then caught a glint on the carpet. 'Is this key yours?'

The Doctor came over and took it from her. 'No. It looks like the key to a small box or briefcase. Liz's perhaps – I'll ask her when she gets back.'

The Doctor didn't have long to wait. Liz, feeling happily full from the meal, even if the company she'd kept had been less pleasant, came in about ten minutes later. 'Any luck?' the Doctor asked.

Liz shrugged. 'Some. He did ask questions about our "stolen property" – even which of us had a key.' She tossed her coat aside. 'I think you're right, Doctor. He knows something about what happened to the TARDIS.'

'Oh, by the way,' the Doctor added. 'Is this key yours?'

'No,' said Liz, 'I've never seen it before.'

Many of the hospital trains that drew into Warsaw Station were owned or subsidised by members of the Imperial family, or by prominent politicians.

One of the longest, pulled by the most powerful engine, belonged to Vladimir Purishkevich. He liked the idea of having something so formidable and strong under his control; that was the sort of thought that made him laugh.

A luxury carriage had been added for the benefit of the high-ranking officers who occasionally went along, or for the owner when he needed a ride. This one was furnished like any other plush drawing room, with leather armchairs and mahogany tables. Purishkevich welcomed Felix aboard, then Dmitri. Two other men followed them on to the train: one was Ivan Sukhotin, a fresh-faced young officer who was recuperating at the Anglo-Russian Hospital, which had been set up at the Belossielsky-Belossievsky Palace; the other was a thin and nervous civilian, Doctor Lazovert, who had treated Sukhotin's wounds.

Sukhotin was a friend of Dmitri's, and Felix was glad that that was as far as their relationship went. He doubted he could bear to share Dmitri.

Once the train's motion had settled into a steady rhythm, Dmitri settled down into his chair. 'Well, gentlemen. We know our task. How exactly should we go about...?'

Felix shifted uncomfortably. The idea of cold-bloodedly killing a man was one he wished he didn't have to consider. But he also knew that, as with so many things, if an unpleasant act was absolutely necessary, it was better to get it over with as quickly and simply as possible. 'I will take a revolver on my next appointment, and shoot him there in his apartment. The quicker the better.'

Dmitri, Sukhotin and Purishkevich exchanged glances of disbelief, and Purishkevich laughed suddenly. 'No, Felix, be serious. How will we –'

Felix couldn't understand this reaction. How much more straightforward could he possibly be? 'I just said, I will keep an appointment he has already made, and shoot him.'

Purishkevich blinked. 'You're serious, aren't you?'

'Of course,' Felix exclaimed. 'If we weren't, none of us would be here.'

'That isn't what I meant. Rasputin's apartment is filled to bursting with his whores and his followers. Then there are the Ochrana guarding the doors. Even if you managed to shoot him, you'd never get out in one piece. No... It'd be better for him to just –' Purishkevich made a vague waving motion – 'disappear.'

'The killing ought to be a secret,' Dmitri agreed, drawing Felix's attention. 'He is favoured by cousin Nicholas, and his murder *might* be seen as a protest against the Tsar.'

Felix shook his head hurriedly. 'You're right, we must avoid that at all costs.' Saving the Tsar and Tsarina from the monster who preyed upon them was to be his greatest gift to them, not an attack. He shuddered at the thought that anyone could imagine his motives to be anything other than to protect Nicholas and Alexandra. 'How then?' he asked, as much to forestall anyone from asking him to speak during this troubling thought as to actually get suggestions from the others. Right now he needed his own silence as much as others' voices.

'The first thing is to get him away from those damned Ochrana vultures,' Purishkevich growled. 'We can't do much with them looking over our shoulders.'

'Kidnap him, you mean?' Sukhotin asked.

'Lure him away,' Felix said slowly. 'The Ochrana watch him and his visitors constantly, but that shouldn't be a problem, given the right circumstances. His resistance to temptation isn't that high – he'll follow a pretty girl anywhere.'

'He's always had his eye on Irina, hasn't he?' Dmitri put in.

Felix nodded. 'But she's away in the Crimea.' He shrugged; pretty girls to lure a common lecher such as Rasputin could be found anywhere.

'The English woman who visited you with Kuznetzov,' Dmitri suggested. 'Elizabeth Shaw.'

Felix thought about that. She was certainly striking enough, and had expressed a dislike for Rasputin… 'Perhaps. I'll speak to her later, but the specific girl isn't that important. Rasputin would follow *any* girl straight into the jaws of Hell if he thinks she'll spread her legs for him. The more important question is what we do with him once we've got him.'

Purishkevich laughed again, and drained a gulp of gorilka. 'Why, then you can shoot him, of course!' He put the glass down, momentarily becoming more thoughtful. 'The body should not found anywhere near either his home or the site of his murder.'

'The Front?' Sukhotin suggested. 'There are enough corpses there – who would notice one extra?' Felix nodded slowly. Since Rasputin was doing irreparable harm to the war effort, that seemed appropriate.

'We can bring him out on this train,' Purishkevich said. 'Nobody would notice any bloodstains...'

'All right,' Felix interrupted. 'Mrs Purishkevich is on duty here at nights – she can burn any evidence. Tomorrow, I'll visit Miss Shaw, and invite her to join us.'

Chapter Eleven

The morning sky was grey and watery, a very English sky, thought Jo.

She had breakfasted on jam and bread, when the Doctor came into the lounge of their suite. 'You're up with the lark, Jo. Still, the early bird catches the worm.' The Doctor seemed impossibly alert and cheerful for so early in the morning. Not for the first time, Jo wondered how he ever managed to get enough rest. He didn't seem to sleep much, yet he was always alert even at the earliest hours of daylight.

'I suppose I'm just learning what you've always said.'

'Well, never too late,' the Doctor agreed approvingly. He passed through on his way to fetch his own breakfast, and Liz emerged from her room a moment later.

Liz was still in nightgown and robe, but nevertheless looked fresher than Jo felt. Jo had never been one to be instantly alert after waking up.

Liz smiled. 'You're –'

'Up with the lark,' Jo finished. 'I know. The Doctor just said so.'

Liz nodded understandingly. 'I should have known he'd be up. He never did seem to sleep when I was at UNIT...'

'He still doesn't,' Jo agreed, and they chuckled together.

'Do you?'

'Oh, I do. But I had to get up early today.'

'Any particular reason?'

'I'm going to see Rasputin.'

Rasputin... She had intended to stay away after his

parting remark last night. While he might not be a demonic despot, he was certainly an inveterate womaniser. But then she decided that the drink was probably making him talk nonsense. He seemed to pride himself on attracting girls, not forcing them. She supposed he didn't see any challenge in that.

Liz's expression was horrified. 'You can't be serious – Rasputin? The "mad monk"?'

Jo nodded enthusiastically. 'I met him yesterday – he brought those files the Doctor wanted. You know, he's not as bad as all the stories say,' she insisted.

Liz shook her head. 'Haven't you read your history books, Jo? This is the man who rules Russia from behind the throne. He's a philanderer, a manipulator, a rapist…'

'You haven't met him,' Jo said defensively. 'I've heard the stories, and I've seen the film, but he wasn't like that at all.'

Liz didn't think that was very reassuring. 'I don't need to meet him – I saw his eyes yesterday, and they were undressing both of us.' She certainly wouldn't trust him around herself, or any woman.

'Now, that's…' She was about to say 'ridiculous' but caught herself. She had noticed that too, but… 'That's not exactly proof that he's the devil incarnate.'

Liz sat back, looking at Jo with a mixture of horror and concern. Jo found it quite patronising. 'He's also a notorious hypnotist – he must have got at you…'

Jo blinked. 'I have been hypnotised before, and by more of a hypnotist than Rasputin could ever be. Look, I'm grateful that you care, but you've got it all wrong.' With that, Jo left.

Liz remained seated for a moment. She knew the Doctor

well enough to know that he'd be concerned. She went through to the kitchen, where the Doctor was patiently instructing the chefs how to prepare his breakfast.

'Doctor,' she said. 'Have you spoken to Jo this morning?'

'Just to say good morning, why?'

'She tells me that she's off to see Rasputin again today.'

'Yes, she met him yesterday. She is old enough to live her own life. And I think she's sensible enough to be careful who she talks to.'

'Look,' Liz said defiantly. 'You know history, remember, so you must also know what sort of man Rasputin was – is. If he could twist someone as single-minded as the Empress round his finger, then surely you can see how easy it would be for him to overpower a girl like Jo.'

The Doctor looked at her levelly. 'She's not quite as dizzy as you might think, you know.'

Liz nodded, a little embarrassed. 'But what was it Nietzsche said? That someone who challenges monsters might become one in turn. That if you look too long into an abyss, the abyss looks into you.'

'That's something of a paraphrasing, Liz. But yes, I know what you mean.'

'You know the history books better than I do – you know what he stands for. He's at the heart of darkness.'

'And you think that Rasputin's darkness is dragging Jo in?'

'Yes, that's exactly what I think, Doctor. And I also think that you see that yourself.'

'Evil has always had an allure for humans,' the Doctor remarked. 'Historical atrocities become entertainment for the descendants of perpetrators and victims alike. The most brutal butchers and dictators become almost cult figures, from museum exhibitions about the Roman arenas, to endless documentaries about Hitler. But, Liz, none of that turns people into the disciples of those butchers.'

'Maybe, and maybe not. But there's a difference between watching a TV programme about one of the most notorious manipulative criminals in history, and actually meeting him in person. Distance protects us from that, but now it's gone.'

'Look, Liz, Jo *is* one of UNIT's trained agents. She's seen and faced a lot of very nasty creatures during her time at UNIT. Even nastier than our friend Rasputin.'

Liz nodded. 'I'm not denying that, but she admits herself that she's been hypnotised into working against you before.'

'By a Time Lord,' the Doctor said pointedly, 'capable of all but totally subjugating the human will. Rasputin may be a rather unsavoury man, but that's all he is. A man! Besides, as I told Jo last night, the stories you heard were told by Rasputin's enemies, so they're hardly a reliable source of objective information.' He smiled reassuringly. 'Believe me, I care about Jo as much as anyone. She knows what she's doing.'

The Ochrana building on Kronversky Prospekt looked more like an apartment block than a prison, certainly less fearsome than the granite fortress. Appearances could be deceiving, however, and frequently were.

Academician Kuznetzov's leg twitched with impatience. He tried not to fidget but couldn't help himself, and it was a failing he hated.

He was sitting in the office of Viktor Vasiliyev. Sombre panelling and carpeting gave the place the funereal air of an undertaker's office. Kuznetzov doubted, however, that an undertaker's office would be so rank with the tang of cigar smoke.

'This is what you called me out of bed for?' Vasiliyev asked from the other side of the desk. He certainly showed all the signs of having been wakened when he didn't want to be: red-rimmed eyes and an unshaven jaw. He squinted at the piece of paper Kuznetzov had given him.

'It *is* in Rasputin's handwriting, isn't it?'

Vasiliyev regarded the spidery scribbles coolly. 'Yes... But Rasputin gives these notes to anyone who pleases him.'

'That note,' Kuznetzov said coldly, 'was found in Arkady Morovich's pocket. It's addressed to Manus, the "Swedish banker", whom we both know is a German agent.'

'All it says,' Vasiliyev protested, 'is, "Rasputin would be grateful if this man is allowed entry." It could be to the public baths, for all we know.'

Kuznetzov nodded. 'Or it could be to border guards, or guards at Headquarters, or Tsarskoe Selo.' He leaned forward, trying to put more urgency into his words. 'This is a note from Rasputin, granting access to some unknown place to a German agent, and was found on a murdered body.'

'Our investigations suggest suicide.'

'Well, of course they want it to look like that...'

Vasiliyev sighed, but Kuznetzov sensed that his doubt had wavered. He knew that Vasiliyev would at least consider the possibility now. He forced down the urge to smile at the way his plan was falling into place. 'All right,' Vasiliyev said. 'I'll investigate.'

Kuznetzov spread his hands. 'That's all I ask. There's no point in having informants if you don't accept their information.'

'No... No, I suppose not.' Vasiliyev folded up the note, and put it in a drawer. 'You can collect the... Academy donation, on your way out.'

'Thank you,' Kuznetzov replied, rising with a half bow.

Kit had reached the coffee lounge first this morning. More accurately, he had arrived last night, and whiled away the evening in the company of a couple of majors and some expensive prostitutes. When the officers and the girls had gone off to a room somewhere, Kit had picked the lock of a vacant room and slept there. Even without his fidelity to Ashley, he'd not have risked compromising himself with women of the night who were probably also in the pay of the Ochrana.

His stolen rest meant he didn't keel over in the street with exhaustion, even if it also meant he didn't have the chance to say goodnight to Ashley's picture. That was a little ritual he had; it made him feel a little more comfortable, and made her absence more bearable.

By the time Vasiliyev arrived, Kit had the samovar waiting for him. The Ochrana chief looked somewhat puzzled and worried.

'Something wrong?' Kit asked, once Vasiliyev had settled into his seat.

'Perhaps. Things are very odd these days...' He handed over a piece of paper. 'What do you make of that?'

Kit looked at the horrendous handwriting. 'One of Rasputin's notes to the favoured. There must be a million of them by now. Manus isn't exactly a great choice of follower, but...'

'Apparently this note was found in the pocket of Arkady Morovich.' Kit froze, wondering if this was where his role ended.

122

'That's the man who fell off one of the rostrals the other day?' he asked, careful to keep his voice level.

Vasiliyev nodded. 'If Morovich took the note from Rasputin, it makes good, if circumstantial, evidence for Rasputin having murdered him. I wondered if you agreed.'

Kit felt quite tongue-tied. The honourable thing would probably be to come clean, and tell Vasiliyev what had happened at the rostral, but honour and self-preservation weren't always the best of bedfellows.

It would also be a greater dishonour to endanger his job here than to keep his mouth shut about that death, or so he told himself. That seemed to satisfy both his conscience and his desire not to be implicated in murder.

'That would be a fair assumption,' Kit said finally. 'And I've no doubt it's Rasputin's handwriting...' Though a good forger could forge anyone's hand. Vasiliyev would know that as well, of course.

Vasiliyev nodded to himself. 'This is certainly a golden opportunity to put our own credibility ahead of Rasputin's...' He folded the note away. 'Thank you, Kit.'

Academician Kuznetzov had gone straight to the Moika Palace from the Ochrana HQ, and handed Felix another note. In fact, it was the same note, identical in every way. He was quite proud of the forger who had created them for him.

His spirits lifted by Vasiliyev's belief, Kuznetzov had expected even better results from the man who had already laid plans to kill Rasputin. It was a bit like preaching to the converted, but Kuznetzov didn't mind doing so from time to time, to reinforce opinions.

It was a considerable shock when Felix tore the note up.

Kuznetzov shook his head in disbelief. 'What's wrong with you, Felix? You've just been handed evidence that the man you plan to kill is a traitor. You should be glad!'

'Please, don't understand me so well,' Felix responded drily. 'Do you think I'm so uncomplicated as to see things so conveniently black and white? And what makes you think I have any such plans?'

'Oh, come now, Felix Felixovich! That old sot Purishkevich has been telling anybody who'll listen in the lobby of the Duma that you and he are going to be heroes.'

Felix turned away, visibly biting back the curse that rose in his throat. Purishkevich was a worse drinker than Rasputin; not as temperamental or violent, but even more dependent on it.

'Don't worry. You *will* be heroes,' Kuznetzov pointed out, 'when everyone sees that Grishka Rasputin has been selling our strategies to the Germans.'

'No,' Felix said quietly.

Kuznetzov lost track of what he was going to say next. 'What? Don't tell me you believe he's innocent?'

'Of course not!' Felix snapped. He knew Rasputin had been a member of the German Party, and that some of his supposedly Swedish friends were certainly German agents. 'But nor do I believe your "evidence" is genuine. Neither will anyone else who matters, because Rasputin is many things – crude, selfish – but he is not stupid. That means two things, Kuznetzov,' Felix went on, levelling an accusatory finger at him. 'One, it means that there would be a danger that people might feel that *all* of the case against Rasputin was equally false; and two, it means that we would be allowing the real source of this *other* trade in secrets to continue betraying the Tsar and Russia. And I will not allow either of those things to happen.'

'But Felix,' Kuznetzov protested, 'this is –'

'I'm taking this course to protect the Imperial family,' Felix said sharply. 'My duty is to protect them from any harm, not just to exchange one threat for another. So, as I said, no.'

Jo went looking for the Doctor, and found him crossing off locations on a map. Apparently these were places which Kuznetzov was known to frequent, but didn't contain the TARDIS. 'Doctor,' she began. 'I've been thinking. We've come back in time, right?'

'Right.'

'So, what if we could change things – say we saved Rasputin –'

'No, Jo.'

'Why?'

The Doctor shook his head curtly, a faint smile playing across his face. 'Why? Because you can't, that's why. And even if you could, you'd only succeed in causing the most horrendous consequences for the future.'

'But it's just one man, Doctor –'

The Doctor looked momentarily angry, but then sighed. 'I know, Jo. It seems a very small thing, doesn't it? Saving one man's life can't do any harm, can it?'

Jo nodded eagerly. 'Exactly.'

'All right, then. Let's say you prevent Rasputin's murder – what then? His death was one of the key triggers for the Russian Revolution.'

Jo frowned. History wasn't really her strong point, and she hadn't even taken the subject at O level. Still, she did know a few basics... 'Without the Revolution, the Tsar and his family would be saved. Anastasia would definitely survive. And we'd have a lot more peace in our own time.'

'Would we?' The Doctor shook his head. 'No, without the Revolution, Hitler would have no Communist enemy to distract him from his plans to invade Britain. Russia's own military would be too scattered and ill-equipped to fight back when he finally invaded. Nazi Germany would roll in and claim Russia's oil reserves and industrial strength for itself. By the time even America realised the scale of the problem, they would too late to resist, and Hitler would have the world.'

'But you can't *know* that,' Jo protested. 'You can't be sure that that's what would happen.'

'Not a hundred per cent, no,' the Doctor admitted.

'And we know that *doesn't* happen. Just like the Daleks don't invade Earth in the twenty-second cent–'

The Doctor cut her off. 'That's different, Jo. In many ways that was simply a theoretical abstraction made real by a temporal anomaly.'

Jo threw up her arms. 'You know I can't answer back to your gobbledegook, Doctor. But you saw the strikers and protesters in the city. There's just as likely to be a Revolution even if Rasputin doesn't die.'

'Very probably. The web of time is quite resilient, but you can be sure that there would be some kind of unexpected side-effects to any changes you tried to make. And in my experience, unexpected side effects are never positive, Jo. Never.'

Kit had slipped quietly into the Winter Palace to see the Doctor. Security was supposed to be tight here, but with the Romanovs away, and so many wounded in the palace,

Kit had found that the occasional bottle of malt Scotch opened most doors in St Petersburg.

'Ah, there you are,' the Doctor said, as Kit met him on the main staircase. He must have been about to go out. 'I was just about to go and look for you.'

Kit nodded. 'I wanted to talk to you too, Doctor. I just had a rather interesting conversation with Vasiliyev.'

'Interesting? In what way?'

'He had a note, which Kuznetzov gave him as evidence that Rasputin is a German spy. He says it's evidence that Rasputin murdered a man called Morovich, who knew his secret.'

'But you don't believe this alleged evidence?'

'No.' Kit grimaced. 'Rasputin was nowhere near when that man died – I know because I was there. He was spying on me when I met a contact at the Volkhov rostral. We heard him move, and he fled. We followed him up to the platform at the top, since we certainly wanted to know who it was and what he had learned. When we got there, he had climbed over the rail. I think he meant to jump down in stages, from prow to prow – there are several set into the column – but missed. I made a grab for his hand as he slipped, but...'

The Doctor regarded him curiously. 'You mean the man hadn't been hypnotised by Rasputin into jumping?'

'No! I mean, I wouldn't put it past Rasputin to do such a thing, but no. The man was simply terrified of being caught by us. I imagine he thought we would have killed him.'

'Would you?'

Kit grimaced. 'I wouldn't, no, though I couldn't swear the same for my contact. I'd have rather offered him money to keep his mouth shut.'

'Good. Systems of rewards are always better than punishments. And speaking of rewards, I found out something else about our friend Kuznetzov. He has several million roubles hidden in his apartment, and someone placed a key to a case in our suite. I haven't found the case it fits yet, but I've no doubt that there's one somewhere – no doubt in case he needs evidence of my "crimes".'

'Was there anything else incriminating in his apartment?'

'There were some illustrations of the equipment stolen from me, but nothing linking him to Germany, if that's what you're wondering…' The Doctor scratched his nose. 'Just a minute, there was one thing – the telephone rang, and the man who called Kuznetzov referred to an associate called "Koba". Does that name mean anything to you?'

'Koba?' Kit echoed. 'Vasiliyev occasionally makes deals with criminals – let a small fish go to catch a bigger one –'

'Yes, yes. I am familiar with the idea.'

'One of them was a "Koba", though I never met him.' Kit looked up, thinking of the Doctor's mention of the inordinate amounts of money Kuznetzov had hidden. 'And if I remember rightly, that Koba was a bank robber, who robbed banks for the SR Fighting Section.'

'A mixture of the personal and political,' the Doctor said ironically. 'Rob a bank in the name of revolution for a political statement that stirs up the authorities, and keep the money for yourself.'

'Sounds like he picked a better business to go into than we did, Doctor.' Get yourself rich, and blame it on a political cause if you get caught; it sounded like an ideal situation to Kit. It was a shame that truth never matched up to ideals. 'Do you mean to suggest that Kuznetzov is Koba the bank robber?'

'No.' The Doctor paced around in a tight little circle. 'No, I'm sure I've heard of this Koba before, but Kuznetzov is a total stranger to me. It certainly seems likely that Kuznetzov and Koba are working together, though. Besides, the man said that this Koba had approved Kuznetzov's plan.'

'I don't suppose he happened to mention what that plan was?' Kit asked hopefully. That would make his life a lot easier.

'No.'

Kit wasn't the least bit surprised. It seemed that an easy life was doomed to be as alien to him as the other side of the moon. 'Where do we go from here?'

'I'll go back to the Academy, and see if there's any sign of the TARDIS in any of the labs or workshops –'

'If they've discovered your last break-in they'll be watching for you,' Kit pointed out. 'I'll take care of that search.'

'You don't have to go to all that trouble on my account –'

'I'm afraid I do, and it makes more sense.'

The Doctor nodded. 'All right. I'll go and see how the authorities are getting on with their search.'

Chapter Twelve

When the large car drew up in the Winter Palace's courtyard, Liz had expected it to contain Kuznetzov. She was quite surprised when Prince Felix Yusupov emerged.

'Miss Shaw,' he said politely. She smiled at his charming air. 'I wonder if I could press you to join me for a chat?'

'Of course.' She didn't have much interest in hobnobbing with royalty even in her own time, but nor did she want to pass up the chance to learn anything; Kuznetzov was one of his friends after all, and perhaps a more oblique approach was wise. Perhaps that was what they thought too.

'Miss Shaw... Academician Kuznetzov tells me – and I noticed myself – that you have no love for Grigory Rasputin.'

Liz began to get the uncomfortable feeling that at some point she had said something she shouldn't. 'That's true...'

'There are some of us who feel the same way,' Felix said softly. 'I'd like you to come and meet them, at the Moika.'

'Now?'

'No time like the present.'

Liz wondered how Felix would react if he knew how ironic that statement was. She was no expert, but she did know that Rasputin was fated to die within the next couple of weeks. She was reluctant to agree, but also didn't want to risk becoming a target by refusing. Besides, it might still lead her closer to both the truth and the TARDIS.

'Very well.' What harm could it do?

* * *

This time Felix showed Liz into a much more sumptuous drawing room, filled with treasures from Asia and the Near East. Felix made the introductions quickly, though Liz already recognised Dmitri.

Purishkevich reminded her vaguely of Lenin, though it was probably just his fashionable – for the era – beard and haircut. Sukhotin seemed the very image of a nineteenth-century Guards officer, lacking only the duelling scar. Lazovert seemed nervous, and she suspected he was only involved because he was too scared too refuse. Kuznetzov wasn't there, and Liz wasn't sure whether to be relieved or disappointed.

Purishkevich laughed, waving his drinking hand around and almost spilling his vodka. 'Sometimes I don't know why she doesn't just marry him as well, or at least make a public ceremony of handing over the keys to her bedchamber.'

Liz recalled the song that was just becoming popular back in her own time. 'Lover of the Russian queen... That's what they *say*, at least.'

Purishkevich fixed a drunken beady glare on her. 'Of course, and it's true. Why else would she be so desperate to keep her liaisons with him a secret?' Liz had to admit that this was a bit of a mystery. Alexandra certainly seemed to be engaged in some sort of illicit relationship, and there was no smoke without fire... Purishkevich frowned momentarily. 'Where is that letter that Felix had...?' He put his drink down, and started raking through the papers in the desk drawer. 'I'm sure it was here somewhere... Aha!' He straightened, brandishing the letter triumphantly. 'Let's see what you make of this...'

Liz sat uncomfortably. Reading someone else's mail was not a particular hobby of hers, and the fact that this was from Alexandra to Rasputin meant it was clearly stolen. That wasn't a comfortable feeling. Still, she could hardly tell Purishkevich to shut up…

"*My Beloved, unforgettable teacher, redeemer and mentor,*" he simpered in a warbling falsetto that he obviously found overly amusing. "*How tiresome it is without you. My soul is quiet and I relax only when you, my teacher, are sitting beside me. I kiss your hands and lean my head on your blessed shoulder. Oh, how light do I feel then. I only wish one thing: to fall asleep for ever on your shoulders and in your arms. What happiness to feel your presence near me. Where are you? Where have you gone? Oh, I am so sad and my heart is longing. Will you soon be again close to me? Come quickly, I am waiting for you and I am tormenting myself for you. I am asking for your Holy Blessing*" – Pah, I've never heard quite heard it called *that* before – "*and I am kissing your blessed hands. I love you for ever.*"

'It's certainly pretty explosive stuff,' Liz agreed. 'This could do great damage if it was made public –'

'It would also damage the Empress and the Tsar,' Felix pointed out. 'We want to save them from Rasputin, not make things worse for them.'

'Then why did you ask me here?'

Felix's features tightened, and he glanced at Dmitri for what looked like support. 'Tomorrow night, we want to bring Rasputin here.'

'To kill him?' In her own mind it was a rhetorical question, though she knew that they couldn't see it that way.

'To… deal with his threat as is best appropriate. He has a… particular interest in my wife –'

'And any other female so long as she's still living and

breathing,' Purishkevich added.

'We had hoped to lure him here with the promise of meeting Irina, but she is in the Crimea. I'd like to ask if you would...'

'Be the bait in her place?' Liz wished he hadn't asked that. What was she supposed to say in answer to a proposal that she join in a cold-blooded murder? How could she live with her conscience if she accepted? 'No, I won't be a party to murder.'

Felix made a calming motion. 'You don't have to be. All you have to do is be here tomorrow night. If Rasputin will see sense and agree to leave the city, we can all celebrate together.'

Liz considered. If they hadn't found the TARDIS by then, she'd probably have to come to keep an eye on Kuznetzov anyway.

She turned back to Felix. 'Very well. I'll visit the palace, but I won't take part in the –'

'Of course not,' Purishkevich exclaimed cheerily. 'What sort of men would we be, if we asked you to do our dirty work for us?' Liz didn't waste her breath with a reply.

'Thank you,' Felix said, his voice warm with deep feeling. Liz felt unaccountably pleased about that. 'If you'll honour me, I would like to show around the city. To make up for the burden I've placed upon you.'

'The honour is all mine,' Liz replied.

Vasiliyev had been worried when he had been called to the Winter Palace, fearing that some of the country's treasures had been stolen, or that there had been an assassination. He and the troop of black-coated Ochrana agents who accompanied him had not expected to find something valuable that had been added.

A man in the uniform of the palace guard, called Mischa, had discovered a briefcase full of money in one of the guest suites.

'Is anyone using this suite?' Vasiliyev asked.

'Yes sir, some foreign dignitaries. A man called the Doctor.'

Vasiliyev knew that he was one of the new arrivals who had turned up unexpectedly at Tsarskoe Selo. The one who had reported his property stolen. He also recognised the serial numbers of these wads of money as being on the stolen list. But what would the man want with it, if he was so affluent as to be able to travel the world anyway? Unless it was for pay-offs to locals...

'Miss Shaw?' A voice called from outside. Kuznetzov's voice, Vasiliyev recognised. He went outside to where the Academician was knocking on the door of a neighbouring suite.

'What are you doing here?'

Kuznetzov appeared surprised. 'I could ask you the same question. I have an appointment with Professor Shaw.'

'How convenient. I wonder if she has any stolen money in her rooms.'

'Stolen money?'

'We've just discovered a bag full of it in the Doctor's rooms.'

'Professor Shaw did call me to say she was suspicious of him... Do you want me to, ah, hint at some questions to her?'

Vasiliyev nodded slowly. He should really have all three arrested, but Miss Grant was with Rasputin, which made her all but immune for the moment, and sometimes subtlety was better. If she was already talking to Kuznetsov, she might simply clam up if brought in. 'Yes… If she doesn't know he's been brought in, we might have more luck getting an honest story out of her.'

Kuznetsov nodded an agreement. Then he frowned. 'The Doctor, you say?'

'Yes.'

'You know, a man answering his description tried to burgle my train.' Vasiliyev's ears pricked up. Why hadn't Kuznetsov reported this already? 'The thing is… when the guards tried to arrest this man, Kit Powell intervened to save him.'

'Kit?' Vasiliyev echoed. 'You say Kit rescued the Doctor?'

'That is what I said,' Kuznetsov replied.

'I don't believe it.' Kit was an invaluable member of Vasiliyev's team, not a common criminal.

'Then you're calling me a liar?' Kuznetsov asked softly.

'No,' Vasiliyev said slowly, though he wouldn't hesitate to do so if he did think that. 'No, I just don't believe your people are competent observers.'

'You should hope they are, since they're also informers for you. I still believe this Doctor is a spy.'

'Oh, I *know* he is,' Vasiliyev agreed.

Kuznetsov blinked, taken aback. 'You do?'

Vasiliyev thought, then turned to an aide. 'Put the word out – I want the Doctor brought in immediately. And Kit Powell.' He turned away, returning to his examination of the bag of stolen money, and so missed the look that passed between Kuznetsov and Mischa.

It had taken the Doctor some time to go all the way to Ochrana HQ. He doubted they had had any luck finding the

TARDIS, but it couldn't hurt to ask. Before the Doctor could get inside, however, the surprised-looking guard on the door had drawn him aside. 'You are the Doctor?'

'Yes, I am. Now, if you'll excuse me, I have some urgent business inside –'

'You certainly do.' The man produced a gun. 'Chief Vasiliyev wants you.' Two more agents in identical overcoats joined him. The Doctor considered making a break for it, but changed his mind. There must be some reason why they were looking for him, and since he hadn't broken any – well, many – laws here, perhaps it related to Kuznetzov. In that case, he might learn more by going with them. And he was going inside anyway.

'You know, you could just have said "please". The guns are simply rude.'

'Come with us.' Instead of taking the Doctor inside, the agents led him to a car, which was soon speeding through the city. They drove south for a short distance, and over a long bridge that led to a sprawling medieval fortress built on its own island.

The Doctor recognised it at once as the Peter and Paul fortress, and saw that they had finished building the central basilica since he was last here.

The Ochrana agents escorted him to the eastern end of the island. 'I thought you said Vasiliyev wanted to see me. Shouldn't we be at the Ochrana headquarters?'

'He wants you segregated. He'll come to visit you soon enough.' The agents handed him over to the Specials, guards in green cloaks who ran the prison. 'Hold him with no visitors until Chief Vasiliyev arrives.'

'Understood.'

The Specials ushered the Doctor into the medieval

tower. The Doctor was surprised at the thick carpet that graced the floor of the Trubetskoy Bastion. He had scarcely expected to find an early-twentieth-century Russian prison so well furnished. As the guards escorted him along, he began to realise the truth. Neither his boots or theirs made any noticeable sound against the carpet, as they would on planks or flagstones. Clearly the carpet was there so that prisoners wouldn't hear their captors coming to spy, interrogate or even execute them, and therefore keep them in a more constant state of suspense.

When the guards stopped and opened a cell door, the Doctor saw that the cells themselves *were* much as he expected: cold and damp stone, with moss growing on the walls. From the scale of the dampness he guessed that the cells were below the level of the river.

The door slammed closed. Shaking his head, the Doctor settled down to wait.

Vasili Maklakov wasn't entirely surprised by Felix's return to his office, though the fact that he was accompanied by a rather striking woman was more unexpected.

Felix got straight to the point. 'You said that if I decided to deal with Rasputin myself, you would be able to help with advice...?'

Maklakov looked Liz over coldly. He didn't know where *she* fitted in but, if Felix trusted her enough, then it was his funeral. He nodded. 'All right. I presume from the fact that you've brought someone with you, that you have formed a small cadre of conspirators?'

Felix nodded. 'Vladi-'

'No!' Maklakov snapped hurriedly. 'Do not tell me who they are! Don't tell anyone. The most important thing you must remember is to guard your own safety in this.' He calmed somewhat. 'Don't tell me, because then – if the worst comes to the worst – I can stand as your legal counsel. If I am already involved that would be difficult, to say the least.'

'I understand. You'll forgive me if I hope it doesn't come to that…'

'Make sure that you can shrug off any suspicion that may come your way, and send it elsewhere. Distance yourself from the crime…' He trailed off in thought. 'Book a table for yourself and Rasputin at the Villa Rode for after when the deed is to be done. Afterwards, telephone there to ask if he's arrived. That way people will know you expected to see him alive.'

Maklakov hesitated, then opened a drawer in his desk, and drew out a vicious-looking club – a thin steel bar, wrapped in padded leather. 'Take this,' Maklakov said, handing it to Felix. 'Its use may become… appropriate…'

Felix looked at the club with a mixture of distaste and weariness. 'Thank you, Vasili.'

Outside, Liz looked at Felix as they emerged onto the street. 'You don't sound like you've done much of this before.'

'Killed anyone?' Felix shook his head. 'No. No, I couldn't.' He allowed himself a faint smile. 'Well, not before, anyway.' He looked at the club. 'When I was a boy, my father used to force me to take part in hunts and shoots at Rakitnoe. It's part of the noble way of life, you see, Miss Shaw.'

Liz understood that; even in her own time, hunts were conducted by the upper classes. They were living examples of the past, when the king had the choice of the tastiest animals for his banquets.

'I never liked it,' Felix went on. 'Not from the first. But my father wanted to raise a good little prince to hunt and carouse and lead troops… So we shot. I wounded a hare once.' He seemed to wince, as if reliving the moment, and looked into the distance. 'It screamed, on and on… So human. I never thought animals could do that. I haven't been back to Rakitnoe since, and I gave away all the guns that were bought for me. Eventually my father gave up buying them.' He paused. 'Did you know my brother was killed in a duel?'

Liz shook her head. This wasn't what she'd come to hear, but it looked like something he needed to say.

'He, ah… He was courting a girl, Countess Marina Heyden. She was already engaged to an officer in the Horse Guards, Baron Manteufel. Nicky wanted to marry her. Mother and I both told him that she was too fast and loose, and that he wasn't thinking, but he didn't listen. Manteufel married her, but six months later, she and Nicky were seeing each other again.'

'And got caught?'

'Inevitably. Manteufel challenged Nicky to a duel, but our families talked him out of it, and they settled more amicably. Manteufel would divorce Marina.'

'But you said there was a duel… What went wrong?'

'The military mind, Miss Shaw.' She could understand that all too well. More boys playing soldiers, as if the world didn't have enough of them. 'To the other officers in Manteufel's regiment, not fighting a duel was… Was throwing away his and his wife's honour. So, to save face among his brother officers, he reissued the challenge. Nicky told us he refused it, but…'

'But he lied so that you wouldn't interfere.'

Felix nodded sadly 'They fought on July the fourth, 1908, and Manteufel killed Nicky. In doing so he almost killed my mother. She was... insane, with grief, for a very long time.'

'And what about you?' In spite of herself, Liz found that she was concerned about him.

'Me?' Felix looked into the fireplace, and his eyes reflected the flame that burned both there and within him. 'I wanted to kill Manteufel.'

'But you didn't do it, did you?'

Felix shook his head, a little too sharply.

'If you couldn't kill Baron Manteufel even after he killed your brother, surely you can't kill Rasputin.'

'The situation is different,' Felix said steadily. 'Where the fate of the whole Russian people is concerned, personal concerns must take second place. My hatred of Manteufel is merely personal, but killing Rasputin is a duty. It *has* to be done, to save Nicholas and Alexandra from those who think them weak. And to save Russia. We are at war, Miss Shaw, and we cannot afford to be derailed by the madness of one ambitious criminal.'

Rasputin took two large bites out of his sandwich, then handed it to the nearest guest. 'You can finish that off.' He could feel Jo's eyes on him, and sense her distaste, but he also knew she was too fascinated to leave. She was different from the others here, in some way he had yet to fathom, but she was still only human.

Feeling amused, he dipped his finger into a pot of jam, and held it out to her. 'Perhaps you have a sweet tooth?'

Jo looked disappointed in him, which he found surprising and quite fascinating.

'I don't think that's very hygienic,' she said primly.

141

Rasputin laughed, as a woman in a Parisian dress leaned past Jo, and took his finger into her mouth, shaving off the jam with her tongue. 'You see, Josephine, some know how to humble themselves before God.'

'I don't see any sign of Him at this tea,' she replied. 'Just a dirty old man.'

Rasputin pulled his finger from the woman's mouth. 'No sign of Him?' he echoed darkly. How dare she blaspheme in this way? 'The Lord is everywhere, girl! Don't you go to church?' He gulped down a swig of wine. 'You have displeased me,' he snapped. 'Go now. You may come back tomorrow, but I will see you no more tonight.'

'Suits me fine,' Jo retorted, as Simanovich gently escorted her out of the room.

Rasputin watched her go, already regretting his temper. That was twice he had snapped at Josephine, and he wasn't sure she'd give him a third chance. The room seemed much dimmer without her presence. He would give her a hundred roubles tomorrow, to make up for dismissing her. As it was, however, he still needed companionship for the night. He took the hand of the woman in the Parisian dress, and rose from his seat. His other visitors paused respectfully as he led her out towards the bedroom.

'Come with me,' he said. 'If you please me, I will purify you.'

Chapter Thirteen

The Doctor was whistling tunelessly, knowing it would irritate the guard, who he was certain remained outside. 'Decided to show some basic rights at last, have we?' he asked, when the door was finally opened.

'Vasiliyev is ready for you.'

'I'm sure I wouldn't want to keep him waiting.' The Doctor pulled on his jacket and strolled casually out of the cell. 'I could do with a bite to eat. Breakfast's the most important meal of the day, you know.'

'You'll be fed when it's time.'

The guards marched him back along the carpeted corridor, to a small office. It must have been some sort of guard captain's office, as there were rows of keys, and a locked gun cabinet in addition to the small desk and filing cabinet.

'Do sit down, Doctor,' Vasiliyev said. He nodded to the guards, who withdrew. 'I'm sorry I couldn't speak to you last night, but I was unavoidably detained.'

'I know the feeling,' the Doctor said acidly.

'Quite.' Vasiliyev placed a briefcase on the desk. 'Do you recognise this?'

'No, but I imagine it was planted in our suite at the Winter Palace. And it was also full of stolen money.'

Vasiliyev grinned unpleasantly. 'Convenient of you to "imagine" so accurately. Assuming that you're about to protest your innocence, how could you know what it contained?'

'Because I found the key to a briefcase that didn't belong to any of us, in our rooms. It seemed logical to assume the case was also put there, but I didn't find it. As for the contents: that depended on who put it there, and if it was planted by who I think planted it, then it would logically be full of stolen money, because he has plenty to spare.'

'You are a veritable Sherlock Holmes, I'll give you that…'

The Doctor looked at him thoughtfully. 'Is this money the only reason I've been brought here?'

'No, I have a few other questions. Firstly, who do you work for?'

'I don't work for anybody, old chap. I'm what you might call freelance.'

'A mercenary.'

'Hardly!'

'Do not go back on your word, it does not become you. Where is Kit Powell?' Vasiliyev asked before the Doctor could protest.

'Don't you know? He does work for you, after all.'

'Well, I had thought so too, but with him rescuing you during a burglary, and then you being found with a pile of money for pay-offs…'

'Burglary?'

'Kuznetzov's train.'

'Kuznetzov again… I might have guessed. Mr Vasiliyev, you do realise that you're being manipulated by Kuznetzov? Or are you too blind to see that?'

'Academician Kuznetzov is –'

'Academician Kuznetzov is involved with criminals, stole the property that I reported stolen and, I believe, planted that briefcase.'

'He is one of my best informants, Doctor. I trust him more than I trust you. Guard!' The door opened. 'Take the Doctor back to his cell, until he decides to tell us where Kit Powell is.'

'Vasiliyev,' the Doctor protested, 'you are making a very large mistake. Neither Kit nor myself is your enemy –'

'Out!'

The guards hauled the Doctor out of the room.

Once they were gone, Vasiliyev relaxed. It didn't really matter whether the Doctor talked or not; Vasiliyev knew all of Kit's haunts. Since it wasn't unusual for Kit to vanish for a day or two, it was unlikely that he knew they were after him. Sooner or later he would have to turn up.

And then there was Kuznetzov who had so conveniently appeared at the Winter Palace to incriminate the Doctor... Vasiliyev didn't believe in that degree of coincidence.

The Special duty officer came in. 'It's all arranged, sir. I sent my best executioner – he'll make it convincing.' The Special hesitated. 'I just hope this Doctor doesn't kill him.'

'I don't think so,' Vasiliyev said. 'He's not the type, more fool him.'

The Special unlocked the door, and ushered the Doctor forward. The Doctor didn't like the look of this at all. He knew that under the Soviet system, there would be an executioner waiting inside to deliver a shot to the condemned man's head without time for fear, but would someone have thought of that already?

He abruptly sidestepped, bumping into the Special, who stumbled into the cell. As the Special went in an arm emerged from behind the door, levelling a pistol at the entrant's head. There was a curse from behind the door, the executioner realising at the last moment that this wasn't his prisoner.

By that time the Doctor had grabbed his arm, pulled him

out into the open and dealt him an arcane karate blow to a vital nerve point. The executioner slumped, paralysed, and the Doctor neatly swung him around and into the second Special. 'Sorry about this, old chaps,' he said, bundling them both into his cell while they were too dazed to resist.

With the cell door safely closed, the Doctor looked both ways along the carpeted corridor. He heard no sounds from any of the other cells, and presumed they were empty. In any case he didn't have the keys to open them.

He paused to pick up the executioner's fallen pistol, and opened it up to take out one of the bullets. It was a blank round. 'Yes, I thought as much...' He shoved the gun through the peephole in the door of an empty cell before he started along the corridor. The Doctor had found it odd that Vasiliyev made no reaction to his pointing the finger at Kuznetzov. Presumably he was hoping that the rival suspects would eliminate each other, or at least lead him to them...

Felix didn't want Liz to have any doubts about what they were doing, so he had persuaded Lazovert to drive them in a closed car through the Larva district in the southeast of the city. They were safe in the car in daylight.

The Larva district was as squalid as he remembered it, but Felix prided himself on how he had become hardened to the horrors of poverty. He had first come here before he began working with Aunt Elisabeth to help the poor. He and a couple of his friends had gone there disguised as beggars, to see how people lived. His friends had thought it all a great joke, and prided themselves on their good fortune, but Felix had been horrified. His shock was not just at the conditions, but even at the realisation of his own feelings: when jewel-draped ladies and cigar-smoking gentlemen ignored him as they went past, he found himself becoming indignant. To be so ignored, to count for so little...

When they had failed to attract any money, the trio had gone to a local dosshouse, where they were given lice-ridden blankets with unidentifiable stains. Men and women mixed, drank, fought with bottles they had drained in one long swig, mated, and were sick over each other.

Felix had fled, his stomach rebelling at the stench that filled the air. 'I could hardly believe that I really saw those things,' he murmured. 'How, in this day and age, could a government allow human beings to be reduced to such abject misery?' He had relived that day many times since, though he was no longer sick at the thought. 'Things were even worse when Aunt Elisabeth and I went to Khitrovka district in Moscow.'

There, the buildings were almost exclusively taverns, dosshouses or rancid whorehouses. Anyone who had a coin for a bed for the night either had the sense to flee at sundown, or his body was collected with the others on the police's morning rounds. Screams punctuated the night, but no one ever responded to them. Thieves would kill a man for the dregs of a vodka bottle, then strip him of his clothes overnight. Whores that didn't stay in the brothels would be added to the cartloads of bodies that were taken to the anatomy classes at the University in the mornings.

With so many women selling themselves, there were also lots of children in the Khitrovka. Scabby three-year-olds were rented out to female beggars for ten kopeks a day. Infants were more highly prized, going for twenty-five kopeks a day. The more sickly the child, the more valued it was to the beggars, so they would starve their children in order that their cries would be more anguished, and thus attract greater charity. Babies were sold to professional beggars by auction at the weekly Khitrovka Market.

Liz shook her head in horror as the picture unfolded before her. 'And if the babies died?'

Felix shrugged. 'If they did, then they would carry the corpse to beg.' Those who survived their infancy knew no other life. Ten-year-old prostitutes, too drunk to stand, sold themselves for half a rouble a night, or were auctioned off to the pimps for fifty roubles.

Even younger beggars quickly learned to ruin their filthy clothes and hide their shoes before begging in the snow outside the city's nightclubs and theatres.

Liz took a moment to recover. 'Where were the police during all this? Surely a city the size of Moscow has a large police force?'

'Of course,' Felix agreed, 'but no policeman is stupid enough to enter Khitrovka after sunset. That is Rasputin's Russia.'

'This country is not unique,' Liz said steadily. 'Even England has such –' She stopped. 'Has' she had said. Not 'had'. And it still did, even in her time; how was she supposed to improve Felix's mood by predicting that such things would still happen in sixty years' time? 'Even England has such areas.'

'I understand that our situation is not unique,' Felix admitted, 'but I believe that the cause of it is.'

'You blame Rasputin for this?' Liz couldn't really see how. She had seen enough evidence that Rasputin was a womaniser, a corrupting influence, and a drunken boor, but he could hardly be responsible for the way people lived.

'Yes. The Empress will make no appointments to the

government without Rasputin's agreement – he has admitted as much to journalists, and anyone else who'll share a drink with him. The man makes decisions on a whim, based on the bribes he gets, or the favours he is owed, or probably the auguries in the entrails of a sheep. None of those timeservers are even remotely competent; they're just puppets, stooges of his, there to provide Rasputin's plans an easier path through the Duma.'

'Rasputin himself is a peasant,' Liz said reasonably, 'a man of the people. I hardly think it would be in his best interest to do so much damage to his own supporters.'

Felix smiled, as if to a child who makes the simplest error by approaching things from its own inexperienced viewpoint. 'Professor, Russian politics are not the easiest thing in the world to navigate through. With these incompetents in charge, the people demand even more changes, which they hope he can give them.'

'And you?'

'I had lived purely for pleasure until then,' Felix admitted. 'I was raised to produce an heir and not look at the suffering around me.' He smiled. 'In many ways seeing those things, and realising that there are more essential values than money and power, were what gave me the freedom I had always sought. I was myself, and not my father's image of a son.'

The tunnel had started to rise, and the Doctor soon found himself at a dead end. It was hardly logical that someone would build such a route to nowhere, though, and the Doctor immediately started searching for a secret door of any kind.

A small piece of stone moved under the Doctor's hand,

and he suppressed a sound of triumph. With admirable silence, the wall facing him swung inward, allowing access to a narrow exit, which the Doctor had no qualms about taking advantage of.

Outside, he found himself in a candlelit mausoleum. In the Doctor's experience, such places were normally small and intimate for family members, but this one had quite a high vaulted ceiling. It also had no sarcophagi, and didn't seem to have been put to any use yet. Behind him, a section of marble wall slid back into place.

The Doctor wished he didn't have more important things to do than stay and study the room. A little regretfully, he moved to a more mundane door at the far end.

Through the door was a corridor that led out into the nave of what the Doctor realised must be the Peter and Paul Cathedral, still within the fortress. Bluish-tinted marble pillars supported a dome of golden leaves.

Below the image of a dove was the ikonostasis, surrounded by curtains, and guarded by the Archangels Gabriel and Michael. Sarcophagi were installed around the nave, and both a pulpit and the Tsar's modest throne flanked the ikonostasis.

The Doctor made straight for the door, passing by the sole bust in the room, of Peter the Great, whom the Doctor had always thought looked somewhat like a young Marlon Brando. The Doctor had a certain regard for Peter; his curiosity and intelligence would have made him a fine explorer, but – much as he had tried – the Doctor had never quite been able to cure him of that strange fascination he had for methods of torture. As with so many figures in human history, the Doctor sometimes found it difficult to reconcile the convivial host he remembered with the man who later tortured his own son to death.

He wondered what Peter would have thought of Rasputin, or Felix Yusupov. He didn't doubt that Jo was reporting the facts as she saw them, and perhaps Rasputin wasn't the ogre everyone thought him to be... But if he was not, then it would be so much more difficult to leave him to the fate that awaited him. The Doctor wondered how Jo would face up to learning that lesson. Or how Liz would equate Felix the charming prince with a cold-blooded killer.

None of it was new to the Doctor. None of it at all.

Felix had had Thesphe arrange for workmen to move furnishings and carpets into a normally disused basement room at the foot of a side staircase. He wanted Rasputin to be at ease, and so it would be better if the room looked lived-in.

Before he went down to pay them off, he saw that a letter from Irina had been delivered. He had written to her about his intentions, of course. She had always understood everything about him, and he was sure she would understand this too. He opened it, and began to read.

Dear Felix, it said *Thank you for your insane letter. I could not understand the half of it. I realise that you are about to do something wild. Please take care and do not get mixed up in any shady business.*

Felix gently folded up the letter, his heart sinking. He could all but hear her voice asking him to change his mind. That was something he couldn't do; not now. Descending to the basement, Felix watched as the workmen left. He was not truly looking forward to this, but nor was he willing to leave his duty undone. For once in his life, he would follow it through.

The prospect of inviting a human being to his death – even someone as perverted and depraved as Rasputin – horrified him. The man might be the very incarnation of crime and vice, but he was still a *man*. He was still a flesh and blood creation of God's, with all the rights to life and privileges that Felix would consider for any man.

Even just contemplating being a host to Rasputin's last supper gave him the shivers. At least he could draw some strength from the convictions of Purishkevich and the others. Where the destiny of all Russia was concerned, Felix felt that all personal considerations should be set aside.

While Felix was out of the Moorish room, Purishkevich, Sukhotin and Dmitri were filing in. 'It's all arranged with my wife,' Purishkevich was saying. 'She'll dispose of his rags, and we can dump the body –'

Liz rose to leave; she had known that Rasputin was fated to be murdered, but it hadn't sunk in until now that it was these men who would do it. 'I'm sorry,' she said, a little stiffly. 'I should go. I think you'd be more comfortable if this was a more private conversation between you.' It was difficult enough to not try to stop their planning, let alone sit in on it.

The air seems somehow fresher outside, but only for a moment, before she realised that Kuznetzov was before her. 'Perhaps you're being too hasty, Professor Shaw. You said yourself that we'll be well rid of him.'

'That doesn't mean I have ambitions to do it myself. I think roast chicken is a good thing, but I wouldn't like to be the one who kills the creatures.'

Kuznetzov nodded understandingly. 'I know it's difficult for a member of the fair sex, but I thought that *you* –'

She stopped him with a raised hand. 'Don't patronise me, Kuznetzov.' She had enough of that from the budgetary appropriations boards back at Cambridge. 'As it is, I have enough objectivity to not mention your plans to anyone who might try to stop you, but my patience only goes so far.'

His manner cooled, and she realised that of the two possible effects of a threat, hers had had the wrong one. 'I suggest you stretch it a little more, for the sake of the prince, yourself, and your friends.'

'My friends?'

'What would they say if I told them you'd been conspiring with us? Or if I told the Ochrana you'd been conspiring with each other?' He approached slowly. 'Or if they simply… died.'

'Don't think for a moment that you're impressing me –'

'I've had you and the Doctor and Miss Grant followed since you arrived in that police box. The *yi-lei lone-mo* Doctor, luckily for him, is somewhat out of reach, but it would take only one word from me for Miss Grant to be…' He waved the fingertips of his free hand across his throat. 'Or worse,' he added. He smiled, and now Liz realised that there was no warmth in his smile at all. 'But I can also guarantee Miss Grant's safety – if you do something for us.'

'Such as?'

'Rasputin is partial to a pretty face, of course, and would follow one just about anywhere. He has been invited to a… last supper, if you like, at the Moika Palace. If you persuade him to come, then you and Miss Grant will be safe, and allowed to leave the city alive. Naturally if you should attempt to warn Miss Grant…' He made a shooting gesture with his finger.

'What about our transport?'

'Ah…' Kuznetzov shook his head. 'I don't think so. I have no idea how that box can transmigrate itself instantaneously, but I will find out, eventually.'

'I think you'll find that a very long investigation,' Liz said defiantly.

'Then it can give me something to do during my retirement, can't it? Professor Shaw, I'm not asking you, and I'm not making a charitable deal: I am telling you that if you don't ensure Rasputin's presence tonight, Josephine Grant dies slowly, and you get to watch.'

Chapter Fourteen

Kit was atop the Volkhov rostral once again. The icy wind clawed at him as the young man who had been spying on him plummeted to his death. The man's mouth screamed accusations so loudly that they must have been heard in Moscow.

Kit lunged for him, grasping desperately, but he was too far away. The wind tore at him, and Kit suddenly realised that it was *he* who was falling: falling an impossibly long way...

He sat bolt upright, a cold sweat soaking his skin. His apartment was silent, the only screams being those of distant trains and factory whistles. There was also an insistent knocking on the door of his apartment. 'All right, just a minute, dammit.' Unscheduled disturbances that woke him never brought out the best in him.

He had awakened on his back, which was mildly irritating. There was a picture of Ashley on the dressing table, and he always fell asleep facing it, in the hope that he would wake up to be greeted by her face. But he always found that the first thing he saw in the morning was the cracked paintwork on the ceiling.

He didn't feel at all rested, and anyway rarely felt refreshed until he'd been up for an hour or so. It played hell with his work, but he learned to live with it.

He opened the door to see the Doctor. 'Come on, Kit,' the Doctor said urgently. 'I have the nasty suspicion that I was followed here.'

'Followed?' Kit's sleep-fuzzed brain had yet to stumble into full wakefulness.

'By the Ochrana. Academician Kuznetzov has framed the two of us.'

'Oh, hell and damnation,' Kit muttered with feeling. 'Vasiliyev…'

'Has already arrested me. I managed to escape, but I can't help feeling it was too easy – he wanted me to lead them to you –' There was a crunch from downstairs. The apartment building's front door being forced open, Kit realised.

'Thanks so much. You know, Doctor, I do actually value my life. In fact, I don't know what I'd do without it.'

'I'd rather avoid the possibility of having to find out the answer to that. Is there another way out of here?'

'The roof.' Kit had dressed in record time, and jumped up on to a chest of drawers. From there he opened a trapdoor in the ceiling. 'Come on then.' He pulled himself up into the mouldy attic space, then helped pull the Doctor up after him.

By the sounds of footsteps several people had barged into the room below, and Kit scampered along a wooden beam to the hatch cut in the tin roof. He knew the movement would be heard below but that couldn't be helped.

He and the Doctor emerged on to the frosted tin roof, and immediately started towards a narrow alley between this building and another one. A shot cracked past them, and Kit had jumped before he even realised what he was going to do. He was beginning to wonder if his subconscious had his best interests at heart, the way it had got into that habit.

He slammed into the lower roof of the neighbouring building, and slid on the ice. Luckily there were plenty of handholds, and he could steady himself as the Doctor also leapt across.

He and the Doctor bolted along this roof, shots banging into the tin tiles. Risking a glance back, Kit saw an Ochrana man make the jump. The agent slipped on the ice, and dropped off the side of the building until only his hands remained. The next two agents to jump had to stop to help their comrade up, and by that time Kit and the Doctor had made it to a third roof.

Before long, they had gained enough distance to slip inside a building without being noticed, and descend to street level. 'I know a safe place,' Kit said. 'One I've never used before, so Vasiliyev won't know it.'

Together, they went to a disused shop on the other side of town, in the Smolny district. Like all agents, Kit had been briefed on certain safe houses in the city, and how to get to them. Once inside, Kit put a kettle on. 'Coffee, I think. Now, tell me – why have I been risking my valuable life jumping over rooftops?'

'It seems I've underestimated Academician Kuznetzov,' the Doctor admitted drily. 'Apparently, he has convinced Vasiliyev that we are German spies acting as links between Rasputin and Manus.'

'He's what?'

'Look, do try to listen, old chap. It's vitally important that –'

'I heard what you said, Doctor. It's just ridiculous.'

'Ridiculous or not, that's what's happened. And now we have to do something about it.'

'I'll kill Kuznetzov,' Kit muttered darkly.

'That would be an extremely foolish thing to do – it would just make us look more guilty.' The Doctor's tone softened. 'Besides, I don't think you really *want* to do that, do you?'

'Not really, I suppose,' Kit admitted. 'But the thought keeps my spirits up. Kuznetzov is a traitor... A German spy.' Kit shook his head. 'It hardly seems credible, Doctor. Ourselves and the Russians have both kept a watch on Manus. We know he's German Intelligence's link here, and that all their information goes through him. But Kuznetzov has never passed anything to him as far as we know.'

'That's because you were approaching this from the wrong angle,' the Doctor said severely.

'If you mean we should have been watching Kuznetzov, before we know he should be watched –'

'No, man! The mistake is in the assumption that a spy in your midst must be working for Germany. The Romanov family does have other enemies, you know.'

Kit started to frown, but caught himself. 'The SR?'

'That's right,' the Doctor agreed with a nod. 'The Socialist Revolutionary Fighting Section, to be precise.'

Kit shook his head more firmly. 'Not their style. Their way is to put a bomb in your car, or send an armed mob round with sledgehammers and axes. Kuznetzov's manipulations are too subtle for the Fighting Section.'

'People do evolve new techniques.'

'Very well,' Kit said dubiously. 'Let's assume you're right. What does Kuznetzov think his anarchist friends have to gain from a plot against Rasputin?'

'Shock in the Royal household. The Empress is very fond of him for looking after her son – she'll be practically destroyed by his death.'

Kit could see what the Doctor was getting at now. 'And he's still popular among the lower classes... Everyone knows that the aristocracy despises him. If that aristocracy was seen to get rid of him, it would provoke more anger in the peasantry…'

'Precisely. And since the ruling family are friends of Rasputin, who would be distraught and thrown off-balance by his death, their government would be more ripe for overthrow.' Kit had to agree with the Doctor's assessment. You could almost scent revolution in the air some days. '"It was carried out in the manner of a moving picture scenario designed for people of bad taste."'

'What?'

'Oh, nothing. Just something Trotsky will say… Of course!'

Kit blinked. 'Of course what?'

'I should have realised at once… We're all in more danger from Kuznetzov than I thought, Kit. You see, I just remembered who Koba is.'

Kit sighed. 'Don't keep me in suspense.'

'His real name's Iosif Vissarionovich Dzhugashvili, but these days he calls himself the "man of steel" – Josef Stalin!'

Kuznetzov had been recalled to the Ochrana HQ by an urgent phone call from Vasiliyev. 'I trust this is good news? The spies have been arrested?'

Vasiliyev made a dismissive motion. 'You know how I like to work. We took most of them at dawn. Anyone who even met Manus has been pulled in for questioning.'

'And the Doctor and Powell?' Kuznetzov asked with practised mildness.

Vasiliyev's mouth turned down. 'They've gone to ground.' He shook his head. 'They can't stay out of sight for long – all my most important people know Powell by sight, and the Doctor isn't exactly inconspicuous.'

'I'll ask around. Perhaps Professor Shaw will have some ideas.'

'My thoughts exactly,' Vasiliyev agreed.

Vasiliyev watched from his office window as Kuznetzov got into a waiting car and drove off. He nodded once, and the driver he had had stationed below set off after Kuznetzov.

Vasiliyev, of course, had never trusted anyone fully, and Kuznetzov less than some others. So what if the trust he had in Kit was misplaced? That merely meant he should be more vigilant with his other informants.

There was also the matter of two informants trying to pin something on each other. It happened from time to time, but it was always even more suspicious than anyone or anything else. In such instances, Vasiliyev had found, it was often better to jail both of them, even if one is innocent, than to free both when one is guilty.

He had heard that it was better for a hundred guilty men to walk free than one innocent go to the jail or the gallows. That always made him laugh; he was dealing with the real world, not ideals. And in the real world, the reverse was most definitely true.

Rasputin looked at the black clouds with loathing. Normally they didn't bother him, but lately… Lately things just didn't seem right.

In the summer, he thought, he might go back to Pokrovskoe for a while, to get back in touch with his roots. That was always valuable for a holy man such as himself. Those who came to see him at his apartment were mostly devoted enough, but the villagers back home were his true flock, even if he didn't preach to them.

It occurred to Rasputin that if he told the people at home the things he told the journalists here to impress them – about the Tsar bowing to his whims, and the Empress madly in love with him – they would probably beg someone so worldly and wise to deflower their daughters… in a pure fashion, naturally.

That thought reminded him of his wife, Praskovia Dubrovina. She was no longer as young and pretty as he liked, but he did still love her. She was sent by God to be his wife, he thought. She must have been, because marriage was a holy thing, yet she also understood that it was necessary for him to test his resolve with women, and sometimes purify them with himself. 'He has enough to go round for everybody,' he recalled her saying once.

Yes, he would take the children and visit home in the summer. And he would ignore the part of his mind that added 'if I live that long'.

Kit was still trying to understand what Kuznetzov wanted. 'A link between us, the Germans, and Rasputin…'

'Yes,' the Doctor agreed, stroking his chin. 'We've caused him trouble, so I can understand his desire to get at us, but why Rasputin?'

'We know that Rasputin guides the Empress…'

'On the contrary,' the Doctor retorted. 'All we know is that he tells her what she wants to hear.'

'What?'

'You do take notes of these conversations, don't you, old chap?'

'Yes, of course.'

'Then I suggest you check over them. Start with your transcripts of their discussions and you'll find that

Alexandra proposes exactly those ideas that Rasputin later supposedly suggests. He just slips them back to her, to make her feel she has an independent confirmation that it's the best way to proceed.'

'Doctor, are you telling me that Rasputin is… a fraud?'

The Doctor hesitated. 'Well, not a fraud exactly, but someone who firmly believes that the Empress knows best and wants to prove it to her. Don't you see?' the Doctor said impatiently. 'Rasputin is Russia's Janus figure. To the Empress he's a loving and loyal subject who saves her son; but to the public he's a drunken lecher. They can't understand why else the Romanovs would tolerate him unless he was controlling them, because if the knowledge of the Tsarevitch's haemophilia got out it'd cause a struggle for the throne.'

December 16th dawned with the usual abandonment of the trams. The snow overnight had locked up the points, and there just wasn't enough power to shift them.

Felix had never really thought much about the weather before, since this was perfectly normal for a winter's day in St Petersburg. Today, though, he felt it was strange. Maybe it was because everything reminded him of cold and death. The whiteness of a corpse in its shroud, the chill of unliving flesh…

He shuddered. His stomach churned with the thought of how the day might end, and he tried to turn his attention back to the study papers he was revising. He knew he should be taking in all the important details he would need for tomorrow's exam at the Corps des Pages. Knowing it didn't make it happen, unfortunately.

Felix's father had long ago tried to force his son into a

military academy, but Felix had deliberately failed the entrance examination. He had no taste for soldiering and fighting. When war broke out, he escaped conscription because he was an only son. At least, he was an only remaining son.

Irina and most of his friends had therefore been surprised that he wanted to join the Guards now. Felix himself didn't see that much of a contradiction. He had no intention of being posted to the Front, and his position would make that impossible unless he volunteered anyway.

Just as he had been quick to convert the palace into a hospital, he also felt it was his duty to lead by example in this regard too. Well, in a way. Most of the rest of his generation were already in the military anyway, but it was still important to Felix that he be seen to be doing what was right and proper.

That was something else he had learned from his aunt, the Grand Duchess Elisabeth.

Much as he wanted to immerse himself in the studies that would give him entrance to the Guards without being sent to the Front, his mind kept returning to the imminent prospect of killing Rasputin.

Partly it was an irritating distraction, but it was also exciting. By this time tomorrow, he and the others would be heroes throughout Russia.

He would also be a murderer. But if he did nothing, and knowingly allowed Rasputin to drag the country and its rulers further down into the abyss, wouldn't he be a far worse criminal?

He told himself so, repeatedly. Sooner or later, he knew he would believe it.

* * *

Dmitri woke in a cold sweat, the image of his mother drenched in blood receding only slowly. He had been fourteen when it had happened for real. An anarchist's bomb had devastated his father's car, blowing off his limbs. Both Dmitri and his sister Marie saw their mother gathering pieces in the folds of her dress, her mind as much a ruin as the shell of the vehicle.

He had joined the Third Guards Regiment, but it hadn't helped him deal with the nightmares. He often wondered whether Marie suffered from them as he did. She never talked about it in her letters, and Dmitri himself felt that it would be too painful to bring the subject up. So he could only wonder.

He also wondered whether Rasputin's death would simply add to his nightmares, or ease them. He wished he could go and see Felix, who would surely be able to ease his mind. He knew the plan, though, and knew that they were not to meet until after sunset.

He wasn't sure why, other than it probably appealed to Felix's sense of the dramatic. He had always been a great one for the theatre, and for dressing up. For the playing of parts, and the execution of scenes.

Purishkevich rolled over in bed, and saw the morning light slipping in through the gap in the curtains. It stabbed at his eyes, and he knew that today's hangover would be a bad one. Still, he had nothing important to do until nightfall, so he could afford to turn over and go back sleep.

Rasputin woke suddenly, heart pounding in his chest, as if he had been running for his life. He was in bed, safely at home. He could feel the warmth from the visiting girl's breasts pressed against his side, and relaxed slightly as he recalled falling asleep.

He lay awake now, disappointed. It had taken several glasses of muscat to enable him to sleep at all, and he had hoped that he would be granted a proper rest for a while.

He rose anyway, knowing that he wouldn't get back to sleep. At least the day held some promise: He and Felix were going to meet, and there was always the hope that Irina, Felix's wife, would be there. Yes... he would enjoy a night with her. He was certain he could give her the pleasure that Felix reserved for Grand Duke Dmitri...

Rasputin's spirits lifted. Yes, this was going to be a good day after all.

Chapter Fifteen

The telephone buzzed, and Rasputin stumbled over to it. 'Yes, what is it?'

'A friend, Grishka,' an unfamiliar voice said. It sounded young but worldly. 'You are in danger today. If you're wise, you'll get out of the city for a while. If not... I doubt I would be able to help you.'

Rasputin sighed. This was a tale he'd heard often over the past few months. 'Let me guess: I am to be assassinated?'

'You have a choice now,' the voice repeated. Then the line went dead. Rasputin looked at the receiver as if it were a rotten apple he had just bitten into. Rumours of his assassination were nothing new to him; it was simply something that one as public as he had to get used to. People were jealous of his rapport with the Tsar and Tsarina, or his prowess with women, and wanted him out of the way. They felt that they would be happier if there was not someone so obviously more notable than themselves. Such hubris was a common problem, even since biblical times. Rasputin was sure there was a quote about it somewhere in the Bible, but didn't recall it off-hand. Holiness wasn't just a matter of memorising words by rote, it was in one's bearing and actions.

Rasputin put the receiver down, and fingered the line of the scar that had been left by the whore Gusyeva two years ago. As if on cue, it was starting to ache. He fetched a bottle of muscat, and settled down in his favourite armchair. He would be safe enough here, with the Ochrana guarding the doors, until Felix came. Once, a pair of irate husbands whose wives were sleeping with him had tried to burst in and shoot him, but the Ochrana had tossed them into some dungeon somewhere. If anyone was stupid enough to think they could be rid of Grishka Rasputin, then let them suffer the same fate.

Liz had been astounded by the number of people waiting outside Rasputin's apartment. Even though he lived on the third floor, the queue of followers, journalists, and what would be called groupies in a later time stretched all the way down to the front door.

Liz had waited relatively patiently for her turn, and Rasputin's diminutive secretary eventually ushered her through the double doors and into the dining room. The room seemed too small for its oaken furniture. Rasputin was waiting for her, his pale blue eyes intense but also strangely distant. She noticed the end of a scar at his hairline, and wondered what had caused it. If his brain had been bruised through some injury in the past, it might explain the ambiguity of that gaze.

Like Jo before her, Liz was surprised that Rasputin was only of average height, having expected a much more imposing figure. When his eyes focused on her, Liz suddenly felt what Felix had described as his magnetism. It wasn't attraction *per se*, but it was a sense that if he was paying so much attention to you, then there must be some link between you. She wondered if it was simply an inherent trait, or whether it was one he had deliberately cultivated to impress people.

Liz remembered Felix expressing bewilderment at why the ladies of his class were so taken with Rasputin, but she thought she could make a good guess at the answer.

Rasputin was brutally straightforward, with no airs and graces. His treatment of the girl who had preceded her had been nothing short of what in her day would be described as sexual harassment.

These people didn't know that, or at least didn't think in those terms. To them, he was simply *different*, a refreshing change from men who had been brought up to see their wives as no more than means to continue the family line, and who would run off with their mistresses at every opportunity. Rasputin was as promiscuous, far ruder, uncouth… But he was honest about it. Liz didn't consider any of these things to be particularly attractive, but now she could see understand how it affected others.

Rasputin laughed. 'The lion shall lay down with the lamb…'

'I wonder which of us is which,' Liz said drily.

He laughed again. 'Does it matter? The important thing is that the scriptures say they should lay down together.' He came round to stand behind her. 'Take off your clothes.'

Liz would rather have had root canal work done without anaesthetic. 'That bluffness may work on the Russian ladies, but I am immune.'

Rasputin shook his head. 'You think I am too close to nature? You should come out to Siberia in the summer, and work in the fields. When you see a stallion take a mare in the street, you have nowhere to hide from that simple fact of nature.'

Liz considered turning around and walking straight back out, leaving Rasputin to face his fate blind. She knew that she was risking a temporal paradox simply by coming to deliver the message she had been given, but it seemed logical to assume that since the message originated with

Felix, it was part of history anyway. That being the case, Rasputin would still die tonight. She stiffened. If only none of them had ever got involved… The scientist in her was beginning to feel very lost and alone in the face of this terrible inevitability.

'I do have a question, though. Do you know how much harm you're doing to Russia and the Tsar?'

'Harm?' Rasputin echoed. 'I do no harm.'

'That's what I thought you'd say.'

Rasputin's eyes flashed with anger, and for a moment Liz thought he was going to hit her.

'Why should I listen to a damn word you say?' he railed. 'How could anyone think I could ever mean my beloved Tsar and Tsarina any harm? Did I not save their son? Do I not agree with their policies? You've been baiting me since you walked in through that door. Women come to me for favours or pleasure, yet you come to bait me. Why is this?'

Liz knew that telling the truth was the last thing she should do… and yet she couldn't help herself. His voice was certainly persuasive, even though it didn't attract her. 'Because I have to, that's why! Do you think I enjoy lying and trapping you?'

'I don't know – do you?' he asked bluntly.

'No!' The man was infuriating. She was half tempted to punch him.

'Then what makes you do it?' His eyes narrowed in thought. 'Or should I be asking *who* makes you do it?' He circled her, like a panther deciding which prey to spring at. He wasn't undressing her with his eyes this time, though. 'That's it, isn't it…? Someone put you up to this.'

'A friend of Felix Yusupov's – Academician Kuznetzov. They want to make sure you accept Felix's invitation to come to the Moika Palace tonight. They said to say Irina will be there –'

'My fondest wish,' Rasputin said, with feeling. Liz could hear the desire in his voice.

Liz nodded. 'And if you don't come, they'll kill a friend of mine and the Doctor's. Jo Grant.'

Rasputin froze. 'Josephine?' He beckoned Simanovich over from the anteroom. 'No more visitors today.'

Simanovich looked surprised. 'Is something wrong?'

Rasputin hesitated. 'No, I just feel tired. I didn't sleep much.' Simanovich nodded after a moment, and went to shoo away the hopeful. Rasputin sank slowly into a chair. 'You come claiming to be a friend, and yet you bring me only this dilemma…'

Liz felt vaguely ashamed, even though she knew she had done the right thing. She just hoped Jo wouldn't suffer because of it. She wished she could hope for Rasputin to survive since, seen like this, he was no monstrous ogre. He was just an aging hellraiser with a big mouth, who had picked too many fights over the years. 'Believe me, I would much rather not be here like this. But Jo is my friend, and I gather she's yours too. I'm just trying to find a way –'

Rasputin waved her comments aside. 'Go back and tell Felix to pick me up at eleven o'clock.'

From the window of his study, Rasputin watched Liz get into a waiting car. She probably wondered why he had agreed to go, or even thought he was lying. Rasputin didn't mind that; people had been misjudging his motives for things all his life. What difference did one more make?

He had felt the shadow of impending death hovering near him for some time, and if it was God's will, then so be it. Not that he really thought Kuznetzov or Purishkevich could succeed in killing him. He was a working man, and strong, not like these consumptive politicians and aristocrats. Knowing that he was walking into a trap, he should be able to draw his enemies into the open, and then fight his way free. The Tsar and Tsarina would then waste no time in creating suitable punishments for them.

And if, since he would have to wait until they made their move in order to find out what it was, they did manage to injure or kill him, well... He was a religious man, after all; and what could be more fitting than to give your life for your flock? If truth be told, perhaps it was time anyway. Every day the wine dulled his pains less than before, and those pains grew. And besides, he would be made a martyr. Perhaps he could turn the death he had already foreseen into something that would strike at his enemies, so that by killing him, they would be killing themselves.

As if prompted by the fears about his fate, Rasputin's stomach wound was beginning to ache again. Perhaps it was trying to warn him to change his mind, but Rasputin enjoyed his reputation for stubbornness. Some wine would dull the pain, he hoped...

Vasiliyev left the Ochrana building as dusk was falling. He would have dinner, and then head home. His car was waiting for him outside, the engine already running. His driver knew that it wasn't wise to keep the Chief of the St Petersburg Ochrana waiting.

Vasiliyev got into the back seat. 'The Villa Rode today, I think.' The driver did nothing for a moment, then Vasiliyev was pushed sideways as someone got in the car beside him. Before he could protest or call for help, two bony fingers pressed into his chest, and Vasiliyev found that he suddenly couldn't move.

'I'll take that, if you don't mind,' the Doctor said, pulling Vasiliyev's revolver from its holster, and handing it to the driver. Vasiliyev saw that the driver was Kit Powell.

'What have you done to my usual driver?' Vasiliyev demanded, as Kit started the car moving. 'Killed him?'

'He's feeling the cold a little too keenly today,' said the Doctor. 'He's at home, and he's staying there.'

'We gave his landlord fifty roubles to keep him locked in,' Kit added helpfully. 'Don't worry. We're not taking you far.'

The pain had long since dissolved into a throbbing pulse, and now that was resolving itself into an insistent knocking. It was the front door, Rasputin realised, and Simanovich had gone home for the evening.

Blinking the tiredness out of his eyes, he opened the door. It was Anya, and Rasputin's mood rose slightly. 'Come in, come in…' He kissed her on the cheek, and led her through to the drawing room. 'Matriona,' he called, bringing his sister out from the kitchen. 'Fresh tea.'

'Thank you,' Anya smiled. 'Alix sent this for you; she knows things have been difficult for you lately.' She drew a carefully wrapped package out from the bag she carried. 'I think you will like it.'

Rasputin unwrapped it cautiously, despite the effects of the wine. Inside was a small silver-framed icon, inscribed to him by Alix and her four daughters. It was quite beautiful, and Rasputin knew he would find a good spot for it on the bedroom wall. 'A greater gift than the altar. I will thank her personally tomorrow.'

'There was to have been a letter with it, but that has

vanished,' Anya said as Matriona brought a steaming samovar through. She poured tea for both of them.

'Vanished?'

'Strange things are happening, Grigory. Alix is sure she must simply have lost the letter, but I suspect it may have been stolen. I don't know what it says, but…'

He shook his head. 'Don't worry, Anya. Letters cannot harm me.'

'All the same, there are rumours at court, that you are in danger –'

Rasputin grimaced. 'Rumours are simply that: rumours. Not truth. Mine ear hath heard and understood this many times today. It's nothing.' He almost told her about Miss Shaw's visit, but managed to keep it to himself. What sort of friend would he be, if his last words to Anya and Alix were simply to cause them pain and worry?

'Perhaps,' Anya said doubtfully. 'But Her Majesty would probably feel better if you stayed safely home for a day or two – and I know I would.'

Rasputin shrugged. 'Maybe I will, but I have an appointment with the Little One tonight.'

'Yusupov?' Rasputin could hear the disdain in her voice. He wondered how she'd feel if she was as certain as he was, that Felix's friends hated him so much. She'd probably take some guards and raze the Moika Palace to the ground. It was so tempting to tell her, and find out.

'Yes. He invited to me to meet Irina and perhaps some others, at the Moika at midnight.'

'Midnight?' Anya echoed. 'Is he afraid to be seen with you in daylight? Why should he want to see you so late?'

'I don't know.'

'I don't like this,' Anya stated. 'Some of Felix's friends say unkind things about you – inflammatory, even. I don't think you should go.'

Rasputin could have argued the point with her, but he still felt sleepy from the wine, and she knew him too well to be bullied by him. He also knew that if he prolonged the conversation, he would almost certainly end up telling her the truth. 'You may be right,' he said. 'I'll stay in and read to my daughters.' She smiled at him, broadly.

It was simpler this way…

Vasiliyev was nervous for the whole trip, but not really frightened. Real anarchists or spies would have simply killed him by now. He didn't want his captors to know he was so sanguine about it, though, and tried to look haunted as they drove through the city.

Kit guided the car neatly around to a disused shop in the Smolny district. Though unused, the floor and shelves were clean of dust, suggesting that Kit and the Doctor came here frequently. Kit ushered Vasiliyev into the shop at gunpoint, and bade him sit on a wooden box.

'Why have you brought me here?' Vasiliyev demanded.

'We want to make a deal, of sorts,' the Doctor told him.

'Deal?'

'Yes. Our freedom, for an anarchist infiltrator.'

Vasiliyev's eyes narrowed. 'Two German spies for one anarchist? Not a good deal.'

Kit pressed the muzzle of Vasiliyev's own revolver to the Ochrana chief's cheek, while the Doctor spoke. 'Vasiliyev. If Powell or myself were really agents of a hostile foreign power – in this case Germany – I think you'll agree we could kill you now, and leave your body in some suitable spot where it would never be found.'

Vasiliyev considered retorting about how they'd never get out of the country alive, but he knew Kit too well to think that would impress him, and the Doctor didn't seem the type of man to be easily disturbed either. He nodded stiffly. 'Yes, Doctor, that would be a fairly reasonable assumption.'

'Then I hope you'll accept our good faith,' the Doctor said. He took the gun from Kit, tipped out the bullets, then handed it back to Vasiliyev.

Vasiliyev didn't touch it. 'And make it appear that I was killed in self-defence?'

The Doctor sighed. 'Good grief – you really are a most paranoid chap…'

'I *have* just been abducted. You must forgive me if it makes me a little dubious as to your intentions.'

'A gun with no bullet for a gun with blanks,' the Doctor said pointedly. 'Fair exchange is no robbery.'

Kit sighed. 'What if I were tell you we're not German spies? I work for Bertie Stopford, the British Ambassador. The Doctor here works for Stopford's friend Lethbridge-Stewart, from the Intelligence room of the British War Office.'

Vasiliyev looked doubtful. 'And you can prove this?'

The Doctor nodded. 'Yes, I will, if you listen to what we have to say.'

'Very well.' In fact Vasiliyev already believed him. It fitted with his own observations, and those of his informants, as well as providing a reason for them to be both wary of discovery and anti-German. But there was never any harm in getting a confession to corroborate things.

The Doctor put his hands on his hips. 'Well, the first thing you have to know is that Academician Kuznetzov has had you completely fooled. He's not working for you, or the Germans, but for the SR Fighting Section.'

Vasiliyev felt a chill. 'The SR…?'

'That money which he tried to use to frame us comes from a supply he got from a man called Koba. Which means it's stolen.' Vasiliyev could work that out himself; the bank robber Koba was notorious.

'Koba is in exile in Siberia, safely out of the way.'

'Oh, come now,' Kit interrupted. 'You know as well as we do that half the revolutionaries in Siberia still run their gangs by messenger from their gulags, and that's not counting how often Koba escapes.'

'Either way,' the Doctor went on, 'it seems that he's been cooking up some kind of scheme to destabilise the ruling class here in St Petersburg.'

'You mean Yusupov's plot to kill Rasputin?' Everybody who was anybody knew about that. It was the worst-kept secret Vasiliyev had ever heard of.

'Well, I suspect that would happen anyway. But I imagine that Kuznetzov's intention is to use that stolen money to fake some kind of deal between the aristocracy and foreign spies –'

'Us,' Kit added drily.

'Yes, precisely: us. To cause further unrest and stir up a little revolution.'

Vasiliyev looked at them for a long moment. 'Just before you brought me here, my agents reported that Kuznetzov has gone to the Finland station. Apparently he bought a ticket to Vyborg…'

'Less than an hour from the Finnish border,' Kit said quietly. 'Now this would be a very odd time for one of your informants to try to flee the country –'

'I suppose we can assume he's not just visiting Vyborg,' said Vasiliyev. His instincts had been well-honed by his length of service in the Ochrana, and they were all telling him that Kuznetzov was frightened and running.

'Maybe he is,' the Doctor said, 'but isn't it strange that he leaves town just after implicating a rival informant in treason? Some people might think that was a sign that he knew there was danger of being proved wrong. Or proved to be lying outright.'

Vasiliyev knew what the Doctor was saying made sense, though he almost wished it didn't. He still didn't know enough about the man, and Kit clearly had loyalties other than to the Ochrana. But if he had thought Kuznetzov was so innocent then why had he had him followed in the first place?

'Why would Father Grigory go to see Felix tonight?' Empress Alexandra was asking in her mauve boudoir.

Anya shrugged. 'To see Irina. You know he has desired her since they first met, and it's not as if Felix has the tastes to satisfy her.'

Alix frowned, shaking her head. 'I could believe that, but Irina is in the Crimea with Felix's mother...' Alix began to feel an insistent foreboding, though it could simply be that her last medicinal dose of cocaine was wearing off. She tried to ignore the uneasiness that was seeping through her.

'I saw the Doctor's friend, Miss Shaw, with Felix,' Anya said slowly, 'and Miss Grant was with Grigory earlier. Perhaps the four of them are planning to meet.'

'Perhaps,' Alix agreed, for the sake of saying something. 'But I don't really believe that, and I don't think you do either.'

'Not really,' Anya admitted, 'but that doesn't make it impossible.'

'It must be a mistake of some kind... You say that this Josephine Grant is a friend of Grigory's?' Anya nodded. 'Then perhaps she can ask Professor Shaw what's going on.'

Anya nodded. 'I'll have her picked up the next time she goes to see him.'

Chapter Sixteen

The Finland station was smaller than the huge and chaotic Warsaw Station with its succession of trains from the Front. The platforms were sheltered by red and gold archways, which were only mildly stained by the smoke and steam from the trains.

Kit was somehow amazed that they were still alive, let alone here with Vasiliyev and a dozen Ochrana agents in those imaginatively matching overcoats. Vasiliyev had arranged for troops to be put at his disposal at a moment's notice as well.

Kit was rather uncomfortable with the circumstances under which they were here. Mainly it was that his position was no longer a secret, which meant he wouldn't really be able to continue in his usual job after this. That saddened him, not just because he hated change, but because he'd miss the people he had got to know, whether they were contacts, friendly rivals or civilians.

He also thought his and the Doctor's current status was rather odd, to say the least. Vasiliyev had placed them under arrest, and in the custody of the agent in charge, but had allowed them to come along. Kit wasn't stupid enough to think that could be for any reason other than that Vasiliyev didn't trust them enough to let them out of his sight. And since they had proved their ability to escape from incarceration – or at least the Doctor had – Kit wouldn't put it past Vasiliyev to be thinking that a stray bullet in a crossfire was a more certain means of dealing with problematic loose ends. In many ways, Kit had always admired him.

He had been watching the people milling around the station. Most of them were civilians, since those hospital trains came in from the west rather than the north. So far he hadn't seen Kuznetzov, but he hadn't really expected to. The Academician had enough of a lead on them that he was probably aboard a train already. But looking and listening were Kit's specialities, so that's what he did.

Suddenly the Doctor pointed. 'There, d'you see? In that carriage.'

Kit squinted at the train to which the Doctor was pointing. Lights were reflecting off the window, but it did look like Kuznetzov, all right. Vasiliyev must have thought so as well, because he and the Ochrana agents made a beeline for the carriage door.

Kuznetzov relaxed in the well-populated wooden carriage. In about three hours he'd be in Vyborg, then in Finland an hour or so after that.

His plan had taken a few knocks, but he was glad to see that the fail-safes he had thought of had worked perfectly. Rasputin would soon be dead, if he wasn't already, and the aristocracy and foreigners would be blamed. The Russian people would look for new leaders who could protect them from such assassins… And new leaders from whom he could get better scientific budgets, to hire new technicians. He wouldn't have to defraud the government to pay for an education for *his* sons, he promised himself. That could only be good for the country.

He was half tempted to announce his plans to the rest of the carriage, but they didn't seem very interested. They were looking at some sort of commotion outside, and Kuznetzov allowed his eyes to follow. They almost popped out when he saw Viktor Vasiliyev, Kit Powell, the Doctor, and a knot of Ochrana agents running along the platform towards his carriage.

The first thing that passed through his mind was the childish protest that this wasn't fair. That was followed a moment later by the fleeting hope that they were after someone else.

Trying not to move too quickly, for that might make his fellow passengers point him out to the Ochrana, Kuznetzov rose from his seat, and walked up to the door to the next carriage. As he reached it, the train jerked into motion. Kuznetzov's hopes rose; perhaps the Ochrana hadn't made it in time? But the door at the far end of the carriage opened, and Kuznetzov knew otherwise.

He went through into the next carriage before anyone could spot him.

The train was starting to move as the Ochrana men spread across the platform. There was a sudden mad dash to catch up with one of the doors of the last carriage. More damned running, Kit thought sourly, in between moments of certainty that he was about to suffer heart failure.

The Doctor's long legs carried him forward easily, with Vasiliyev and one of the Ochrana agents close behind.

Kit was annoyed now; there was no way he intended to be left behind while others dealt with the man who'd messed up his job here. That thought spurred him on to a last desperate effort, and at the last moment he managed to swing himself aboard. A passenger caught him just in time to save him from falling back out the door, and the Ochrana agent pulled it closed.

The Doctor was already at the seat where he said he had

spotted Kuznetzov. He turned to the people sitting opposite. 'Excuse me, did you see a man sitting here, with grey hair? Where is he now?'

A woman pointed through the door to the next carriage. 'He went in there.' Kit glowered slightly. If she'd been a bit less co-operative, it might have given him time to get his breath back. As it was, Vasiliyev was already shouldering his way through the door, checking his gun.

The Doctor pulled Vasiliyev's gun down, glaring into his eyes. 'Don't be a fool, man. There are dozens of innocent people in each of these carriages, and if you start a firefight in there, many of them will get hurt.'

Vasiliyev glared right back, not willing to be influenced by anyone. 'I'm not letting Kuznetzov get away.'

The Doctor held his gaze. 'Yes, well you just remember which of you is supposed to be the anarchist. What would you rather report back to Interior Minister Protopopov? That you prevented an anarchist from causing havoc, or that you caused some yourself?'

Vasiliyev looked away for a moment, and Kit thought he might have to jump in to save the Doctor again. Vasiliyev put away his gun, however. 'Don't think I won't shoot back if he starts something.'

'No, I don't imagine you won't.' The Doctor threw the door open, and led them through into the next packed carriage.

Jo was just about to enter 64 Gorokhovaya Ulitsa when one of the Ochrana guards stopped her. Jo was worried by this; they might not be the KGB yet, but she was sure they were the next best thing. 'Miss Josephine, someone wishes to see you,' he said.

He nodded to another agent, who took Jo's arm, not too roughly. 'Come with me, please.' He ushered her to a waiting car.

Jo wanted to run, but knew she'd never break free of his grip. Heart beating as quickly as it could, she allowed herself to be bundled into the car. There wasn't really anything else she could do.

Rasputin had been woken yet again, this time by Interior Minister Protopopov. Rasputin wondered what ghosts Protopopov was seeing in the shadows this time.

Protopopov looked around nervously. 'I tell you Grigory Efimovitch, that something is going on. Several Ochrana reports have passed my desk with warnings of a plot. Dammit, Vladimir Purishkevich has been boasting in the Duma itself about how he's going to celebrate when you're gone.'

'I'm sure he has,' Rasputin scoffed, more to convince himself than Protopopov. 'But he will have a long wait, I assure you.' He thrust a drink into the Minister's hand. 'It won't be the first time that someone has wanted Grishka Rasputin out of the way, but I am still here.'

'There is a considerable difference between the drunken husbands wanting to kill the man who's screwing their wives, and a Member of the Duma promising reform on the back of a murder!'

Rasputin turned away, ignoring Protopopov's warning. Rasputin quite liked Protopopov, but felt he had no honour or real guts. All that mattered was that he wasn't a threat, and so Rasputin had agreed with his appointment over that of those who were threats to him. He didn't care that the people believed he had had Protopopov appointed, but he did care that Protopopov also believed it, because up till now Rasputin had expected his gratitude could be useful some day.

Tonight, however, his fears were merely irritating. 'I'm perfectly safe. The only thing that will strike me down after tonight is a hangover.'

It was just after six in the evening when Felix turned off Nevsky Prospekt and reached the Cathedral of Our Lady of Kazan. The cathedral's colonnaded arms, copied from St Peter's in Rome, reached out towards pedestrians on the Nevsky, but Felix turned down the side of the Griboevoda Canal.

The colonnade almost hid the brass statues and bas-reliefs that stood against the cathedral's walls. At either end were larger statues, of the old generals. On the left was Barclay de Tolly, who had been born in Scotland and fought a rearguard action against Napoleon. To the right was Field Marshal Kutuzov, who had taken the field against Napoleon at Borodino.

Felix paused at the statue of the one-eyed Kutuzov. Though brought up in a military family, Felix had never been impressed by the veneration of soldiers and warriors. He often wished humanity had found more sensual hobbies for itself than butchery. Today, however, he *did* feel a certain kinship with the man. Before Borodino, Felix's teachers had told him, Kutuzov came here to pray, and dedicated himself to protecting Russia from the danger that faced it.

He nodded, once, to the statue, feeling that he understood a little better. Then he went inside.

The interior was actually quite subtle, rather than being overloaded with riches. Four pillars of pink granite supported the domed ceiling. In a chapel space on the Nevsky side of the building, Kutuzov's tomb was a solid altar of its own, draped in Napoleonic-era banners.

Felix decided against going in, and instead moved straight across to the ikonostasis. It and its balustrade were solid silver, made from treasures looted and melted down from Moscow churches by the French, then later recaptured by the Don Cossacks. Felix knew that this use of recaptured loot was a symbol of victory over Napoleon which Kutuzov would have found most appropriate.

Sheltered by the ikonostasis was the Virgin of Kazan – a carved and beaten metal icon of Mary and Jesus. It was said to have appeared miraculously in the sixteenth century, and Felix had heard stories of how it supposedly had mystic powers which saved Moscow from Tamerlane's Mongol horde. Its powers reputedly came to Russia's aid in times of danger.

Felix knelt before it as Kutuzov had before facing Napoleon at Borodino, but in his heart the act did not inspire much confidence. Perhaps because he knew this wasn't the original icon – that had disappeared nine years earlier, and this copy replaced it.

Yes, he told himself, that was why his heart still trembled with uncertainty: because this wasn't the true icon, and not because of any doubts within himself. He had banished them, he reminded himself; they were set aside for a greater need. What were his fears compared to the wellbeing of the Tsar's family and their beloved country? Nothing more than illusions cast by formless shadows. He could ignore their pitiful attempts to distract him.

The candlelight seemd to make the silver and gold ripple and shift. It was odd, yet not disturbing. Rather it reminded

Felix of the calmness of the sea under a midsummer sunset. The sounds of others' soft prayers, and the clatter of movement outside the cathedral all faded from his mind, washed away by those gentle waves that he fancied lapped around him.

It would be so much easier and more pleasant to allow himself to be carried off, drifting gently away on the still waters with their scent of incense... But no. He had a duty, which he owed to all of Russia's sons. If that meant sacrificing his life or freedom after a necessary crime, then it was a sacrifice he was willing to make.

Kit was totally baffled, Vasiliyev looked disgruntled, and even the Doctor seemed a little puzzled. They had searched the train from one end to the other, and found no sign of Kuznetzov. Now they gathered in a rather beaten-up compartment in the foremost carriage.

'I don't suppose he could have jumped off the train?' Kit asked with a sidelong look at the Doctor.

'I suppose it's possible,' the Doctor agreed dubiously. 'But surely someone would have commented on it.'

'You aren't a policeman, then,' Vasiliyev said. 'The first thing you learn is that nobody ever saw anything. Unless you find a way to refresh their memory...'

'I'll have you know I was one of the first men certified by the Pinkerton's agency,' the Doctor said pointedly. 'But if he *has* jumped off, he could be anywhere between here and the city.'

'No,' Kit said. 'He doesn't strike me as the type to risk breaking his neck jumping off a moving train.' This time the look at the Doctor was more blatant. 'He's hiding somewhere. I can feel it.'

* * *

The car hadn't whisked Jo off to some dank Soviet dungeon, but instead took her back to Tsarskoe Selo. Her hopes began to rise, as she realised that these Ochrana agents were the sort of people who'd probably strong-arm you no matter what they were doing. Perhaps Anya had actually found the TARDIS...

As if to bring her hopes even higher, it was Anya who met the car at the door of the Alexander Palace. 'I'm glad you could come,' Anya said.

'The invitation was very strong,' Jo pointed out.

'My apologies, but that is simply the way the Ochrana are trained. You're not in any trouble, if that's what worries you.' Jo relaxed somewhat, as Anya led her into a plush drawing room, where someone had already laid out tea.

'I wondered if maybe your soldiers had found the TARDIS?'

'I'm afraid not,' Anya said. 'Whoever took it has hidden it well.'

'The Doctor thinks Academician Kuznetzov took it,' Jo said. 'He had pictures of it.'

Anya sat down, frowning. She looked very formidable. 'Kuznetzov... Another one of Yusupov's friends... I wish I could say I was surprised. In fact he might have some bearing on why Her Majesty asked me to bring you here.'

Jo looked around. 'Is the Empress going to be joining us?' She quite looked forward to meeting the Empress again.

Anya shook her head. 'Her Majesty is on nursing duty over at the Catherine Palace. She believes in leading by example. Now... I gather you and I have a mutual friend: Father Grigory.'

At first Jo wondered who she meant, but then realised that Anya meant Rasputin. 'Yes. He could do with some better manners, but he isn't the monster everybody says he is...'

'Indeed not.' Anya smiled, a rare event. 'When my husband died, it was Father Grigory who brought me back to my senses. I shall never forget that. Of course I feel that I owe him a great deal, and one thing I owe him is to make sure he remains safe, unharmed by his enemies.'

Jo nodded sympathetically. 'He does seem to have a lot of them.' She decided it was best not to let Anya know that she already knew that he would be killed by those enemies.

'Sometimes,' Anya said thoughtfully, 'it is difficult to tell who those enemies are. Or even whether friends can accidentally seem like enemies because of mistakes...' Jo was beginning to wonder what Anya was referring to. Whatever the case, it sounded like she was building up to something delicate.

'Grigory has been invited to a party tonight, at the Moika Palace owned by Felix Yusupov. The Empress and I both feel that there is something odd in holding a tea party at midnight. Many of Felix's friends who will be there have spoken against Rasputin in the past...'

With a start, Jo realised that Anya was talking about Rasputin's murder. Wasn't that how the film had ended, with him being invited to a late-night tea party, and murdered?

'Josephine,' Anya said slowly. 'I brought you here to ask if you would go to the Moika, and look around, to see if everything is... legitimate, or not. If not, call me, and I shall send guards to keep the peace. I would go myself, but Felix and the others would recognise me immediately, and that might simply put Grigory in more danger.'

Jo didn't know quite what to say. She didn't want to be anywhere near Rasputin's murder. Let it stay in history, not be played out for her.

Even so, this was a request from the Empress of All Russia ... That was kind of an honour, wasn't it? She knew Anya could command her if she wished, and yet was simply asking this of her as a personal favour.

'Miss Grant,' Anya continued, as if realising Jo's resolve was wavering. 'I'm not asking you to challenge anyone, just to see whether those at the Moika Palace mean any harm to Rasputin.'

'Perhaps the Doctor would –'

'The Doctor isn't here. He and the Ochrana are pursuing the man who stole your cabinet. Professor Shaw will probably be there tonight too, and that's the other reason I ask this of you – you can also warn her, if there is any danger.'

Jo thought hard. If Liz was in danger and the Doctor was out of the way...

'All right,' Jo agreed, finally. 'But how will I get in?'

Anya considered a moment. 'Naturally, you will need to look inconspicuous. Perhaps you could dress as a nurse – most of the palaces in St Petersburg have had some wings converted into hospitals. The nurses' uniforms we use here at Tsarskoe Selo are just the same as the ones used in the hospital wing at the Moika.'

Jo looked doubtful. 'I might be asked to do something actually medical, and I'm not sure...' she demurred.

Anya nodded decisively. 'In that case, it would be safer if you appeared to be just a member of the domestic staff. If you are dressed as a maid, you should not attract any undue attention.'

* * *

The icy wind threatened to freeze Kuznetzov to the spot, as he lay flat on the roof, hanging on for dear life. His eyes were stinging from the smoke and steam flowing along the rooftops, and he could barely make out the dead trees that lined the track on either side. This wasn't the way he had anticipated making the journey, but he wasn't going to let the Ochrana take him, not while there was a breath left in his body.

There was a clatter from the front end of the carriage, next to the coal tender. To Kuznetzov's dismay, the Doctor pulled himself up onto the roof. He adopted a cautious defensive stance as Kuznetzov rose. 'Yes,' the Doctor said in self-satisfaction. 'I thought you might be up here.'

'You are not calling for your friends?'

'We're both scientists, Academician –'

'Besides,' Kuznetzov went on mockingly, 'you want your police box back.'

'Yes,' the Doctor admitted. 'It contains some very important equipment of mine.'

'I'll wager it does... I'll tell you what, Doctor; give me the key, and tell me how it transports itself from one place to another, and I'll provide evidence that you and your friends are innocent.'

'I'm afraid any evidence you produce now wouldn't be believed anyway. You've cried wolf once too often.'

Kuznetzov nodded. 'Then I'll just have to take it from you.' He lashed out with a hand, but the Doctor dodged, bringing up his own hands. Kuznetzov ducked, sweeping his leg round to knock the Doctor's feet out from under him.

The Doctor let himself roll aside, out of Kuznetzov's way, and got back to his feet. 'I must say you're keeping spry for your age.'

'You forget, Doctor, I've been travelling along the trans-Siberian railways for years. I've been all over Mongolia and northern China, with and without official permission.' He lunged again, aiming the heel of his hand for the Doctor's nose. The Doctor ducked so that the blow merely grazed the side of his head, and struck back at a nerve cluster. Kuznetzov's whole right side suddenly went numb, and he could feel himself fall backwards.

An instant before he fell off the edge of the carriage roof, the Doctor grabbed his jacket, and pulled him to safety. 'And perhaps you don't realise that I was once a student of Wong Fei Hung himself,' the Doctor said.

The numbness faded as Kuznetzov coughed through the smoke that was enveloping them from the engine. His mood suddenly lifted, as he recognised the flaw in the Doctor's strategy. He was trying to merely subdue his opponent, and also making efforts to ensure that Kuznetzov didn't fall off the train... Since Kuznetzov had no such qualms about the Doctor's wellbeing, the advantage was all his.

Reinvigorated by his realisation, Kuznetzov lunged forward, carefully keeping his balance against the juddering of the carriage and the icy wind, pummelling the Doctor with rapid punches. The Doctor blocked them all well, as Kuznetzov had expected. Without breaking the rhythm of his movements, he swung around, spinning a reverse kick at the Doctor's head. The Doctor swayed aside and jabbed at a nerve point on Kuznetzov's knee.

Kuznetzov landed painfully on his back, icy fire blooming throughout his left leg. The Doctor looked down at him disparagingly, his hair whipping back in the chill wind. 'You know, there's really no need for all this.' Behind the Doctor,

Kuznetzov could see a low bridge approaching.

Kuznetzov got a foot under the Doctor's chest, and grinned, grabbing the Doctor's throat. All he had to do was hold the Doctor's head up a little, and the bridge would take it off.

The Doctor stopped struggling, and must have realised that something was up. He couldn't press himself flat, or pull away, but at the last moment he flung himself sideways. They broke apart, the Doctor rolling across the carriage roof, and over the edge. Kuznetzov saw his hands grab at the roof, and heard the meaty sound of the Doctor slamming into the carriage wall.

Carefully, not wanting to overbalance or be hit by a branch, Kuznetzov pulled off a shoe, and with a grip around its toe smashed its heel down on the Doctor's hands in turn.

The Doctor was being constantly buffeted by the wind, as well as choked and blinded by smoke, and knew he couldn't hang on much longer. Especially under the pounding from Kuznetzov's shoe on his knuckles. He also knew it was surely only a matter of time before a tree branch clipped him. Holding on as tightly as he could, he pushed himself out from the side of the carriage with his legs, and kicked out sharply at the window.

The astonished passengers who had been watching him shielded their faces against the flying glass as the Doctor swung inside feet-first, moments before a gnarled set of branches seemed to claw the side of the train.

Kuznetzov pulled his shoe back on, and started along the train's roof, trying to get as far as possible from the carriage which held the Doctor. He knew that in minutes his pursuers would come up here after him.

Up ahead, he could see the approaching lights of the Tarkhova Halt. It was just a small local station serving the town of Razliv, but he knew the train would stop there. Already, he could hear the brakes start to screech as the train slowed.

Kuznetzov flexed his muscles slowly, trying to bring them back to life without cramps. It didn't help that his lungs and eyes were full of smoke from the engine.

The train slowly ground to a halt, and finally bumped to a full stop. Carefully, so as not to make any sound in the carriage below, Kuznetzov made his way along the roof of the train, to the last carriage. There, he climbed down the door jamb, and on to the platform.

There were some sympathisers in this town, he recalled, who had a house with a barn. If he could just find that, they'd be able to get him across to Finland, and safety. Not to mention a warm welcome for the success – mostly, in all the important areas – of his mission.

The train was starting to pull out of Razliv when the Doctor burst into the compartment with Kit and Vasiliyev. 'He's on the roof.'

The two men were on their feet at once, but before they could reach the door at the end of the carriage, an Ochrana agent pointed out the window. 'There he is!'

The Doctor and the others darted for the door, but Kit had no intention of jumping off another moving train, especially a fast one. That would truly be tempting fate. Instead, he reached up to just under the luggage rack, and tugged sharply on the communication cord.

The brakes kicked in again almost instantly, sending passengers stumbling around. The Doctor had flung open the door already, and leaped out, followed by Vasiliyev and the Ochrana agent.

Feeling a lot safer, Kit followed them out, in time to hear Vasiliyev order his agent to call for military backup.

On the road into town, Kuznetzov was now openly fleeing.

Chapter Seventeen

The murder room had been decorated by the time Felix returned to the Moika Palace. The gentle curves of Chinese porcelain vases sat in the corners, as if to resemble truncated pillars. Most of the room's floor was covered by Persian carpet, but a gorgeous white polar-bear-skin rug was splayed out in the middle. Some attractively carved chairs, with a mellow leather upholstery, were arranged around the rug, particularly on the fireplace side, where a small table could hold trays of food and drink.

To one side of the fireplace was an inlaid ebony cupboard, whose interior was a labyrinth of miniature bronze columns and tiny polished mirrors. A seventeenth-century Italian crucifix, encrusted with cut crystal, stood atop it.

Felix nodded distractedly. Everything was perfect, just as planned, but it all reminded him that he was about to break the most important of laws. He wondered whether he would be able to bear looking at any of these things again after tonight.

He realised after a few moments that Thesphe was watching him concernedly. 'I am well. Have the servants prepare a light meal for eleven o'clock. Tea, cakes and enough wine for six people.'

'Yes, Highness. And yourself?'

'I'll be with Colonel Fogel, preparing for tomorrow's examination papers.'

After Felix had ascended the spiral staircase to the lounge, the door on the middle landing opened. It led to the courtyard, and it was from there that a small feminine figure in a servant's uniform slipped into the palace.

Jo Grant looked around. The palace was huge and labyrinthine, and she got the impression that she could search around here for days and might not find Liz or Rasputin. If this was to be a tea party, there must be food to be arranged, and so the kitchen was where it would be done. All she had to do, then, was hide by the kitchen, and follow the servants when they took the food to whichever rooms were occupied.

There seemed to be just the one room downstairs, so she went up and into the palace.

This palace was also truly sumptuous, and Jo felt a little sad that she wasn't affected by it as much as she might have been if she hadn't already seen the other palaces over the past few days. She marvelled at how the Doctor kept his eyes continually open to wonders.

Jo hid when a couple of servants went past, and then followed them discreetly. They went to a linen cupboard first and Jo saw that it contained, among other things, some aprons like the ones they wore. She paused just long enough to add one to her disguise before following them again. Eventually they passed a doorway that Jo could see led to a huge kitchen. Unfortunately there were still some people working there – a few cooks and a black butler.

Jo knew how to be patient, though, and moved into an adjoining room, to pretend to do some cleaning while she awaited her chance to find out what was going on here, and call Anya.

Footsteps from the corridor outside made Jo scuttle round to be closer to the door. 'What poison are you using,

Doctor?' a man's voice asked.

'Potassium cyanide,' a slightly younger male voice answered. 'There is enough in each of the cakes on this plate –' Jo peeked through the crack in the door to see which ones he was pointing at – 'to kill a man in thirty seconds.'

The second man, whom Jo thought looked rather like Lenin, nodded. 'Good. Perhaps you should dust some of these glasses also.'

Jo shrank back away from the door, horrified. This didn't look much like a plot to kill one man, but everybody at the party! And Liz, she knew, would be there too…

Kuznetzov ran, his heart pounding in his chest. Every painful beat reminded him of the fate that awaited him if his steps faltered. Whatever else happened, he himself had to get away. He couldn't even go to the barn now, not without leading the authorities there.

How the hell had this happened?

Ordinarily Kuznetzov might have been as afraid to return to his own comrades as he would be to be caught by the authorities. It had taken him considerable effort to persuade them to rely on such a subtle plan, and he knew that Koba would waste no time in getting back to the old ways in his punishment for failure.

So long as Rasputin still died, however, then he would have landed a strong blow against the current administration, and hopefully one which would save his own skin.

First he had to make sure that no one interfered with Felix's plan, and if that meant distracting them by letting them chase him, then so be it.

* * *

The night was clear and frigid as Dmitri's sedan car pulled into the courtyard of number 64 Gorokhovaya Ulitsa. Felix opened the car door, letting out the heat that had built up in the car. 'Are you sure you're ready?' Lazovert asked.

Felix wasn't, but could hardly put this off now. So he nodded, pulling his hat down over his face. He was nervous enough already without Lazovert provoking his fears. He took a few deep breaths to calm himself, and walked across the courtyard to the door of the apartment block. With each step, he reminded himself that he was doing what he must, for the good of his beloved Tsar and Tsarina. They were family, just like Nicky was.

A doorman stepped out, a suspicious look on his face. 'Who do you want at this time of night?'

'I have an appointment with Grishka Rasputin,' Felix answered, surprised at how calm he sounded.

'I might have guessed,' the doorman grumbled. He unlocked the gate, and ushered Felix through. Felix went straight up the stairs to the door of Rasputin's apartment. There, his hand paused over the bell, for just a few seconds, before ringing it.

'Who's there?' Rasputin's voice demanded, sounding a little tired and, Felix thought, a lot drunk.

'It's me, Grigory. I've come for you.'

The door opened, and Rasputin stared out at him. He was wearing a white silk shirt embroidered with blue cornflowers, and black trousers. A raspberry-coloured cord was tied around his waist. He seemed unusually clean and tidy to Felix, and stank of cheap soap. Even so, Felix tried not to recoil from the power he sensed emanating from the man. It was both alluring and repulsive. Rasputin looked at Felix's hat as the Prince entered the apartment. 'Why are you trying to hide yourself under that?'

Felix winced. 'Didn't we agree that no one was to know you were going out with me tonight?'

Rasputin looked momentarily vague, then nodded. 'True, true... I haven't told a soul,' he announced proudly.

'Good,' Felix said, greatly relieved. 'Why don't you finish dressing, and –'

'Can't find my boots,' Rasputin grumbled, peering under a chair. 'It's those children again – they've hidden them. They don't want me to go out, I think.'

Felix nodded, and looked around the room. He felt a wash of pity for Rasputin, that did nothing to strengthen his resolve.

'Ah, there they are,' Rasputin said in satisfaction. He started pulling on the snow boots. 'Perhaps we should go visit the gypsies again tonight, my son,' he suggested. 'The snow won't cool their women...'

'Perhaps,' Felix agreed blandly, 'but we visit the Moika first. Miss Shaw and Miss Grant are waiting for you there.'

'Both of them?' Rasputin sobered up, eyes glinting alertly.

'Both,' Felix confirmed. 'Come on, we don't want to disappoint them, do we?'

'No,' Rasputin agreed with a lecherous grin. 'That we don't.' His grin froze slightly. 'Not that I'd want to offend you, my son, but your mother isn't going to be at this supper, is she?'

'No,' Felix said with a smile. 'She's in the Crimea, enjoying a milder winter than we are.' He didn't bother to mention that Irina was there as well; if Rasputin thought he might encounter her as well, he'd be even more willing to visit the Moika palace.

'Good, good. I wouldn't want to cause any trouble.' He

slapped Felix on the back, almost hard enough to knock him off his feet. 'Lead on then, my son. Don't want the tea or the women to grow cool.'

'Indeed not,' Felix agreed drily. He allowed Rasputin to lead him down the back stairs, closing the door quietly so as not to wake the rest of his family. Lazovert opened the door for Felix and Rasputin. Once inside, he started the car, and set off on a circuitous route that Felix had already given him. Rasputin already knew where he was going, but Felix didn't want the police to follow them successfully.

Kuznetzov turned off Razliv's main street, trying to double back to the station. They wouldn't expect that. The lack of people around at this hour made his flight faster, but also left him more exposed to the pursuers who *were* here. Kuznetzov had never before felt quite so alone as he did now, passing from one pool of lamplit snow to the next.

He could hear his footsteps, too loudly. Even his heartbeat was the sound of a bass drum, though he was sure it was one others couldn't hear. Then there was the sound of an engine. He barely skidded to a halt at the end of the street before an armoured car turned the corner.

Its machine-gun turret swivelled towards him, and he bolted off between the trees that surrounded the small town. At least there, the terrain was too rough for the armoured car to follow him. He had to get away. He just *had* to.

Jo listened carefully for the kitchen staff to go off-duty, and deserted her adopted cleaning duty. There was some food and drink loaded on to a serving trolley, ready for Thesphe to take it down to the room where they would sit.

Listening to make sure that she wouldn't be discovered, Jo removed the poisoned cakes from their plate and dumped them into a rubbish bin. Then she took some similar-looking cakes from the larder, and carefully arranged them on the plate instead.

That done she removed the poisoned glasses, putting them in one of the sinks with some other dirty dishes and setting clean glasses on the trolley in their place. Rasputin would still get killed – she didn't dare try to stop that, though she desperately wanted to – but at least Liz and the others wouldn't be poisoned. Now Jo had to do two things – find a telephone to call Anya, and find Liz.

Kuznetzov's heart was now pounding at the inside of his chest with insistent fury, as if it were a caged animal desperate to break out. Around him, the hoofbeats of Cossack lancers' mounts mockingly echoed that beating in his ears, driving him one way and then another through the dead black branches.

A shout came from ahead, and he saw some soldiers running towards him. He shouldered one aside as he emerged from a small copse, and kept running. He had no choice but turn once more, plunging headlong back towards the road to the station. He vaguely sensed that the Doctor, Kit and Vasiliyev were running towards him from the left.

When he risked a look to check, not only were his fears confirmed, but he saw a soldier aiming a rifle at him too. 'No!' the Doctor called out. He pushed the soldier's rifle skywards just as the man fired, the shot splitting the air harmlessly. 'You mustn't –'

The harsh clatter of machine-gun fire punched through

the night from the armoured car's turret. It had been waiting for the men and horses to herd him back to the road where it waited. Bullets stitched their way across the yellow-tinted street, kicking up little puffs of snow, before tearing across Kuznetzov's back.

Kuznetzov stumbled, and fell to one knee with an audible crack that made even the Doctor wince. Kuznetzov, to his own surprise, didn't feel it. He wasn't dead, so he reasoned that he must be in pain, but he wasn't aware of it. For a moment he wished he was an ignorant peasant. He wouldn't know that he was in shock, that his nervous system was overloaded, that he was dying.

He rolled on to his back as his pursuers surrounded him. 'You're too late, Doctor,' Kuznetzov breathed. 'Too late to save Rasputin, and too late to save your friends from implication in his death…'

'My friends?' The Doctor's face went grim. 'You mean Jo and Liz?'

'They're already with Fe…' Kuznetzov coughed up some more blood. 'One thing, Doctor…'

'Yes?'

'You were wrong.' He allowed himself to smile, feeling he deserved it on the grounds that at least he had fooled his enemy about one thing. 'I *did* go to Tunguska in the summer. I saw the forest smashed flat from horizon to horizon… Except at the heart. The trees still stood at the heart…' He blinked, as if the forest were before him now.

The Doctor's face hardened. 'Where is my TARDIS? The blue box.'

Kuznetzov used the last of his consciousness to force a smile. 'Why should I tell –' He never even knew that he hadn't finished the sentence.

* * *

Kit had listened intently, and caught the Doctor's sleeve. 'We might still be able to save Rasputin.'

'I suspect you'll find we're too late for that, old chap. What's more important is getting Jo and Liz out of the Moika Palace. If they really are there, they're almost certainly in the most terrible danger. Besides, whatever else this plot may be, it isn't a German one, and nor does it affect Britain's war effort.'

Kit didn't like what he was hearing. 'Are you saying we shouldn't try to prevent it?'

'That's right,' the Doctor said firmly. 'At present, this is purely an internal matter. If we don't get Jo and Liz out, their presence could make it international.'

'The Moika Palace? Are you sure that's where they'll be?'

'Absolutely certain,' the Doctor said firmly. Kit felt dismayed. His hopes of charging to the rescue would be dashed, since in this weather, and with the railway line blocked, it would take hours to reach the Moika. 'What would be our best way of getting there?' the Doctor asked. Kit got the impression that he knew anyway, and was just trying to make him feel needed. He had to admit it worked.

Kit was initially at a loss, but then noticed the Cossack lancers who had arrived to set up a perimeter. 'Have you ever ridden a horse, Doctor?'

Liz Shaw was beginning to wonder if this was all some elaborate hoax. Kuznetzov should have arrived by now, but there was no sign of him. She also didn't like the way Purishkevich was looking at her. He had had a few drinks tonight already, and was behaving no more gentlemanly than Rasputin usually did.

There was a sound of wheels on gravel from below, and

Liz went to the study window. Felix's car had drawn up in the courtyard. 'They're here.'

'Is Grishka with them?' Purishkevich asked.

Liz nodded, as three men emerged from the car. 'Yes.'

'Good,' Purishkevich said happily. Beside him, Dmitri went over to the gramophone, and started it playing. 'Smile, Professor Shaw. You're about to become a heroine, for both helping kill Rasputin, and saving your friend Miss Grant.'

Liz glared at him. She didn't feel like any kind of heroine. Rather, she felt like a coward, who should have had the courage to call their bluff.

Chapter Eighteen

Rasputin shrugged off his overcoat as they entered the cosy little room. Felix handed it to Thesphe with a little nod. The strains of 'Yankee Doodle Dandy' sank down from upstairs, and Rasputin glanced upwards. 'Is someone giving a party?'

'Not really. It's just Irina entertaining a few friends. They'll be leaving soon – perhaps she will join us then.'

'Ah.' Rasputin prowled through the room until he came to the ebony cabinet. With a delighted, even childlike, expression, he began to experiment with the doors and drawers.

'I hear Minister Protopopov visited you today.'

Rasputin nodded, unable to tear his eyes away from the cabinet.

'What was he saying? More talk of conspiracies, I suppose.'

'Why, yes, my son.' Rasputin turned back to Felix with a shrug. 'The aristocracy can't get used to the idea that a peasant like me is so welcome in the Imperial palace. Some of them are as green with envy as they are consumed by fear.'

Felix thought about this. If Rasputin had been warned that his life was threatened, perhaps he would see sense. 'Don't you think you may be best to leave St Petersburg for a while? So that these plotters are foiled?' If he would go, there would be no need for violence, and Felix would have triumphed without harm to his conscience.

'Leave?' Rasputin laughed. 'Never! I'm not afraid of them.

They can't do anything to me.' He grinned cockily. 'I'm protected against ill-fortune, you see. People have tried to kill me before, but the Lord has always frustrated them. I'm sure He will ensure that disaster befalls anyone who so much as raises a finger against me.'

Felix tried not to look as shaken as he felt, but luckily Rasputin's attention was wandering to all of the fine things around him. He knows, Felix thought. It was impossible, but surely Rasputin knew what they planned? But if he had known, why come here? Felix rallied his courage, fending off the fear that was gnawing away at his mind. 'I don't know about fingers, but I will raise a drink to you.' Rasputin perked up at that, and Felix went to the sideboard where some bottles and glasses stood. 'I have a Crimean red here… from the family vineyards.'

Felix began to pour wine into a glass for himself, then his hand reached out to one that had been sprinkled with cyanide powder. His arm refused to move; damn his conscience… He selected a safe glass for Rasputin too.

Rasputin shook his head. 'Thank you, but no… I had something to drink before you came to collect me. And I wouldn't want the drink to make me as incapable as it makes me willing…'

Felix ground his teeth, but had begun to anticipate such pitfalls. He turned. 'But I've already poured…'

Rasputin's piercing eyes fixed on to the wine glasses. 'Well, in that case…' Felix handed him a glass, which he drained immediately. Felix refilled the glass, then sat down in the chair opposite.

'Cake?' he suggested, holding a plate of sugar- and cyanide-crusted cakes towards Rasputin.

'They're too sweet. Not to my taste.'

Felix put the plate down carefully, and offered another one, with plainer cakes. 'These aren't so sweet.'

Rasputin hesitated, then took one, and ate it experimentally. It must have tasted fine, as he then grabbed another three. Felix could feel his own features set into a sickly and false smile as Rasputin gobbled down the poisoned cakes. If Lazovert's estimate was right, the poison from even one cake should take effect in about thirty seconds. Four should kill him in a minute or so...

Felix daren't even lift his own wine – much as he could have done with its assistance to his courage – in case his hand shook so much as to betray him. Rasputin seemed quite happy with his snack, and now drained the rest of his wine. 'I don't suppose you have any Madeira, dear boy?'

Felix swallowed hard. 'Of course.' Was that it? He asks for Madeira? The poison *must* have taken effect by now... And yet Rasputin sat happily in front the roaring fire, the very figure of health. Even the drink itself didn't seem to be affecting him. Felix returned to the sideboard, collecting a bottle of Madeira and a poisoned glass, which he set on the table.

'Just pour it in that one,' Rasputin instructed, indicating the glass from which he had drunk his wine.

'Grigory, you can't mix Madeira and red wine –' Even though Felix was consumed with horror at the idea that Rasputin might be on to his plan, some part of his mind truly recoiled at the idea of using the same glass for different drinks. For the life of him, he couldn't think why that should bother him right now. But it did.

'Drink is drink. Why dirty another glass?'

Felix shrugged. 'All right.' He made as if to pour into the safe glass, but tapped it with the bottle, so that it fell off the table in an apparent accident. 'Sorry.' He poured the Madeira into the poisoned glass, and handed it to Rasputin.

'You break a glass rather than reuse it without etiquette… Very aristocratic of you, my son.' He drank the Madeira. Felix tried to contain his excitement, certain that the poison would take him this time… The peasant rubbed his throat thoughtfully, and Felix could feel the confidence rise within him. 'The Madeira's good,' Rasputin suddenly announced. 'Give me another.'

Felix closed his mouth with a clack of teeth, in case he gaped at the peasant's failure to succumb to the poison. He poured some more into another poisoned glass and handed it over. Rasputin downed it in one gulp.

Felix almost physically reeled at the lack of reaction to the poison. His careful planning was all for nothing… Rasputin's eyes met his. The peasant was grinning, but Felix got the impression that it was a grin of hatred, by a man facing down an enemy. Felix was suddenly certain that Rasputin knew he had been poisoned.

Rasputin's gaze was strong enough that Felix could feel it pressing upon him. He fought back with all his willpower, struggling against Rasputin's power, just as he had when he had first visited the peasant. He could feel his self-will flee under the pressure, leaving only numbness. Felix rose from his seat, his muscles poised to launch him at Rasputin's throat and strangle the bastard, if that's what it would take.

His legs betrayed him, stepping instead towards the door to the staircase. 'Excuse me a moment, Grigory,' Felix managed to say stiffly. 'I'll go up and see whether Miss Shaw and Miss Grant are ready to join us yet.'

'Good,' Rasputin said, eager but a little slurred. 'You do that.'

* * *

'Yankee Doodle Dandy' was still playing, as it had for the past hour. It was getting to the stage where Liz couldn't imagine *not* hearing it. 'Why don't we put something else on?' she grumbled. 'Anybody would think you don't have any other records.'

'We don't,' Dmitri admitted.

Liz looked at him, wishing he hadn't said that.

Felix emerged from the stairs, his eyes a little wide for Liz's liking; he was obviously under considerable strain. He was as white as a sheet, though she couldn't tell whether it was with fear, rage or just stress.

'This is impossible,' he snapped, and Liz could hear the quiver in his voice. 'Just imagine it – he drinks two glasses of poison, eats several poisoned cakes, and nothing has happened. Absolutely nothing!'

'There must be something,' Lazovert insisted, though Liz thought he sounded almost relieved.

'He's getting a little sleepy from the alcohol, that's all. I can't think what we can do…'

Purishkevich looked ceilingwards, as if seeking divine inspiration. 'All right, Felix. Calm down. Go back. The poison is bound to take effect eventually –'

Liz had been wondering about that. Cyanide was a very quick-acting poison under most normal circumstances. 'Rasputin's a heavy drinker, isn't he?'

'Wine rather than vodka,' Felix said irritably, 'but yes, why?'

'There is a possible reason,' she suggested. 'Acute alcoholic gastritis. That condition thickens the lining of the stomach,' she explained, 'and could delay the absorption of cyanide into the bloodstream.'

Lazovert nodded slowly. 'She's right. The cyanide could simply be delayed.'

Purishkevich patted Felix on the shoulder, in the way men do when they're half drunk and trying to be encouraging. 'There, you see. If the poison has still been useless after another five minutes, come back up, and we'll decide how to finish this, and him. The last thing we need is for morning to catch up with us, and be found with Rasputin's stinking corpse still in your palace.'

Felix took a deep breath. 'You're right, of course. Thank you, Professor Shaw.'

'Don't mention it.' She wished she hadn't. 'If you'll excuse me, I need to go and… powder my nose or something.' It was a stupid phrase, she knew, but she had no idea how ladies excused themselves in this time and place, when they wanted to get away from uncomfortable company. Knowing how to get away from her conscience would have been nice too.

She left the room, and went along to the main entrance hall. She heard something from the kitchen, a faint bump from a walk-in larder, but thought nothing of it. Then there was a muffled cough, and she realised someone was in there.

Cautiously, she moved over to the door, lifting a cleaver as she went, just in case. She whipped the door open, to find a cleaning girl huddling amidst the bags of flour and grain. Then her brain kicked into gear, and she realised that this was no cleaning girl, it was Jo.

Dropping the cleaver, Liz pulled Jo out of the cupboard. The girl smiled when she realised who it was, but her smile faltered at Liz's expression.

'How did you get in?' Liz asked.

'Through the door at the side of the stairs to the basement.' That seemed simple enough, but Liz still wondered why she had put herself in danger. This was no place for a young girl like her, even if she was in UNIT – Liz thought harder. She supposed that this sort of cloak and dagger nonsense was exactly what someone from UNIT would get up to after all.

'But why come here?' If Purishkevich found out Jo was here, or Kuznetzov returned, they would surely kill her as they had threatened. 'You're in danger here, Jo –'

'Anya and the Empress sent me,' Jo interrupted, 'to find out if any harm was meant for Rasputin.'

'There certainly is,' Liz said drily. 'And for you too. Jo, Kuznetzov not only took the TARDIS, but has had the Doctor arrested, and promised to kill you if I didn't lure Rasputin here.'

'Then Anya was right... She said you were in danger.' Jo brightened. 'But the Doctor isn't under arrest any more. He and the Ochrana have teamed up to chase Kuznetzov.'

Liz thought about this. It certainly explained the Academician's absence... And she suspected that only Purishkevich and Sukhotin knew that she was under threat, or would carry it out. 'Did you contact Anya?'

Jo shook her head. 'All the phones are dead.'

'Felix being careful...' Liz looked around. 'Even if you could phone, though, it wouldn't do to change history by letting Anya save him.'

'I know,' Jo said, softly. 'As it is I settled for saving you and the others.'

Liz frowned. 'Me and the others? What do you mean?'

'A young doctor and a man who looked like Lenin –'

'Lazovert and Purishkevich,' Liz murmured to herself.

'They'd poisoned all these cakes and drinking glasses. More than just one person's.' She looked puzzled as Liz's expression changed to one of slowly dawning horror. 'Well, obviously they planned to double-cross their friends, and kill you and them.'

'What have you done?' Though from what had happened already tonight, she could guess.

'I switched the poisoned glasses,' Jo said proudly.

'You little fool,' Liz hissed in disbelief.

'Fool?' Jo exploded. 'But they were trying to murder you all!'

'Jo, Rasputin was poisoned here at the palace, according to the history books!'

Jo paled, as she began to understand what Liz was trying to tell her. 'Oh no.'

'Oh no what?'

Jo tried to speak, but at first nothing would come. 'What if I've just saved Rasputin?'

Liz didn't dare imagine what sort of world they might return to if that was true, but she knew enough about history to know that Rasputin wasn't merely poisoned. For once, Jo's naïvety might actually be a good thing. 'I doubt that, Jo, luckily. But we certainly have to get you out of here.' She thought carefully. She didn't think Jo was in any actual danger, but she didn't want to risk messing up history, or even driving Felix further over the edge. 'I'd better go back up before I'm missed. You stay here. I'll try to find us a way out of here.'

Felix returned to the basement room, and found Rasputin sitting at the gaming table in the middle of the room. All of Felix's fears seized on him again.

'Are they coming down?'

Felix shook his head. 'They're… freshening up first.' What

the hell was he supposed to say to a man whom he had just poisoned – even if that poison had had no effect? His mind was blank. 'Would you care for some tea?'

'Yes, thank you, my son.'

Felix shakily fetched some. As he did so, Rasputin looked around the room. He seemed a bit dazed, but not really harmed. Rasputin sipped the hot tea gratefully, and, to Felix's horror, actually brightened up.

'That's much better. I think those cakes were a little heavy for me.' Rasputin resumed his prowl around the room, and stopped with a little gasp of pleasure. He lifted up Felix's guitar from beside the fireplace. 'Excellent!' He turned back to Felix. 'You have a pleasing voice; why not sing something? Something cheerful, I think – I love the way you sing.'

Felix winced. 'I don't really feel much like singing…'

'Nonsense, my son. Perhaps the sweetness of your voice will even lure the women down.'

Felix took the guitar reluctantly. 'Perhaps one song.' It had been a long time since he had serenaded someone, and that hadn't been since he experimented with women. He barely trusted his voice not to tremble, and wished, fervently, that things hadn't come to this.

But it was too late now.

Chapter Nineteen

Upstairs, Lazovert seemed to have fainted dead away, but Liz was sure it was just nerves, rather than anything physically wrong with him. She couldn't blame him.

'Will he be all right?' Dmitri asked. Liz got the impression that the novelty of conspiring had worn off from him, and he'd rather be elsewhere. She sympathised entirely, but couldn't risk leaving yet, in case Purishkevich or Sukhotin caught up with her and Jo. Besides, much as she detested the idea, she had to make sure that history hadn't been changed – they still had to kill Rasputin somehow.

'I think so. He's been under a lot of nervous strain.'

'Haven't we all –' The door flew open again, and Felix rushed into the room.

'I can't take this any more!' the prince yelped hysterically. 'I just can't. No more. No more.' He looked like he was ready to have a stroke on the spot.

'He's still alive?' Purishkevich asked wearily.

'Alive? He's damnably immortal! I cannot stand to be in that room a minute longer, watching him feed off poison as if it was nourishment. It's just... unnatural!'

It certainly would be, Liz knew, if it were true. She was praying that none of the conspirators would realise what had actually happened. But even half-drunk it couldn't be that difficult.

Dmitri cleared his throat. 'Maybe he really *is* holy. If we let him go in peace today, maybe we'll have better luck with a bomb or something, another time...' He trailed off, looking embarrassed at the suggestion.

'Never!' Purishkevich snapped, his face going purple. Liz could see the bloodlust consume him. He turned to Felix. 'Your Highness,' he said with exaggerated patience. 'Don't you understand that if he gets away today, he'll have slipped through our fingers for ever? He's not going to trust you or come back here again once he realises you tricked and lied to him.' Purishkevich straightened his jacket. 'He cannot, must not, and will not leave here alive.'

'Then what?' Dmitri asked.

Purishkevich controlled his breathing, and straightened his jacket again. 'We show our hand. I'm going down there myself. You can come too, or leave it all to me.' He turned towards the stairs, but Sukhotin stopped him.

'All right, sir. We'll go, if that's what you want.' He sounded bored, to Liz. Of course he was just a soldier doing what he thought was expected of him. She was glad, though; their absence would give her a chance to look for a way out, now that she knew they were still going to carry out the murder.

At the top of the stairs, the conspirators paused. 'Wait a moment,' Dmitri said to Purishkevich. He looked at Felix. 'This is simply causing us intolerable agitation. If he has to die, let's just shoot the bastard and be done with it. The simplest and most straightforward things are usually the best.'

Felix calmed down a little. As always, Dmitri was wise. 'Would anyone object to changing the plan like that?'

'No,' Purishkevich said. 'It doesn't matter who kills him, or how, so long as he dies tonight.'

Felix smiled with relief. Now he had a way to both secure any credit that might arise if the story should come out, and teach Rasputin a lesson for being so infernally unaffected by the poison. Also, it was only right that Felix, who at least had some care about Rasputin, should be the one to do it. It would be something of a sacrifice, knowing that he would never sense the moujik's magnetism again, and that was supposed to be good for the soul.

'Give me your gun,' Felix requested, and Dmitri handed over his Browning revolver. 'I'll deal with him.'

The others exchanged looks, and Felix knew that Dmitri, at least, would understand why he needed to maintain control of this night. They went back up to the lounge, while Felix descended alone.

'Where's Professor Shaw?' Purishkevich asked. They all looked around. 'Perhaps she's gone down to the kitchen to get some safe food,' Sukhotin suggested. 'I'll go and look for her.'

Purishkevich nodded. 'Just make sure she doesn't leave yet. Nobody leaves the palace until that peasant bastard is dead.'

Sukhotin nodded. 'I'll convince her.'

When Felix re-entered the basement room, Rasputin was slumped by the table, resting his head on the wood. His breathing was heavy and unhealthy. Felix brightened; the poison was taking effect after all. 'Is something wrong? Are you ill?' he asked as innocently as he could manage – which wasn't very, but Rasputin didn't seem to notice.

'My head feels choked, and my stomach burns.' He straightened with a wince. 'Give me another drink, that should ease the pain.' Felix was only too happy to oblige with another poisoned glass. Rasputin drank it quickly.

'That's better.' Felix's last reserves of patience and confidence vanished. Somehow Lazovert must have bungled the poison. 'Perhaps we should go and visit the gypsies,' Rasputin suggested again. 'With God in thought, but mankind in the flesh,' he added.

Felix didn't risk his voice with an answer. Instead, he went over to the ebony cabinet that had the cross on top of it, and tried to gather his thoughts. He remained motionless, staring at the cross as he tried to persuade his body to take action. 'What are you doing?' Rasputin asked. 'Is something wrong?'

Felix shook his head faintly, unsure if Rasputin would even notice. 'I love this cross,' he said eventually. The remark surprised himself, as he really had no idea what he was going to say. 'It's a very beautiful thing, don't you agree?'

Rasputin rose, and joined him at the cabinet. 'Yes, it's a very nice thing. Cost a lot of money, I'm sure. How much did you pay for it?' Felix turned to answer, but Rasputin continued speaking. 'This is what takes my fancy most, though.' He patted the ebony cabinet. 'It's quite fascinating, my son. If it were in Pokrovskoe I might have stolen it, long ago.'

Felix nodded slowly. He could see Rasputin reflected in every facet of the jewelled crucifix. A legion of Rasputins... He suppressed an urge to shudder, but the thought had also illuminated something in his mind. Now he understood how the holy devil could have consumed all the poison and lived. Satan looked after his own, didn't he? But if the demon inside him could be exorcised...

'Grigory Efimovitch... Oughtn't you say a prayer before the cross?' He stepped back a couple of paces to give

Rasputin easier access to the crucifix.

Rasputin looked at him, clearly unnerved by Felix's tone. Then his eyes settled into a more gentle aspect, and he nodded. Rasputin turned to face the cross atop the cabinet, and Felix reached slowly into his jacket for his revolver.

Unaware of Felix's silent movement, Rasputin began to cross himself. Felix knew that the devil that protected Rasputin would be driven out by the power of God, leaving the moujik vulnerable. His thumb gently eased back the hammer of the revolver.

Rasputin finished genuflecting, and bowed his head. 'Holy Father –'

From six feet away, Felix pulled the trigger, sending a bullet smashing into Rasputin's back. The prayer aborted itself with a scream as the staretz tumbled headlong on to the white bearskin rug.

Jo hid in the pantry when she heard footsteps hurrying towards the kitchen, but it was only Liz. Jo emerged with relief. 'It's all right,' Liz said. 'They're going to shoot him now.' She looked down sadly. 'I wish I could say I feel relieved at history being protected.'

Jo hesitated, not really sure if she even wanted to say this. 'Couldn't we save him? I mean, he's just one man –'

Liz shook her head. 'You know we can't. The Doctor was right in what he said about getting too close...'

'Close to what?' Sukhotin asked from behind them. When she and Liz turned, Jo was relieved to see that he wasn't holding a gun on them, though he was wearing one in its holster. 'Do you two know each other?'

'You could say that,' Liz said quickly. 'We met when I visited the palace before –'

Sukhotin raised a hand. 'No.' He looked piercingly at Jo. 'I've never seen this girl here before, and her accent... Of course, she is Miss Grant, isn't she? Academician Kuznetzov described her quite well.'

'Yes,' Jo said defiantly, before Liz could answer. 'And I suppose he wanted you to kill me.' That was what had been said, after all. And Jo had no doubt that these men weren't prone to practical jokes.

'Only if Professor Shaw didn't do as she was asked. But she did. When Rasputin is finished, you will be freed. Both of you.' The young officer now had his pistol in hand, but not really aimed at either of them.

Jo sidestepped around the nearest table, where the cakes had been made. 'And what about our property?' Liz asked, looking Sukhotin in the eye. 'That must also be returned.'

'You'll have to take that up with Kuznetzov. I think he has plans for your police box.'

'Oh.' Jo smiled, lowering her hands slightly. 'I don't suppose you'd happen to know where he keeps it?' she asked breezily.

'I might do.' He eyed Liz thoughtfully. 'Now, what would it be worth to you to know?' Jo recognised this game, of course, and was certain Liz did too.

Liz stepped a little closer to Sukhotin, but didn't quite come between him and Jo. 'I'm sure we can come to some arrangement,' she said with a smile. Sukhotin nodded, and Jo used the moment to scoop up a handful of flour from the table, and hurl it into Sukhotin's eyes.

As his head twisted away, trying to protect his eyes, Liz kneed him in the groin. Hardly ladylike, but a useful technique to know when one spent most of one's life surrounded by students who liked a drink.

Sukhotin's gun went off, the bullet shattering a window, as Jo wrestled it away from him. 'We were talking about arrangements,' Liz said to the groaning man. He nodded painfully. 'Good. Firstly I want to know where the police box is.'

'You won't shoot…'

'Didn't your friend Kuznetzov tell you that Miss Grant works for a… unit of British Intelligence? And I'm a scientist – I assure you that the study of reactions to pain and injury is something that we scientists are used to viewing with clinical detachment. And we're used to administering it too.'

Jo glanced nervously at Liz in the silence that followed.

'It's at the old Stock Exchange building. The building was being refitted until it was given over to the Academy as an extra work space for the war effort.'

'There,' Liz said, 'that wasn't so difficult, was it? Now, we're leaving – I suggest you don't try to stop us.'

'Just a minute,' Jo said, thinking about how they'd get out of the palace. 'Do you have a car?'

Sukhotin hesitated, then nodded.

'I think we'd find the keys very usefu-'

Jo broke off in confusion, wondering just when car keys had been invented, but Sukhotin's eyes showed that he knew he was defeated and he muttered, 'It's around the back. The mews -' as if he'd barely heard.

Jo and Liz exchanged triumphant grins. 'Thank you.'

'Don't worry, we won't damage it,' Jo added. Liz was breaking out some hanks of the cord palace servants used for lashing the laundry hampers shut.

Purishkevich bolted from his seat at the shot, excitedly

plunging down the stairs. He didn't realise there had been two shots, thinking that the second was merely an echo. The others followed. In his haste, he bumped against the light switch, and the room went pitch-dark. Dmitri snapped the light back on, and now Purishkevich saw Felix standing over Rasputin's body.

Felix was watching with a mesmerised expression and levelled gun, as Rasputin covered his eyes and twitched slightly. They could hear the peasant's painful gasps for breath, and Purishkevich hoped the stench of the blood that soaked Rasputin's shirt was only a figment of his imagination.

Dmitri went over to the fallen peasant. 'Help me pull him off the rug before his blood stains it.' Purishkevich joined him, knowing that the less evidence of violence that was left here, the better. Taking a leg and arm each, they dragged Rasputin over to the tiles at the edge of the room.

When they put him down there, the twitching had stopped. Lazovert approached nervously, and knelt beside him. He checked Rasputin's pulse, and heartbeat, then pulled up his eyelids to examine the pupils. Finally, he looked up and shook his head. 'He's dead. It's over.'

Purishkevich sighed with relief. Now they were heroes. Even if it did feel more as if Felix had shot a rabid dog than a man.

Sukhotin had given them directions to his car while they tied him up in the kitchen. The women hoped it would take him a some minutes to get loose, and by that time they would be long gone.

Not quite as long as they'd hoped, though – the car had taken a few nerve-racking moments to get started. After some fumbling with an archaic dashboard, Liz had realised this model could be fired up with just the ignition switch – so, thankfully, no need to crank up the starting handle in the freezing cold. When the engine was turning over with a steady breathy whispering, Liz made sure all the car's pedals did what she'd expect them to, then guided it smoothly out of the Moika Palace gates.

The old Stock Exchange building, resembling an acropolis, was in darkness of course. Liz thought that was just as well, since it mean no one was likely to be working inside. 'How do we get in?' she asked Jo.

Jo held up a large metal ring with a couple of dozen keys on it. 'Skeleton keys. First thing they taught me in the UNIT agent's course,' she said proudly. It didn't take her long to open one of the large main doors.

Liz took a pen-torch from her pocket and shone it around the marble hall. There were numerous tables and worktops scattered around, and the odd divan. In the middle of a cluster of such benches was a large dark shape, and she could hear a vague electrical hum... She almost yelled with joy as the narrow torchbeam illuminated the words 'POLICE Public Call BOX' on top of the TARDIS.

'At last!' Jo exclaimed.

'Now we just have to find the Doctor and let him know...'

'If he's dealing with Kuznetzov, I'm sure he'll get him to say where the TARDIS is. In fact he's probably inside already.' To test her theory, Jo knocked on the TARDIS doors. 'Doctor?'

There was no response, and Liz sat on one of the tables. 'He's not back then.'

'We must call Anya too,' Jo reminded her.

'Let's give it until dawn,' Liz said. 'You know why.'

Jo nodded. 'I suppose.'

Liz had thought that visiting the past would be a good source of study. Instead she felt more like a vivisectionist. She felt as if she had poked and prodded the citizens of the past, seeing which way they'd jump... Just like seeing how a chimp reacted to electrical stimulation. She shuddered. Was that what time travel was? A voyeuristic show, to be in at the kill without guilt because it had all already happened?

She went through to where Jo was curled up on a bench, still in her servant's uniform. 'Sorry,' she said. 'About everything.'

Jo hugged her.

Purishkevich had finally been able to turn off that damned 'Yankee Doodle Dandy' record when Sukhotin returned, his face and uniform speckled with flour. 'Vladimir, Professor Shaw has escaped, with Miss Grant –'

'Dammit,' Purishkevich muttered. 'Never mind, it's done anyway.' He handed Sukhotin Rasputin's coat and hat, while Lazovert put back on his chauffeur's coat and cap. Everyone's spirits had been raised by the undoubted good they had done for their country tonight.

Everyone except Felix, anyway. He left Purishkevich smoking a celebratory cigar in the lounge, and went into his parents' wing of the palace. He felt the need to be away from his own things, after what Rasputin had made him into. Murderer and hero; a difficult pairing to live with.

Felix had intended to lie down and try to calm his nerves, but something kept him on edge. He could practically feel that familiar magnetic pull from downstairs, an irresistible force compelling him to go down and face his own actions.

Slipping past the lounge without disturbing Purishkevich – who would not understand – Felix went back down to the murder room.

Rasputin's body was slumped on the tiles where it had been left. Felix went over, with the unwilling compulsion that leads people to probe a broken tooth with their tongue. He took Rasputin's hand, feeling for a pulse at the wrist. He couldn't find one, though the body hadn't cooled much yet.

There was no doubt in Felix's mind that Rasputin had forced his hand by not leaving the city long ago. Part of him was also saddened by the sacrifice not only of his own conscience and morals, but of someone so powerfully alluring as Rasputin. In the end, Rasputin had not just stripped Russia of decency and just government, but he had even stolen himself away from Felix.

Suddenly enraged at this cheating of fate, Felix exploded, grabbing Rasputin by the shoulders and slamming him hard against the tiles. Trying to hurt the dead was a waste of energy, but Felix didn't care, he just needed that outlet for his rage.

Rasputin's eyes opened, glinting with a viperish cold and staring at Felix with an expression of diabolical hatred.

Felix's blood turned to ice, and his muscles to stone. He desperately wanted to run away, or call for help from Purishkevich, but his legs refused to obey his frantic instructions, and his throat remained equally paralysed.

'Felix!' the broken man snarled, his flailing hands tearing at the Prince's tunic. Between the blood on his lips, and the coarseness of the snarl, Felix imagined for a moment some great bear had a hold on him. Except this was worse –

more like wrestling some spawn of Satan himself... Such a demonic adversary would never let go of his soul, but drag him down into Hell. Terror-struck, Felix kicked out, entirely on instinct.

Rasputin collapsed to his knees, coughing dark blood, and Felix bolted for the spiral staircase. He had to get out before the creature attacked him again.

Purishkevich exchanged glances with the others at the roar from below. Rasputin's refusal to just give it up and die was becoming damned annoying. He put his cigar down in the ashtray, and marched through to the anteroom to see what was happening.

As he did so, Felix burst through from the other side, raving eyes bulging from his bloodless face. 'Shoot!' he screamed wildly. 'He's escaping – shoot! Shoot!'

Shaking his head, Purishkevich drew his revolver, and made for the stairs, listening for any sign of an approach from the cellar below.

There was nothing, and he was about to go back and try to calm the prince, when he heard the clunk of the landing door opening. He descended the stairs two at a time, and saw the concealed door to the courtyard was ajar.

Amazingly, Rasputin was indeed out there, limping towards the iron gates in the middle of the low wall that enclosed the courtyard. 'Felix!' he was roaring. 'You bastard!'

Purishkevich darted out the door, and shot at the stumbling peasant. It must have missed, for Rasputin didn't even seem to notice it. Hurrying to catch up, Purishkevich fired again, with no luck. He stopped with a curse in the middle of the courtyard, and took more careful aim. With the gun held in both hands, Purishkevich fired for a third time.

The shot took Rasputin in the back again, bringing him to a halt. Purishkevich wasn't taking any more chances, and fired again. This time a wet spray bloomed from the peasant's head, and he pitched forward into a snowdrift a few feet from the gate. Purishkevich remained standing in the classic marksman's position, almost reluctant to believe his target had fallen. The sound of the shot seemed to hang in the air, and Purishkevich was suddenly very aware of the silent rows of houses on the far side of the Moika.

He barely realised he had started walking, until he found himself looking down on the twitching peasant who had all but destroyed his beloved country. Rasputin was lying face down. Even in the death throes he violated the peace here, Purishkevich noted, staining the pristine snow with his filthy blood. It steamed slightly in the freezing air. He still clung to life too, his fingers feebly clawing at the snow as if trying to drag himself on towards the gate.

Where the blood touched the snow, it was like life in the world. First burning away the purity of those flakes it touched, before cooling and leaving a fossilised tint that would be buried under layers of fresh snow the following day.

Angered at the sight, Purishkevich kicked Rasputin hard in the side of the head. The blow was enough to roll him over, and his face twisted into a wordless snarl. 'Just die, you peasant bastard,' Purishkevich spat, kicking him again. He saw that the burning was fading from Rasputin's eyes and his hands were relaxing, no longer dragging at the snow.

Once he was certain that his victim actually was dead, Purishkevich looked around the courtyard. Patches of frozen blood dotted the snow, and the body was very obvious in the middle of its snowdrift. Purishkevich knew that there were Guardsmen on duty at the main entrance, and set off to get their help. With all the excitement of killing Rasputin, he no longer even noticed the cold.

The two soldiers were on their way round towards him as he approached, drawn by the gunshots. 'Boys,' Purishkevich began companionably, if not drunkenly, 'I just killed Grishka Rasputin, the enemy of Russia and the Tsar.' It didn't really occur to him that he could have been more circumspect; this was a time for celebration.

'Thank God,' one of them said.

'About time,' the other agreed.

Purishkevich was delighted. 'My friends, Felix Felixovitch and I rely on your absolute silence. You must understand that if tonight's business comes out, the Tsarina will not understand at first, and will not thank us. Can you keep this to yourself?'

'We won't betray you, Excellency,' one said. Purishkevich embraced them both in a bear hug, and kissed them on the cheek with drunkenly exaggerated formality. 'Good lads. Now, I need your help to get the body out of the way, back to the foot of the cellar staircase…'

Felix had heard the shots, and cautiously came around from the front of the house. There had been no sign of Rasputin making it to the canal, so he presumed that Purishkevich had brought him down.

Felix re-entered the courtyard through the main gate, and immediately saw the two soldiers bringing the body back to the house. They were also leaving a long trail of blood in the snow.

'Your Highness,' a voice said from behind him, making Felix start. He turned, to see a policeman walking in through the gates. Felix hurriedly approached the man, keeping himself between the policeman and the body, as the soldiers ducked out of sight.

'Yes, Officer...?'

'Vlasyuk, Highness. I heard shots. Has anything happened to you?'

Felix almost laughed, and not with humour. 'No. At least, nothing serious, Officer Vlasyuk. Just a stupid business. I had some friends with me tonight. One of them drank too much and began horsing around. But everything is all right here.'

Vlasyuk hesitated, but then nodded. 'As you say, Your Highness.' He left through the gate to resume his rounds. Felix turned back as the soldiers reappeared, but saw that Rasputin's body had moved slightly.

The holy devil was still alive, Felix thought in panic. Now they were all doomed. How could they finish him off with the police hanging around? His stomach could stand the strain no longer, and he forced himself into a run. He bolted up the stairs and into his parents' bathroom, his stomach heaving, and vomited into the sink. Even after voiding himself, he could still smell and taste the scent of Rasputin's blood. Perhaps it would haunt him, he thought fearfully, for ever.

He staggered back out into the study, and fell back against the wall. How had things got this far? It hardly seemed more than a few days since he first came into contact with Rasputin's magnetism, and recognised the dangers inherent in its allure, and now he had been forced to kill. Damn himself for doing it, and double-damn Rasputin for leaving him no other way...

Except maybe he wasn't dead, could never die. How could you kill the Devil? He was sure that Rasputin would find him up here, still shouting 'Felix' as he had before.

He didn't even realise that he himself was gasping out 'Felix, Felix, Felix…' Over and over as if he was possessed. He sensed a presence by his side, and whirled round in fear and guilt, but it was only Purishkevich.

Purishkevich had rapidly sobered when he saw Felix's vomit-stained mouth mumbling his own name like that. For once, he began to wonder if perhaps they had gone too far. He still thought killing Rasputin was the right thing to do, but they should just have shot him to begin with, instead of playing these mind games, which Felix seemed to be losing.

'Come on, Highness. He's dead. The soldiers moved him inside on my instructions. Come and see.'

He put an arm around Felix's quivering shoulders, and steered him towards the stairs. As they went through the lounge, Felix lifted the leathered steel club which Maklakov had given him on that visit with Liz.

At the bottom of the staircase, the two soldiers guarded Rasputin's bloody corpse. Felix took a deep shuddering breath, pulled himself upright, then fell upon the corpse with an unheralded fury. Even Purishkevich and the two guards could only watch in stunned amazement, as the young prince repeatedly smashed the body over the chest and head with the club, screaming, 'Felix! Felix!' as the blood splashed across his face and shirt. When a spray of blood hit Purishkevich, it jolted him to his senses, and he grabbed the prince.

The two guards followed his lead, pulling the struggling

man back. He still screamed out his own name as he fought to batter the corpse even more, but suddenly doubled over, vomit splashing on to the tiles. Then he went limp.

Purishkevich relaxed his grip when he realised the prince had fainted. He had never seen anything like that display of violence before, and was doubly shocked considering Felix's second thoughts earlier. 'Take… take him upstairs and make him comfortable,' he told the guards. When they left, he wished he could go with them to escape the stench of blood and vomit. He suspected, however, that the acrid air would follow Felix and himself around for a long time to come.

Chapter Twenty

Kit was almost frozen solid by the time he and the Doctor rode back into the Finland station at the side of the rails. The horses weren't doing too much better; they were literally steaming in the cold air. He was strongly regretting having made the suggestion that they use these horses to get back. If ever he had to do this again, he would be sure to insist on waiting for a train.

Confound that, he thought. If he ever had to do this again, he would resign.

The red and gold arches that decorated the platform looked downright bloody, as they darkened away from the few lights that were on. A uniformed stationmaster emerged from a little office, his jaw dropping at the sight of horses instead of trains pulling into the station.

The Doctor guided his mount over to the stationmaster, and dismounted with remarkable agility for a man of his apparent age. He thrust the reins into the stationmaster's hand before the man could say a word. 'Look after these animals,' he instructed crisply. 'They'll need to be walked, fed, watered and rubbed down.'

'I am not a stablehand. Who are you?'

'I'm the man who's putting two horses from the Lancer Regiment into your care. A company of them will coming in here later in the morning, and I imagine they'd like their animals back unharmed.'

'But –'

'Now, I shall also require a car or a lorry. Do you have one?'

'But I –'

The Doctor was clearly losing whatever little patience he had had. 'Good grief, man, it's a perfectly simple question. Is there a vehicle I could use?'

'There's a truck in the loading yard, but –'

'Yes, well that will just have to do, won't it.' The Doctor turned back to Kit. 'Come on, we've no time to lose.'

Kit had dismounted rather stiffly, and handed his reins to the stationmaster with an apologetic look and a ten-rouble note. 'We really need it,' he said sheepishly.

'And look after those horses,' the Doctor called back as he marched in search of the loading yard.

Things had begun to settle at the Moika Palace, but the police had now returned, led by Captain Krylov of the Ochrana, and Vlasyuk. The guard showed Vlasyuk and Krylov into the lounge, where Felix lay on the couch. Purishkevich greeted them. 'Officer Vlasyuk, you were here earlier, weren't you? Asking about what happened with the shooting?'

'Yes, Excellency.'

'You know me?' Purishkevich knew the answer must be yes, since the policeman had addressed him properly, but he was thinking rapidly.

'Yes, Excellency. You are state Duma member Vladimir Purishkevich.'

'And you know this gentleman?' He indicated the blood-soaked Felix.

'His Highness Prince Yusupov.'

'Correct,' Purishkevich agreed. 'Now listen to me. Do you love your country and your Tsar, and want victory over the Germans?'

'Of course, Excellency!'

'And you know who is the greatest danger to the Tsar, who has taken every opportunity to hinder our war effort?'

Krylov grunted. 'Grishka Rasputin.'

'Well,' Purishkevich said slowly, 'he is no more. We just killed him. Those were the shots you heard.' The two policemen's eyes widened in astonishment. Purishkevich continued before either of them could ask any questions. 'If anyone asks, can you say that you saw and heard nothing? Can you keep your silence, and not betray us?'

He quietly thumbed the hammer of the revolver behind his back, just in case the pair turned out not to love their country and Tsar. He didn't *want* to shoot anyone else, but he could still hear the blood rush through his ears from having brought down Rasputin, and it felt good. Two more wouldn't make that much difference, he told himself.

Vlasyuk nodded. 'Yes, Mr Purishkevich. I understand. I won't report this, but if anyone asks me specifically whether this event happened, I will not lie.' Krylov nodded an agreement.

Purishkevich thought about this. With no report, there was no reason why anyone would ask about the event. He uncocked the gun, without showing any sign of the movement to Vlasyuk. 'That's good enough for me.'

As the guard escorted the policemen back out, Thesphe approached, his features inscrutable. 'Excellency. The guard downstairs has wrapped your – ah, the remains, in an old blue curtain, in case there are any more visitors.'

'Good. Have your staff clean up the room down there too.'

Krylov and Vlasyuk left the Palace via the front door, and

strolled back to Krylov's car. Vlasyuk spared a last glance back. He could have smelled the brandy on Purishkevich's breath from Moscow. 'Killed Rasputin, indeed! Did they take us for fools that we would believe such a fable?'

'Write it up. The report will embarrass the drunken fools, and perhaps discourage them from causing such a late-night disturbance again…'

The truck had no heating, but at least the seat was more comfortable than a saddle. An abandoned tram had blocked the road to the nearest bridge, and now they were actually heading back north in search of a way round.

Kit was racking his memory for suitable directions. 'Head round Primorsky Prospekt. We can cut down through the Kirov islands and avoid any other trams blocking the roads.'

The snow gave the city an ethereal air, peaceful and crisp. There was no real traffic on the roads as the black automobile sped along the icy streets.

Sukhotin knew they were going much faster than the car should in such frozen conditions, but was clearly anxious to get this particular journey over with. Beside him, the large mass wrapped in blue curtain was a constant reminder of why Dmitri was in such a hurry.

Purishkevich frowned, and bent down to lift something from the floor. 'Dammit,' he groaned, 'What about these?' He held a pair of heavy snow boots.

'They won't burn,' Sukhotin said. 'They're too bulky. I thought we could bury them, or –'

'All right. We'll throw them into the water with the body.' Purishkevich's eyes met the driver's in the mirror. 'Are we there yet, Dmitri?'

'Almost.' By now the car had left the city proper. They were traversing the road across Petrovsky Island. Ahead, the wooden bridge set upon stone foundations stretched out across a largely frozen river. On the far side, the tree line of Krestovsky Island loomed in the darkness.

Dmitri carefully braked as the car reached the Petrovsky Bridge. A small wooden hut was built atop one of the stone supports half way across. 'The night watchman,' he said quietly.

Sukhotin nodded, and opened the car door, letting in a blast of frigid air. He walked swiftly across, thinking of what sort of cover story to give the man. No one greeted him as he reached the hut, however. He considered knocking, but instead gently opened the door.

The night watchman was huddled in front of a fire, snoring mildly. Ordinarily this would have led to a reprimand, but Sukhotin wasn't going to stand on formality this night. He closed the door just as gently, and hurried back to the car.

'Well?' Dmitri asked.

'The watchman's asleep. We can do it here, and nobody will know the difference.'

'Good.' Purishkevich shoved the curtain-wrapped mass towards Sukhotin. 'Take his legs.' Sukhotin did as he was told, grabbing the inanimate limbs that were hidden in the curtain. The sooner this ruffian was in hell and gone, the better. They staggered a little under the weight. Sukhotin was sure they were forgetting something, but it didn't matter; with the watchman asleep this was a simple matter. Hell, even if the man caught them, he'd probably agree with what they were doing.

With an effort, the pair propped the shrouded body atop

the bridge's railing for a moment, then shoved it all the way over. There was a muffled crack and splash from below, and Sukhotin was gratified to see that the body had gone straight through the thin ice and into the river, even without the weights and chains… That was it, he cursed himself. They had forgotten the weights and chains, dammit.

Dmitri must have read his mind, for he emerged from the car with the bonds, and tossed them off the bridge after the body. Then went a bundle of boots and overcoat. Relieved that it was over, Sukhotin and the others got back into the car, and reversed off the bridge. In moments, they were driving more sedately back through the sleeping city, unmindful of the heavy snow boot that lay forlorn beside the wooden bridge rail.

A moment later, another set of headlights fell upon it.

'Jumping Jehosophat!' the Doctor exclaimed, emerging from the delivery truck. 'Those men were trying to drown someone.'

Kit pointed at a dark gap in the ice below. 'There.'

The Doctor was already climbing down the bank. 'We might just be in time.'

He could feel the rope shift from around his arm, but too late. The hole through which he had been delivered into the water was nowhere to be seen, and new waves of burning cold assaulted him with every passing moment. Terror drove his heart faster and faster, but all that did was make the pain burn more.

He needed to breathe, but there was no air to be had. Against his will, he screamed, but freezing water poured into his throat, instead of sound bursting out. He hit out at the ice in blind panic.

While Kit moved the truck off the bridge, closer to the silent trees on the bank in case they needed to carry someone to hospital, the Doctor made straight for the struggling victim.

He dropped to his knees at the edge of the ice, searching his pockets for an implement strong enough to break through. Whoever had been thrown in the river here would last only a minute or two.

He brushed the snow away from the surface, trying to get a look at where the victim was. The ice was thick and white, but he could just about make out a vague form struggling below.

Then he realised that the darkness blurring the man's face was his long hair and unkempt beard. He looked up, belatedly orienting himself in relation to the Winter Palace, the whole of St Petersburg's winter skyline. A moment's thought showed that the bridge was that between the Petrovsky and Krestovsky Islands, which meant that this man so close to death under the ice was Grigory Rasputin.

The Doctor was certain he could break through the frozen water and pull him to safety. Instead he found himself simply staring at the blurred figure under the ice.

Rasputin's vision was fading, and he could sense a long tunnel opening up nearby. Still, he could make out a man above, who seemed to be about to crack the ice. Though the ice was largely opaque, and the night dark, Rasputin would recognise that shock of white hair anywhere. It was

Josephine's mentor, the Doctor, who Rasputin knew was a good man.

She must have sent the Doctor to save him. Rasputin could feel the tunnel recede, even through the pain that gripped him...

The Doctor lowered his hand, and stood. Rasputin gaped; his saviour could not desert him. He was Rasputin, favoured by God, and therefore indestructible! But still the Doctor stood, watching him gasp for air that wasn't available. Watching, no doubt, even after the blackness took Rasputin's vision.

Rasputin's tears mixed with the Neva, indistinguishable from it. A single tear also fell atop the ice, frozen before it even landed.

Kit looked questioningly at the Doctor, and saw the other man's eyes dart fleetingly towards the ice. 'I'm afraid we're too late, old chap.' He started back to the truck, and Kit could have sworn he was hiding something. Then he turned back. 'It was Rasputin, you know.'

Kit nodded, grimly. 'I thought it might be.'

The Doctor returned to the driver's seat of the truck, and Kit paused a moment. He was vaguely troubled himself; in spite of their efforts, Kuznetzov had got what he wanted, even if he wouldn't be able to exploit it as intended. And with that in mind, perhaps the other things that had been said about Rasputin were falsehoods and exaggerations too.

Now they'd never get the chance to find out.

Felix awoke in darkness, feeling both disappointed and elated. The palace seemed like a haunted house to him now; empty echoing chambers filled with material things that meant little to him.

The servants were waiting with the others when he came back into the lounge. After the nerves of the night before, everyone seemed somewhat despondent. Maybe they realised what they had done was not so clear cut as it had seemed before. Maybe it was the natural aftermath to a heightened state of excitement. Maybe they were simply tired after such a long night.

'We must clean up the blood…' He trailed off. 'Wait, the police already know that something happened, so more may come… Go out to the kennels and shoot one of the dogs.' It broke his heart to say that, but it was sadly necessary. 'Then drag it over the blood trail outside. If anyone asks, we can say that a drunken guest shot it, and that's why there is blood on the snow.'

Jo had cried for most of the rest of the night, while Liz sat thoughtfully. Jo wasn't sure what Liz was thinking, but it was clear that she was no longer as certain about things as she had been earlier.

In six weeks or so, the first Revolution would depose the Tsar. In two years he and his entire family would be dead. It was kind of spooky, Jo thought, that she already knew his younger children would die before they were even her age.

Liz watched the dawn seep through the sky outside the Stock Exchange. Appropriately, the clouds had cleared a little, and the sun cast blood on them as it rose. That seemed appropriate enough. She wondered if she'd be seeing bloodstains in things for the foreseeable future. It had taken long enough to stop being haunted by her previous experiences with the Doctor at UNIT…

'Out, out, damned spot…' she murmured. She went back inside to Jo. 'It's dawn. I think it's safe to call Anya now.'

Kit blinked himself awake; he'd just gone twenty-four hours without sleep, and it was beginning to get to him. The Doctor somehow seemed as spry as ever, and Kit was very jealous of whatever it was that let him stay that way.

They were sitting in the delivery truck, watching Ochrana agents swarm in and out of the Moika Palace. 'Their secrecy didn't last very long, did it?' the Doctor said to himself.

'I don't suppose it matters when you're immune from prosecution. And I'm sure Felix has got some explanation for what happened.' Kit nodded in the direction of a dead guard dog which Thesphe was pointing at while talking to several policemen. 'I don't see any sign of Liz or Jo, though.'

'I imagine they'll be kept somewhere fairly secure…' The Doctor opened the truck door. 'Come on then.'

'Where to?' Kit asked, not too willing to move around.

'To speak to those policemen, of course.'

Groaning, Kit hauled himself out of the truck, and followed the Doctor across to the gate. Another car caught his eye as it turned into the Moika Palace courtyard. 'Doctor,' he said slowly, 'isn't that Vasiliyev's car?'

The Doctor looked. 'I do believe it is…' He changed course, heading for Vasiliyev as the Ochrana chief emerged from the car. 'Mr Vasiliyev,' the Doctor called.

Vasiliyev looked round, wearing a calculating expression. 'Doctor… Kit… I hear Rasputin is missing.'

'Yes, we, er, heard something similar ourselves,' the Doctor said. 'Actually my associates, Miss Grant and

Professor Shaw, are also missing –'

'Not any more,' Vasiliyev interrupted. 'Anya Vyrubova is with them at the old Stock Exchange. It seems they've found your missing property.'

'You mean they're not here?' The Doctor sounded surprised – something Kit had already gathered was quite a rare occurrence.

'No.'

Kit tried to grasp this. 'But Kuznetzov said –'

'You're going to believe something *he* said?' Vasiliyev scoffed. 'I'm sure you can drive the Doctor to the Stock Exchange.' He looked sad. 'I certainly won't need you any more.'

Kit nodded sadly. He'd known that his job here had been curtailed by all this. Still, perhaps it meant he could go back to Ashley…

When he had driven the Doctor to the old Stock Exchange, Kit found the location Kuznetzov had chosen ironic. The rostral that Morovich had fallen from was right outside.

Kit managed to dodge out of Jo's path as she hugged the Doctor. He had left the truck's engine running, as he felt a speedy departure might be wise. Vasiliyev now knew that Kit had no loyalties to him, and his cover was long gone.

He also knew that the plot to kill Rasputin had been so widely known that the Empress must have found out by now. Therefore when she stopped screaming, she would start ordering arrests. Felix and Dmitri, as members of the Imperial family, couldn't be arrested, but there was no such restriction on himself.

Oh well. At least now he could go back home in the knowledge that he had acquitted himself well, without going to the trenches. He should be able to pick a nice cushy job in Whitehall if he played this right.

'What about you, Doctor? I think it'd be best if you found a way out.'

The Doctor nodded with a smile, and held up a small pendant. 'I have indeed.' He looked at Jo and Liz, who both nodded decisively. The Doctor led the girls into the Stock Exchange, and Kit was amazed to see a police box there. True, it looked rather different from the ones he was familiar with – more modern, in a way, for one thing – but recognisable nonetheless.

The Doctor opened the door, and Liz and Jo entered. 'I thought you were leaving?' Kit said.

'Oh, we are.' The Doctor smiled mischievously. 'And I imagine it's an escape route you'll remember for a long time to come.' He shook Kit's hand. 'Perhaps we'll meet again some day. Preferably under happier circumstances.'

'Or at least easier ones,' Kit agreed. 'Goodbye, then.'

The Doctor nodded an acknowledgement, and went into the police box. A moment later, he reappeared. 'You know, I could drop you off back at Whitehall...' Kit was sure the Doctor was pulling his leg.

'How?'

'Come in here a moment, and I'll show you.' Kit hesitated, then decided that after all the trouble he'd had chasing this War Ministry box, he might as well see what was in it. He stepped through the doors.

'Hell's teeth!' he said in astonishment.

Anya saw Kit follow the others into the Doctor's cabinet. She waited a moment, expecting them to come out in some kind of disguises. Instead, a strained elephantine roaring started to emerge from the police box, as the lamp on top began to flash.

She realised she could now see the wall of the palace through the police box. To her amazement, and shivers, the box slowly faded away into thin air.

Anya blinked twice. All she could think of was how much Grigory would have loved to have seen that.

Alix took Anya's call in the small office that served as a nurses' station in one of the wards at the Catherine Palace. 'Missing? All five of them?'

'The Doctor, Powell and the girls have probably left to return home,' Anya's voice said. 'Father Grigory… Felix says they thought he would be at the Villa Rode, and called to speak to him, but he wasn't there.'

'Felix says many things, most of them fantasies,' Alix replied. 'I don't like this. Who will look after my son if Father Grigory is away?'

'I don't know. We're searching the river now, just in case.'

'Call me when – if, you find anything.' Alix hung up. She thought a moment, then moved a small desk, to write to her husband Nicholas.

My own beloved sweetheart, she wrote.

We are sitting together – you can imagine our feelings – thoughts – Our Friend has disappeared.

Yesterday, Anya saw him and said Felix asked him to come in the night, a motor would fetch him, to see Irina. A motor fetched him (a military one) with two civilians and it went away.

This night, big scandal at Yusupovs' house – big meeting, Dmitri, Purishkevich, etc., all drunk – police heard shots. Purishkevich ran out screaming to the police that Our Friend was killed... Our Friend was in good spirits but nervous these days. Felix pretends he never came to the house... I shall still trust in God's mercy that one has only driven him off somewhere. Protopopov is doing all he can... I cannot and won't believe he has been killed. God have mercy, such utter anguish (am calm and can't believe it... Come quickly.

Epilogue

Burning blue-white, and too bright to be viewed with the naked eye, the cylindrical fire blazed over the village of Nizhne-Karelinsk, passing high to the northwest. Though clearly moving fast, it took a whole ten minutes to burn its way down to the horizon.

As it finally neared the ground a small dark cloud appeared. This suddenly swamped the blue light, and a huge column of black smoke began to shoot up. Soon, a wave of sound rolled across the village. It was a swelling rumble, quite unlike the sharp report of an explosion. The village shook as the sound blasted through it and, in the distance, veins of fire rippled through the rising clouds.

This was two hundred miles away from ground zero.

Seventy miles from ground zero, the sky over Vanavara split asunder, and fire lashed out. The thunderclap knocked people off their feet in the rough streets, and earth rained from the sky as the village's buildings shook and cracked.

Thirty miles from ground zero, a wall of superheated vapour knocked the trees down like ninepins on the banks of the Chambe river.

The tents of a hunter were cast, burning, into the distance, and he himself was bowled over for what felt like several hundred yards. The reindeer and dogs he had brought bolted in sheer terror, but he couldn't hear their departure: the incredible sound had ruptured his eardrums.

* * *

Ground zero.

A body six hundred yards across, and massing around thirty thousand tons, burrowed into the Earth's atmosphere at supersonic speed. Five miles above ground, the density of the atmosphere finally proved too much for it: flattened against its own shockwave the body abruptly slowed, stopped – splashed, like a lead bullet on armoured steel. It tore itself apart in a gigantic, continuing explosion. Much of the force was expended downwards as well as outwards, into the great Siberian forest.

The trees for a few hundred yards directly under the explosion were stripped vertically of their branches, and charred, but remained standing as the air thickened around them. The earth at this point was slammed into a bowl-shaped depression a mile across, as the underlying permafrost and plant material were vaporised.

From this point, the shockwave spread out at hundreds of miles per hour, flattening the trees as it went. In a matter of seconds, nearly eight hundred square miles of forest were stamped flat.

Thousands of birds and animals were killed instantly, most smashed to a pulp by the shockwave. Every leaf in the devastated area was scorched away to nothing, leaving only hundreds of square miles of skeletal trunks lying bare under the churning smoke and dust.

It was June 30th 1908, and the happiest day of Liz Shaw's life.